FAIRY TALES

and Other Fanciful Short Stories

E. W. Farnsworth

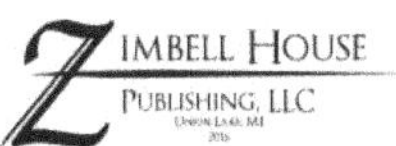

ZIMBELL HOUSE
PUBLISHING, LLC
Union Lake, MI
2016

For permission requests, write to the publisher at the address below:
"Attention: Permissions Coordinator"
Zimbell House Publishing, LLC
PO Box 1172
Union Lake, Michigan 48387
mail to: info@zimbellhousepublishing.com

© 2016 Zimbell House Publishing, LLC
Book and Cover Design by The Book Planners
http://www.TheBookPlanner.com

Published in the United States by Zimbell House Publishing
http://www.ZimbellHousePublishing.com
All Rights Reserved

Trade Paper ISBN: 978-1-945967-29-0
Print ISBN: 978-1-942818-83-0
Kindle ISBN: 978-1-942818-82-3
Digital ISBN: 978-1-942818-84-7
Library of Congress Control Number: 2016944213

First Edition: August/2016
10 9 8 7 6 5 4

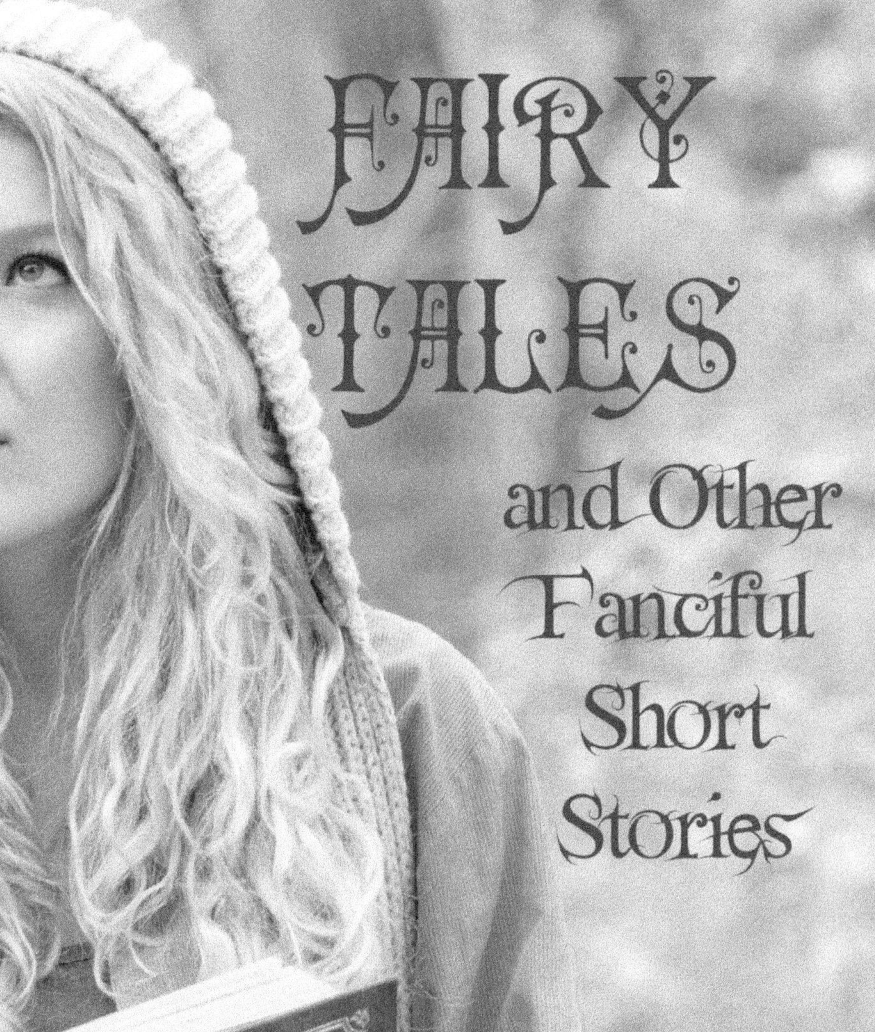

FAIRY
TALES
and Other
Fanciful
Short
Stories
E. W. Farnsworth

Dedication

For Hillary

Acknowledgements

The following works were first published as individual stories in the indicated anthology from Horrified Press in the United Kingdom in 2016.

"Three Trolls Too Many" and "Troll Hide," *Troll Anthology*, edited by George Wilhite, Thirteen O'Clock Press Horrified Press, July 2016.

Contents

Valley of the Giants

Victor Mirabile was the successful location manager for many major films, but his assignment for the new film, *Valley of the Giants*, had him stumped. The film's director wanted a location where scale could be potentially unlimited, and the giant figures would not look out of place or freakish.

The best-selling book by the same name was difficult to visualize because semi-mythical figures like the Yeti or Abominable Snowman, and Sasquatch or Big Foot, had only fleetingly been caught by cameras. The special effects programming team could surely handle inserting the Jolly Green Giant of advertising lore and the ten-foot version of Alice in Wonderland, but the film was not going to become a cartoon—the producer had already nixed that idea.

Mr. Spike Stewart, the producer, a short, fat man with horn-rimmed glasses was fanatical about his vision. He waved his hands when he pitched the vision to Mirabile, and he spoke like a man possessed, "This film has to have the look and feel of the fantastic book. Nothing else will do. Look, Victor, I don't care that we've never done anything like this before. We start shooting in thirty days. You have four weeks to find the location. Find me a location for giants, or I'll fire you and get another location manager who will."

Being threatened constantly was part of his job, so Mirabile weathered the blast and stated deadpan his practical requirements, "I'll need to do some traveling. Will the budget support that?"

The producer had heard plenty of excuses, but he had a film to produce. He was worried about making his deadlines. So in a rising fury of excitement, he acceded, "I'll approve all your travel as long as you deliver a location—or more than one location—that will work. Use your imagination and scour the world. Ask yourself where you would feel at home, and find that place for my film."

Victor nodded sullenly and left the producer's office, careful to duck through the exit door because the doorway was a mere six and a half feet high. Victor was 6-foot-11 ½ inches tall. He was like the giants who would act in the movie, but he had barely missed the cut, which was seven feet tall.

The producer bragged that he had signed contracts with the twenty true giants on the earth for this film, with no disrespect meant to Ole Edvart Rolvaag. He had even signed the Turk Sultan Kosen, the tallest man living at 8-foot-3, for his cast. One reason the producer had chosen Victor as his location manager was that Victor was the tallest location manager on record.

Victor had created a list of the ten places on earth where he thought those afflicted with pituitary gigantism like him would feel at home. He resolved to check out those locations and decide which would be the best setting for the film. His logic was compelling: he would scout the regions where the historical giants were said to live.

At the top of his list was the area of the Himalayan Mountains along the border of Nepal and Tibet where the Yeti were rumored to live. Also called the Abominable Snowman, the Yeti was a huge creature of cryptozoology that inhabited the land of snow, fog, and ice at the top of the world.

In order to scout the area, Victor hired sherpas to guide him through the mountains. They found, tucked in a deep valley among glaciers a place of strange warmth and tropical greenery, watered by snowmelt and heated by brilliant sunshine which sometimes penetrated the rising mist that hovered over the valley in all weathers.

The sherpas refused to go with Victor into the valley because they feared the legendary figures that inhabited it. The lead sherpa spoke for all, "We won't proceed one more foot. The creatures that inhabit this region will kill us all. You go ahead if you like. We'll wait here until you return or until one week has passed, whichever comes first." He snorted and crossed his arms in defiance.

The other sherpas imitated his gestures in solidarity with their leader. Then they all sat down on the ground and began talking among themselves.

Their stubborn actions didn't faze Victor because he was on a mission, so he boldly entered the valley alone. The further he ventured, the warmer the climate became. Freezing temperatures became temperate at first, and then tropical. Victor was obsessed with achieving his goal, so as the temperature changed and the setting turned from ice and snow to green and balmy, he took off his heavy winter clothing, garment by garment.

Not long after he entered the green area, he had shed his arctic clothing and began to sweat. He was exhausted by his exertions in the thin atmosphere but excited by the prospect of the location for the film. The green meadow and scrub turned to forest. Soon, Victor was almost naked in the heat of the forest, but he didn't mind because he thought he had found the place that his producer and director would both endorse. He congratulated himself on his luck and intuition. The sherpas had remained behind, but his insight and initiative about the place proved superior to the sherpas' fears and obduracy.

Victor found a clearing next to a wide, clear pool with a waterfall running down to fill it, and a stream running from the pool into the forest. He tested the water and found it gelid and good to drink.

While he was admiring the scene, Victor saw three huge figures emerge from the forest across the pool from where he was standing. He froze in shock because he had never witnessed anything like them. The figures looked human, but they were covered with hair, and they must have been ten feet tall. Victor knew they were Yeti. He also knew he was experiencing a first. The creatures knew he was watching them, but they didn't flee or try to hide. Instead, they seemed to enjoy having him observe them as they frolicked.

Without hesitation, they all dived into the pool and swam about playing in the water. One of the creatures beckoned to him to join them. Victor was tempted, but he was mindful of the sherpas' warnings. Instead of jumping in the water, he only waved and shook his head. Was he really seeing a group of Yetis playing in the water before him? While he stood next to the frigid water, frozen with shock, he felt a breath on his neck.

He had no other warning before strong hands grabbed him from behind and led him to the edge of the pool. Terrified, he struggled, but he could do nothing to break their hold. Before he could process what was happening, they pulled his remaining clothing away and flung him into the freezing water. He was shocked by the cold, and he tried to clamber out of the pool as fast as possible. The giants who had importuned him to swim ranged all along the shore, and they gestured and mumbled to each other as he stepped toward his clothes all red and shivering.

One of the Yeti walked right up to him and hugged him in its arms, rubbing him all over. The giant felt warm, and Victor realized that it was drying him off with its fur. The creature's breath was sweetly licorice. When the creature had dried him thoroughly, it stood back while he dressed. The others were curious and began to poke him and turn him this way and that. The Yeti that had dried Victor off shoved them away protectively and took his hand. It led him into the forest with the others following behind them.

Victor's head was spinning; he didn't know what to think. On the one hand, he was actually experiencing real Yetis in their natural habitat. This aroused and excited him on account of his mission. On the other hand, he had no idea what the Yetis intended to do to him. He had visions of becoming their feast.

The Yeti village was large enough to house thirty Yeti families. All the dwellings were tall, with enormous entries with varying doorway heights. Yetis wandered through the village doing their daily routines, and children played together until they saw the outsider. Then they gathered around and pointed at the stranger. A boy and girl reached out to stroke Victor's hairless skin. He was making a mental record of the array of the huts and their construction. He tried to assess where he was being led and why.

Victor realized that his escort was a female Yeti and that she had her own dwelling near the center of the village. Nearby hers was the largest habitation, perhaps that of the Yeti chief. As the female Yeti drew Victor toward her dwelling, the chief and chieftainess, both larger than all the other Yetis, emerged from their enormous dwelling and watched silently.

The female led Victor into the interior of her hut and gestured for him to be seated on the floor, which had been covered with cut rushes. She fed Victor a creamy liquid and watched him closely while he drank. Victor tried to communicate with the Yeti, but it was no use. She did not seem to mind the fact that they only sat and looked at each other.

It was not long before Victor heard noises in the square outside the dwelling. He stood and walked outside to discover that the whole village had assembled to gawk at the stranger that the female Yeti had brought home. The chief and chieftainess came forward to parlay with the female Yeti. An argument ensued with both the chief and the female, gesturing wildly at Victor. The chief finally said something and looked like he would strike the female, but the chieftainess intervened and pushed the chief back. Then the chieftainess hugged the female Yeti and pointed to Victor and gestured to the female's dwelling.

Victor suddenly understood what was going on. The female Yeti was the daughter of the chief, who did not approve of her being with a human. The chieftainess, who was the female Yeti's mother, acquiesced with her daughter's wishes to be with the male of her choice.

Victor was horrified by what was happening. He saw right away that he would end up the husband of the female if he did not act immediately. His brain reeled at the criticality of doing just the right thing lest he be killed. He did not want to insult or anger the Yeti community because he still harbored the hope that he could use the location for the film.

He bowed to the chief and gestured that he would be departing. The chieftainess and the female Yeti stood forth and objected. The chief, however, saw his opportunity to get rid of the interloping human. He evidently ordered a group of four young male Yetis to escort Victor back where he came from. One of these Yetis went into the female's dwelling and brought out the rest of Victor's clothes. The Yeti was inclined to keep the clothes as a souvenir. Victor appealed this decision in sign language with the chief, who gestured that Victor should be given back his clothing.

As an afterthought, Victor took out his cellphone and photographed the Yetis and the village with its camera. Later he found this was an inspiration. The hundreds of pictures were the evidence of what he had seen in the Yeti paradise. The Yetis had no idea that he was taking pictures, so they were not self-conscious before his camera.

Finally, the chief and chieftainess gestured for Victor to depart. He was relieved because he did not know their intentions, but still feared they might decide to eat him. Worse, he thought the chief's daughter might rescind the chief's decision to let him go. Victor thought she was desperate for a mate, and he was her choice for that purpose. To be sure he actually left their territory, the chief gestured to a group of males to escort him back where he came from.

Victor didn't look back as he followed the four young Yetis back past the communal pool to the edge of the forest where the path up the side of the glacier lay. Victor put on his cold weather clothing and climbed back up the grade. When he looked back, he saw that the four males were waving to him. They were apparently glad to see him go. As they receded in the mist, Victor thought there still might be a chance to use their home as one of his locations.

He waved back at them, then trekked back to the sherpas' encampment. The sherpas gathered around him to hear about his adventure. Victor decided they probably would not understand what he had been through. He told them that he had been confronted by fearful creatures and only barely escaped.

He told them, "I was lucky. I found what I was looking for, and I wasn't harmed. We should now retrace our steps to your village, so no harm befalls you."

The sherpas had a thousand questions for him, but they had abandoned his quest at the crucial time. He did not think they deserved to know the truth. After they had importuned him without result, the sherpas packed for their journey home. Without a word during their descent, they returned to the sherpas' village.

Victor took stock of what he had seen in the green valley of the Yetis. He reviewed the photos he had taken with his cellphone. He decided that one option he could present was to recreate what he had seen in the green Yeti valley in a stage set made from his photos, but he knew he had to have other options as well.

Victor's second venue was in the vicinity of Mica Mountain in Canada near the British Columbia/Alberta border and the little town of Tete Juan Cache, where the sightings of a female Sasquatch figure had been reported almost fifty years prior. He made contact with a contemporary Canadian cryptozoologist named April Roe, a Canadian Indian known for her expertise with Big Foot sightings, and he paid for her guide services to the best location.

"Mr. Mirabile, people joke that I'm part Sasquatch. I can't prove that I'm not. Look how tall I am. I have a number of likely locations for you to explore. I've camped out in this region all my life. I can honestly say that I've sighted Sasquatches on dozens of occasions throughout the Mica Mountain area. I can help you, but I have to know our constraints."

"Let's pick the optimal location and focus on that. I want the highest probability of a sighting, but I also want to see where the Sasquatches actually live. That would be the ideal film location. Just seeing a Sasquatch wouldn't give us much more than the folklore."

"Well, the best chance of finding the location if you've got limited time is at the center of a range of recent Sasquatch sightings. They're all around Mica Mountain. I've plotted them on this geodesic map. We'll hike there and camp for the night."

Victor and April pored over the map until he understood her logic and the route. They drove until they ran out of paved road. Then they pulled on their backpacks and set out hiking up a steady grade with scree.

In view of Mica Mountain, Victor and his guide pitched camp and built a fire. Seated opposite each other on either side of the fire, Victor and April discussed the background and lore of Sasquatch. The female guide told Victor that she was the granddaughter of the workman named William Roe, who had actually encountered a Sasquatch. Her mother, she said, had drawn a likeness of the creature, but it was discredited because some of the features in her drawing did not correspond to William Roe's published descriptions. For example, the creature's long neck and flowing hair were not in line with his descriptions.

While she described her grandfather's encounter as it had been recounted to her by both her grandfather and her mother, she looked up, and her eyes grew wide in the firelight. She cautioned Victor to remain still and silent with a hand gesture. Victor sensed activity behind him, and two large, hairy and enormous figures sat down cross-legged on either side of him. As if this was the most natural thing in the world, his guide continued her story including the two Sasquatches who had joined them as if their entrance had been planned.

The creatures evidently liked the lilt of her voice. They murmured along as if they were mimicking what they heard. They laughed and jostled Victor as if he were one of them. One Sasquatch was evidently female, but her chest extended lower on her body and was larger than in humans. The other figure was male, monstrously muscular and very smelly. Victor slowly raised his cellphone and took a selfie including his new friends with his camera. At the same time, his guide took a picture with her cellphone camera of the three figures across the fire from her.

The Sasquatches remained seated for a long while after the photo session. Then, just as suddenly as they had appeared, they rose quietly and vanished into the forest. Victor and his guide talked at length about their experience. They were both thrilled and humbled by their close contact with the Sasquatches. Even after the fire died to embers, they talked about having been the first to see this Sasquatch couple.

In the morning, they looked for signs and footprints of the Sasquatches, but they found none. They checked their phone pictures again, and sure enough, they showed what they had experienced. The guide noted that the background of her group picture was somewhat blurred.

"The picture might contain figures in the shadowy background. Perhaps a specialist could improve what actually lurks in the background," she said, sounding hopeful.

They shared their pictures and then set out on the trails to discover where the Sasquatches lived.

They looked for two days but found no sign of a Sasquatch dwelling. They passed nearby an ancient silver mine with danger signs warning of possible cave-ins. On a hunch, Victor decided to enter the boarded mouth of the mine and descend underground.

"Look, Mr. Mirabile, if you want to go underground risking your life, that's your affair. You're the customer, so you've got to be right. I hope you won't mind if I stay on the surface and wait while you descend in the unknown."

"Look, I've heard all this before from other guides who are too chicken to explore things that no one has explored before. If you must sit here and sulk while I make my discovery, so be it. You remain on the surface while I explore the mine. If I don't return within the next twenty-four hours, just inform the authorities that a rescue is necessary.

"I'm reluctant, but, as I said, you're my customer. Your wish is my command."

She pitched camp near the entrance while Victor broke through the brittle, rotten boards and ventured into the mine using his flashlight as he went.

The opening of the mine was narrow, but it gradually widened into a cavern with a dark pool at its center. Along the walls of the cavern were many hollows, large enough for large animals to inhabit. Victor shined his flashlight into the hollows one by one, taking note of the dark surroundings.

In the third hollow, he found two sleeping Sasquatches with their arms around each other. Thankfully, his light did not awaken them. He continued to the other hollows and found sixteen other couples fast asleep. He did not have enough light inside the cavern to take pictures, but with his flashlight shining, he tried to take a few cell phone pictures anyway.

Victor stumbled and dropped his flashlight, and for a moment, the light went out. He was terrified because he was blind and in total darkness. He dropped to his knees to feel the ground for the flashlight and heard a swish above his head. Terrified, he dropped to lie prone on the ground and rolled his body. He felt hands groping to find him, and one enormous foot nudged his side as it shuffled on the earthen floor of the cave.

Victor finally found his flashlight, but he had the good sense not to turn it on right away. Instead, he listened and tried to adjust his vision to see as much as possible in the dark without assistance. After a while, he decided to slither and crawl back to the entrance of the mine. He told himself that if he came to the pool, he could keep on the edge of it and follow it back to the entrance. He heard heavy breathing and the shuffling of bare feet. Then he heard low murmuring.

Not sure what was happening in the cave, he decided to leave right then. The farther he crawled, the more distant the shuffling sounded, and finally, he found the upslope he had used to descend into the cavern. He looked up in the direction of the entrance but saw nothing but black. He started up the incline, feeling his way in the darkness. He felt a hairy foot. The foot moved. A Sasquatch walked down the incline right past his prone body on the grade. Then another Sasquatch passed him, and a third. He was sweating he was so frightened. He was worried they might grab him and take him back into their lair. Yet he continued up the incline ever so slowly. He saw a slice of daylight that must signify that the entrance was near. He deduced that the Sasquatches had been moving away from the light into the darkness.

On a hunch, he rolled on his back and aimed his cellphone camera down the incline up which he had crawled. He snapped on his flashlight and took the picture at the same time. Then he extinguished the flashlight and clambered to his feet to run toward the light. He kept hitting the walls and stumbling on the uneven mine flooring, but he managed to make it all the way to the entrance.

As he broke into the sunlight, he saw his guide was patiently roasting marshmallows on sticks over a low fire. She seemed not to be surprised to see him. In fact, she seemed pleased he had emerged uninjured. She smiled and offered him one of the marshmallows.

"Well?" she asked ironically. She paused to let him tell his story.

"April, I've been through a kind of hell down there. It was intense, but I found what I wanted. As I suspected, the mine is where the Sasquatches live. They're in there now, but they won't come up into the light. I took pictures. Let's look at them together."

Among the pictures, were the dim outlines of the enclosures within the cavern. The final pictures were of dozens of Sasquatches looking in his direction when he had pointed his flashlight and pushed and held the button on his cellphone. The creatures did not try to catch or threaten him.

"An entire city of Sasquatches! This is phenomenal," April said, her eyes wide open with excitement.

"Yes, and they live as couples just as we humans do. They only venture forth at night from a place that has been protected by signs made by humans. If they had wanted to harm me, they had their chance. They did no harm."

"So you have what you came for?"

"I think so, but I'm not sure." Victor was thinking not only of his producer but also of the Sasquatches themselves.

"Why is that?"

"The people I work for want to make a movie about giants. Well, we found a whole underground bevy of giants, but I'm not sure they'd appreciate a film crew setting up in their cavern. And I am sure that the film crew would not like working underground. Anyway, you've earned your bonus, and I'll pay you. In the meantime, I'll ask you not to mention our find because that might ruin the film. Can you hold off announcing our discovery until the film first appears? I'll pay you another bonus if you do."

They agreed on terms, and Victor sent April Roe copies of the pictures he had taken with his cellphone. He decided to return to report on his progress to the film's producer.

"Well, Victor, I hope you've got good news for me. It's only been two weeks, but we'd like to push our production schedule at least a week. So what have you got for me?"

Victor patiently explained what he had found in the Himalayas. He showed the producer his pictures of the Yetis in the misty green valley. He waxed eloquent about how a set might be built from the images in his cellphone pictures.

"I like what I have seen and heard. What else have you got for me?"

Victor then dove into what he had found near Mica Mountain in Canada. He showed the producer his pictures of the Sasquatches in the cavern and their dwellings in the sides of the interior regions of the mine. He spoke of the creatures' non-hostile and nocturnal natures and their habit of living in couples just as humans do.

"Victor, you've certainly had an interesting experience with this. I'm not sure we could get a film crew to go into that cavern in the old mine, and no one can say what those Sasquatches will do if they are invaded. As with your Yetis, we might be able to create their dwelling in the studio. So do you have anything else for me?"

"I plan to explore two more venues, one in the taiga of Russia and the other in the jungles of Venezuela. If I hurry, I can see both before our original deadline has passed. We could economize by my reporting virtually instead of in person."

"I'm not interested in economy right now. I'm interested in time, which we don't have much of. Come with me for a minute and see what I've got brewing here."

The producer walked Victor to a set that had been dedicated to the production of Valley of the Giants. In the middle of the set was a giant beanstalk.

"See that beanstalk, Victor? It's from Jack and the Beanstalk, the story that every kid knows and loves. Here comes Jack, who is a midget we hired—in fact, he's the smallest man in the world as recorded in the Guinness Book of World Records. Over there in the green face makeup and green clothing is the giant of the story. He's the tallest man in the world by the same standard."

"He looks a lot like the Jolly Green Giant in the ads."

"Yes, he does. That's intentional. The cartoon figure will be inserted elsewhere in the film, and the kids will like the fact that it is bigger than life. Our animators are working on the valley for the Jolly Green Garden now. Maybe they can work in some details from your pictures of Yeti City? I just don't know. Artists are prima donnas, don't you know?"

Confused by what was happening, Victor surveyed the work the animators were doing. He saw the outsized imagery and the familiar figures from his childhood with their basic colors and exaggerated expressions.

"As for Yetis, just take a look at our two-dozen-odd extras that'll be Yetis. They'll be doing a choreographed dance routine that'll knock your socks off. They don't look much like your Yetis because, well, no one's really seen a real Yeti, have they? With our release scheduled within twelve months, we haven't time to get the word out and burn it into the imaginations of the audience in time for the initial showing. So we'll have to go with what we have already. I'm thinking the huts could play somewhere, but not the real Yeti figures."

"What about the action figures?"

"We had to go to Korea with our designs for those two months ago. They're baked right in just as the Sasquatch figures are."

"So the pictures I took of Sasquatches won't be used either?" Victor was dejected because all his hard work had been basically done for nothing.

"'Fraid not. Look, Victor, I didn't send you out to get bona fide pictures of cryptozoological figures, did I? You're the location manager. You're not in casting. Let me show you what we've got for Sasquatches from central casting. Come over here."

"You call these Sasquatches? They're way too short and a mile too wide. The bodies of the females are all wrong." Victor was indignant and frustrated.

"Who cares, Victor? They're what the kids will know from all the nonsense that's been shown them on the early Saturday cartoon shows. Speaking of cartoons, we've got a whole line of giants from the comic books inserted in the show as well."

"Let me guess. The Incredible Hulk?" He was irritated and being ironic.

"You got it! We've inserted the Hulk in his enraged mode, and he's one of the action figures by special arrangement with the comic's syndicate." The producer was proud of himself for being creative in a pinch, though Victor thought the idea was beyond ridiculous.

"I've got an inspiration. Want to hear it?"

"Frankly, no. Victor, just get my locations fast. I mean in one week. From what you've just seen, you can tell what we need. So get moving and report back in seven days with what you've found. You've never failed this studio before. You won't fail us now. I know it."

The producer's voice had a threatening edge. Victor's spirit sagged under the immense weight that had been put on his shoulders. He knew he would be fired if anything in his performance was found wanting.

"Oh, one thing more while you're here. You have five brothers, so I'm told. They're all about your size, aren't they? I thought so. When this thing gets rolling into production, I want a group shot in costume so your family can be part of the show."

"We'll see about that. I'm off now. I'll be back as planned," Victor said as he stormed out of the meeting.

Victor understood from this meeting that the location for Valley of the Giants had nothing to do with real giants at all. It had to do with the make-believe world of motion pictures and comics. He did not immediately take off for foreign parts. Instead, he thought about the popular imagination and how the kids of today had been trained to like and to associate with make-believe. Victor went to a few films that struck the popular fancy and did research on the locations that had been used for those films. He also talked with some friends in Hollywood, especially Fred Allston, a director looking for work and thus having a few minutes to spare for his friend.

"So which locations do you prefer above all others, Fred?" Victor asked when he got him on the phone.

"For what kind of film, Victor?" Fred was a director with a vivid imagination alongside a yearning for perfection.

"It doesn't matter. Where do you like to shoot your films for any reason at all?"

"I like Bora Bora for the water and the drinks. I like Zimbabwe for the wild animals—if there are any wild animals there anymore—and the safari culture. I like Belize, except for the black flies, darn them. I like the Grand Canyon because I'm from Arizona."

"You're a big help!" Victor's sarcasm was palpable.

"So go ask someone else, location man. Don't waste any more of my time. I'm busy looking to get hired," Fred laughed and hung up, knowing the frustration Victor was feeling.

Victor canvassed his other friends and associates about what the producers and directors wanted to see these days. He looked through a dozen travel magazines to see what was hot in the editors' minds. Then he decided to see a few monster movies with enormous figures moving through fantasy landscapes. The monsters were not humanoid giants, but they gave the impression of gigantic figures anyway. He liked the Return of the Creature, particularly, even better than The Creature from the Black Lagoon.

Victor tried to imagine the creature as a human-shaped monster. He thought of the pools he had encountered in the Himalayas and the underground mine. He thought of the gigantic figure of St. Christopher, pictured as a giant carrying the tiny figure of Jesus across deep waters in some religious paintings.

Suddenly, he had a revelation: he would boldly go where everyone seemed to be going these days—to New Zealand and to Thailand. He booked his flights and girded his loins for a whirlwind expedition. He would not stay long in either place. In fact, he only wanted to verify what he had already seen.

You never knew what was real and what had been made by graphic design personnel in a film. So he scouted the forest setting for Lord of the Rings and then the island setting for The Man with the Golden Gun. When he returned to the States, he went to work with one of the Imagineering experts at the studio. The two worked for forty-eight hours and produced a mini-pilot for the producer.

As soon as everyone sat down to watch in the private theater, Victor smiled, knowing he found what the producer was looking for.

"I'm not going to take up much of your time today. I've made a pilot that includes your locations for Valley of the Giants. I think we're ready. Play it, Sam!" Victor was all hype now. He was in his pitch mode trying to make his enthusiasm infectious.

A producer always enjoys sitting in a small, private theater. In fact, many producers live in small, private theaters. They only emerge long enough to shake a few hands, sign or deposit checks, eat and relieve themselves. This producer for *Valley of the Giants* was no exception. All ten seats in the theater were filled for this instant production by Victor Mirabile. When the film started, the John Williams' opening music for *Star Wars* played. The New Zealand landscape shown in *Lord of the Rings* was shown with an overlay of the title *Valley of the Giants*. The audience sat up straight in their chairs in anticipation.

Then in quick succession, the film continued with cuts complete with their original music from the critical monster scenes of *Mothra, Return of the Creature,* and *Jurassic Park.* Finally, clips showed the James Bond film figures *Nick Nack* and *Jaws*. The final image was of him smiling with all his metal teeth gleaming. The traditional James Bond denouement music played while the sequence faded to white, and again the title *Valley of the Giants* filled the screen before the final fade to white.

When the lights came on, the producer sat brooding, with his hands folded in a steeple. Everyone awaited the impresario's verdict. Finally, he smiled broadly and said, "I like the settings. If only Richard Dawson Kiel were still alive, I'd find a way to work him into the film!"

"Perhaps there's a way to insert his image into the film graphically."

"Excellent idea, Victor. Make a note of that Becky. So, Victor, let's schedule our venues and get rolling. I want an Assistant Location Manager at each venue starting tomorrow or at latest the next. Advance work, envelopes of cash, the works. Make it all happen. Meanwhile, if you've got a minute, I'd like to show you a few details I'm working on."

The giants who had assembled for the viewing departed from the small theater nodding and muttering among themselves. Finally, Mr. Stewart and Becky, his Executive Assistant, remained with Victor.

"Becky, will you roll our sequences, please."

On the screen, a fanfare from Copeland was followed by the image of the Jolly Green Giant, who with a wave of his hand introduced the rustic dance of the Yetis, whose choreography was lifted straight from the great age of stage musicals. This was followed by a clip showing the studio footage of the story of Jack and the Beanstalk, featuring the tallest and shortest males on the planet. An antic dance of the Sasquatches came next. Wilt Chamberlain appeared talking with two children, each of whom was one-third of the size of the towering basketball player. The finale was the march through New York City by the Stay Puft Marshmallow Man in Ghostbusters.

Mr. Stewart asked, "Well, Victor, what do you think?"

"I think it's going to take a lot of work to mash everything together into a compelling film. Also, I'm not sure Mr. Tubby Soft-Squeeze belongs in a film about giants. Maybe you should consider the Statue of Liberty from the other Ghostbusters film?"

"Maybe you're right, Victor. By the way, while you were gone, we took a message from a woman claiming she was your guide up in Canada on the Sasquatch thing in the mine. She asked that you give her a ring when you got the chance. Right now, we've gotta go. Come on, Becky, let's get over to the studio for that group picture."

"Hi, Victor. I just wanted to call about what we saw here in Canada."

"Yes, April. I'm sorry I was out when you called. I just got back from overseas. What did you want to say?"

"I really don't think we should disturb the Sasquatches that we found. It wouldn't be right for us to blow their cover or invade their space. Do you think you can convince your film people not to use the mine venue as a shooting location after all?" April was deeply concerned because she knew how hard Victor had worked to find the perfect Sasquatch location for his film.

Victor took a deep breath. Under the circumstances, he could make April happy without lying to her.

"April, providentially, we won't use the Mica Mountain venue in the film at all. You're free to publicize the location or not after we release our film."

"Victor, I won't be publicizing the Sasquatches. They have enough trouble staying away from predatory humans as it is. It's a miracle they've survived as long as they have. Imagine having to live in an underground cavern all your life."

"Coming from Hollywood, I can more than imagine that. Anyway, thanks again for being my guide."

"Don't mention it, Victor. Come again anytime. You're the kindest, gentlest giant I've ever known."

"It's good of you to mention that, April, but in the land I live in, I don't even make the cut as a giant. You might make it, just, how tall are you again?"

"Hahaha. Seven-feet one inch in my stocking feet."

"I'll see what I can do to arrange an audition for you."

"Really?"

"Maybe. I'll be in touch."

Lorelei

Lorelei Jenssen was not the most beautiful woman in the world, but she had a most unusual singing voice. When she sang, young men were enthralled, and young women were smitten with envy. She had a reputation for luring suitors who uniformly met misfortune. Over forty handsome men had already died when the famous painter Ronald Stevens decided to try his luck at winning Lorelei's hand. He chose to do so by indirect, devious means, and that is probably why he lived to tell his story.

Stevens was a remarkable painter generally, but as a portraitist he was unparalleled. Beautiful women flocked to his studio to audition for his paintings because a "Stevens Girl" need never worry about attaining fame. Stevens' paintings of women caught the popular imagination that made the advertising moguls salivate. When he painted a "Stevens Girl" beside a product, the sales of that product were suddenly phenomenal. The female subject normally went on to be the poster girl for other products. A few became major actresses.

Ronald knew that he had developed a winning combination. He was in the prime of his professional life. He wanted to find a woman who could stand beside him in the heat of his fame as an equal. Lorelei Jenssen was his pick. He did not rush into the fray. Instead, he bided his time. He studied her history. He recognized patterns others might have missed because he was an artist, and as such, he knew how illusions could be used to trick the mind and heart.

Lorelei's beauty was a matter of illusions that he as a painter could capture on canvas: her copper hair, her flawless white skin, her sparkling blue eyes, the graceful form of her hands, every part of her he sketched from photographs. The more he studied her, the more he loved her and the more he was intrigued by her power over him.

Ronald refused to be rushed to engage the woman even though he felt drawn to her by powerful, invisible arms. Whenever the impulse to rush was about to overcome, the painter went back to painting his matchless subject from her graven images. He finally brought his studies of her parts into a single, integrated figure.

He had a commission to paint a figure for billboards alongside a Rolls Royce automobile, so he decided to use his painting of Lorelei with minute, but significant changes. No one but she would realize that she was the subject. She would be driven wild with the thought that anyone would study her so closely without knowing her and painting her from life.

The Rolls Royce people loved the picture of the woman with their car. Billboard versions of this new "Stevens Girl" went vertical all over England and the United States. In Times Square, the mystery girl standing beside the exquisite automobile stopped vehicular and pedestrian traffic from every vantage.

Among those who became fascinated with the beautifully painted woman was Lorelei Jenssen. She could not believe that the model for the image was anyone other than herself.

The figure did not have her copper hair. Instead, her hair was red. The figure did not have Lorelei's flashing blue eyes. Instead, her eyes were hazel. However, the figure's proportions were clearly hers, and the bone structure was a perfect match.

One of her more recent suitors remarked that she had changed her hair color and worn contact lenses to fool the public. He had become so enamored of the Times Square billboard, that he stepped off the curb to see it from a different angle and was struck by a taxi and died.

Lorelei was no shy violet, and she had a brace of litigious lawyers dogging her heels. She went to Ronald Stevens' studio to demand satisfaction. She wanted him to confess that she had been the model for his Rolls Royce billboard ads. He sent an assistant to the door with a prepared message.

"Hello, my name is Kevin Angland, the painter's assistant. Mr. Stevens is doing a life study now with his newest model. She is the beauty who is featured in the Rolls Royce ads. He simply cannot be bothered with distractions."

When he said this, his nose rose in the air slightly, and he affected a snobby, officious attitude as he continued speaking.

"You can't imagine the number of women who have called claiming to be the mystery woman in his work. Do you have a card? I'll give it to him when he breaks free from his painting. I can't say when that will be, though, since he often paints straight through the afternoon into the night."

Lorelei was not amused at the contrived charade, but she had a game of her own to play.

"I won't leave my card for him, but I'll be at the Rhine Café downtown singing on each of the next three nights. If he wants to see me, he can go there after ten o'clock. I'll recognize him from his publicity pictures. I'll come to his table and sing a special song for him."

She gave Kevin a look that reduced the man to imbecility. He was totally struck by her beauty and her voice. He might have followed her down the stairs and all the way home if Stevens had not warned him about the woman's siren charms.

Ronald did not go to the Rhine Café the first night. He sent Kevin with a pair of earplugs to guard him against the beautiful voice and gave him a bouquet of red roses to present to the singer. Lorelei appeared on stage in a setting that looked like a crag over a river. She wore a dress that shimmered and spangles with her copper hair like stars. She was the only light in the room when she started singing, and the audience was spellbound by her act. Included in her act, were five male dancers who were drawn too close to the treacherous rocks beneath her and perished trying to reach her.

Kevin was affected by the woman's visual beauty, but he did not hear her siren's song because he wore the earplugs. Lorelei came down from her crag and navigated to the small table where Kevin was sitting. He gave her the roses, which she accepted as if they were part of her act. She distributed the roses to each of the other guests before she resumed her position on her crag. She kept her eyes on Kevin while she shifted into another song. As the stage went dark, Kevin saw that she was perplexed that her singing had not had its usual effect, at least on him.

Kevin returned to the painter after the show and told him exactly what had transpired. Ronald praised the young man for his performance and told him that they would go together to see Lorelei's act the following night.

All the next day, the painter worked on his gift for Lorelei. It was a painting of the woman exactly as Kevin had described her on the rocky crag over the Rhine. Kevin reviewed the painting, saying that it closely approximated what he saw the previous evening. When it was time, the two men took another dozen roses and the painting to the Rhine Café. They also both wore earplugs.

The Lorelei's act went precisely as it had the prior night. The singer was gorgeous in her spangling gown. The male figures were drawn fatally to the rocks where they died. Lorelei came down from her crag and made straight for the table where Ronald and Kevin sat. She sang with such expression that both men felt the power of her presence. Still, they sat unmoved.

When her song ended, and everyone rose to applaud her, Kevin gave her the roses. Ronald Stevens raised the painting and tore aside the fabric that covered it. Lorelei was fascinated by the image. She had to shake her head and struggle to keep her composure to finish her act.

She distributed the roses and moved back to her crag and sang the finale as the darkness fell. Ronald saw that the woman's gaze was fixed on the painting. As quickly as possible after the lights went up, Ronald and his assistant left the Rhine Café and hailed a cab.

"Do you plan to go to the Rhine Café again tonight, sir?" Kevin seemed very much smitten by her and hoped his boss would say yes.

"No, Kevin. Tonight, I want Lorelei Jenssen to feel my absence. If you want to go to see the show, feel free to do so. I'd advise that you take the earplugs if you do."

That night, Kevin did attend the show. As on the two previous nights, he took a dozen roses. He wore the earplugs. Lorelei's act had changed. One of the five men who were lured to the rocks by her song was wearing ear mufflers that indicated he could not hear the siren song. He survived the tragic consequences suffered by the others.

Angry, Lorelei came down from her crag and tore the man's ear mufflers off. She continued to Kevin's table and pulled out his earplugs. She took the roses and distributed them around the room. Then she turned and sang the song of her finale as she ascended the crag. The fifth man, who was now without his ear mufflers, perished on the rocks. Kevin, who finally heard the siren song, was pierced to the heart with the sad music.

When the act ended, and the lights went up, the painter's assistant sat as if transfixed in his chair. He loved Lorelei as he had loved no other woman. She came still in her costume to his table and asked Kevin whether he would escort her home. Stuttering, he said he would do so gladly.

The next morning when he went to his studio, Ronald saw that a note had been thrust under the studio door. The note was from Kevin, who wrote that he would not be coming back—ever. Ronald took the note to the john and burned it in the sink. He was upset because Kevin was not coming back. He was not, however, surprised.

He then began working on a new painting, very large, improving on the small painting he had taken to the Rhine Café. Because he had seen Lorelei's act, he was able to recreate the scene with detailed fidelity. He captured Lorelei's face during her finale when she confidently sang the song that would bring all males into thrall.

Ronald worked and reworked her expression until her image replicated what he assumed must be the effect of her singing. The next afternoon, after making the final touches on the painting, he telephoned his agent Bert Stine to drop by to see his new work.

"Bert, I want your opinion about this painting. I'm on the knife edge about it. On the one hand, I think the painting stands alone as a work of art. On the other hand, I believe the painting could have a potent sales message for just the right product."

Without further preamble, Ronald pulled aside the coverlet that hung over the painting and watched his agent closely. Bert Stine was dumbstruck by the beauty of the image. He rushed right up to the painting and was about to touch it when Ronald stopped him.

"Don't touch it, please, Bert. The painting's still wet."

"Sorry, Ronald. She's so real, I feel impelled to touch her."

"What do you think, then?" He was genuinely interested and anxious to know what Bert thought.

"I think this painting will sell anything in the world."

"Why don't you find me a customer who will use this image as the Rolls Royce people used the last one."

"I'm mentally going through my A-list as we speak. I'll make a few calls. In the meantime, don't make a single change to this painting. I don't want another brush mark or accent. This is—perfect!" Bert hurried out of the studio to make his calls. Ronald Stevens pulled the drape back over the painting. He heard a knock on his studio door.

When he answered the door, a man from the Western Union handed him a telegram that read as follows: "I simply must have the picture that you painted of me. Meet me at the Rhine Café with the picture at two o'clock this afternoon. I'll make it worth your while. Signed: Lorelei Jenssen."

Ronald laughed. He wrapped the small painting that Lorelei had glimpsed during her act. He used expensive gift paper, adding a ribbon and a bow. He took a cab and arrived at the Rhine Café at precisely two o'clock. Lorelei was seated at a small table near the back of the café. Seated next to her was Kevin, who could not keep his eyes off the woman.

"Mr. Stevens, I'm glad you decided to come." She rose and walked toward him.

"I've brought the painting. It's a gift for you. Please take it." He handed her the gift-wrapped painting and watched her as she greedily ripped off the ribbon, bow, and paper. She looked at the painting as if she wanted to devour it with her eyes. Ronald saw that she was as smitten by the painting as Kevin was of her.

"Kevin, I surmise that you did not keep your earplugs in place when you went to Lorelei's performance…"

Kevin shook his head from side to side, never taking his eyes off Lorelei. Ronald saw that the man was infatuated in the root sense: he was a fool for love. With her eyes still on her picture, Lorelei addressed Kevin as if he were her servant.

"Kevin, darling, take this painting to my apartment and find a place on the living room wall to hang it. Be a dear and have it up by the time I get home at four. Don't just sit there. Get going. I'm going to talk with the very talented Mr. Stevens in the mean time."

Kevin rose and took the painting from his mistress. He backed away and left the café on his errand.

"Hahaha. Mr. Stevens, will you buy me a drink?" She was glad to be free of her adulator for a few moments. She looked at the brilliant painter as a potentially more worthy conquest.

Knowing how she must feel, Ronald was determined to play his own game. "Ms. Jenssen, why don't we split a bottle of crisp, cold champagne?"

Lorelei signaled for the bartender to uncork a bottle of bubbly and bring it in a bucket of ice with two champagne glasses to her table. The bartender deftly threaded his way through the other guests in the crowded bar hoping for a generous tip for timely service.

"Mr. Stevens, I would like to toast a very fine painter who knows how to make a lady shine in oil." She was stroking him on purpose because the power of his art paralleled the power of her voice.

"Ms. Jenssen, I must have a good subject or, I confess, my art avails little. You are a magnificent specimen." Now he was stroking her ego and causing her to sit up straight in her chair. She could not keep her eyes off his.

"Please call me Lorelei if I may call you Ronald."

"Lorelei, do you intend to make a butler out of my assistant?" He masked his rebuke in a compliment to her attractive power.

"Ronald, he has done that all by himself. I can see why you chose him to serve you. He's so attentive." Lorelei said this offhand as an insult to Kevin as well as a compliment to Ronald's natural superiority to an underling. This implied that she and Ronald were on an equal plane above Kevin.

"Please try not to break his heart." He said this ironically, but she took it seriously.

"That's always the problem, but I don't break hearts, Ronald. Somehow, people become victims all by themselves." She looked down as if to suggest that her powers of attraction were not for her to control.

"At my last count, you've lost forty-one suitors. That can't be entirely accidental." Ronald fired this salvo directly at her, and it might have struck home if she were not convinced of the superiority of her talent over her will.

"I agree it's not accidental, but I don't intend it."

Ronald affected to think about that statement for a moment. Then he addressed her accountability directly. "Did you have any human feelings about any of your suitors?"

"I wasn't particularly interested in any of them. They came to me like moths to a flame. A flame does not intend to do a moth harm, does it?"

"I'm not sure the right comparison is with a moth. Perhaps a praying mantis or a black widow spider would serve the purpose better." Ronald turned the images of predation back upon her. He wanted to see if he could penetrate her air of insouciance.

"I'll not be insulted by you, Ronald. The day is still young, and we're drinking champagne. Let's enjoy each other's company." She sipped her champagne and looked at him seductively over the top of her fluted glass.

"Why were you so interested in having my painting of you?" Ronald was interested in what she would say. She had glib answers for everything else. She did not disappoint.

"I thought you caught me perfectly on canvas. I must admit to vanity, but the likeness was unlike any photograph or painting ever done for me before. Here you painted it without using me as a life model. I found it remarkable. Then I talked with Kevin, and I discover you had a lot of practice sketching my pieces and parts before you composed your painting. You also had Kevin's description to go on. I also think that your Rolls Royce advertisement had something of me in it too."

"When I create, I take things from everything I've seen and admired. Each work is a composite of many elements. Surely you don't have red hair or hazel eyes? When I painted you in your native element on that crag over there, the effect was unique."

"I agree. I think, Ronald, we could be a great team if we worked together."

"What if I said that we'd make a great team if we worked independently? You see, I don't intend to become like Kevin."

Lorelei looked down and fidgeted a little.

"Can I have a cigarette?"

"Of course. Permit me to light it for you." Ronald extended his lighter, and she leaned her cigarette into the flame. She moved her hand gracefully as she removed the cigarette while she looked Ronald over appreciatively.

"So where are we now, Ronald?" she asked with a mischievous smile, thinking she had won the game of repartee.

"I've done another painting of you, much larger than the one Kevin is hanging in your living room right now." This was the bombshell he planned to drop, and she was for a moment dumbstruck. Lorelei's eyes narrowed as she considered the implications.

Her fingers working as if they wanted to grasp something intangible, she asked, breathlessly, "May I see it?"

"It's not ready to be seen yet. I wouldn't want you to see it prematurely." He teased her without mercy now.

"Surely you would want to paint me from the life?" She was jealous that he could paint her from mere description. Perhaps his painting with her as his model might produce even more lustrous results. He decided to take the wind out of her sails.

"You forget that I've seen you in the life. I painted from the memory of my having seen your performance here."

"But you didn't hear me sing. Kevin told me you both wore those earplugs."

"That's true, but an artist can only deal with what he sees. I didn't need to hear you sing to know the power of your song. Your expression told me everything I needed to know about you and your music."

"When can I see the large painting?"

"I will let you know. If we're lucky, it will be within the next week."

The singer and the painter finished their champagne. Lorelei went back to her apartment and found the small painting mounted on her living room wall. She haughtily dismissed Kevin and sat down to admire her image. Kevin went to a nearby bar to drown his sorrows.

Ronald went back to his studio to find a telephone message from Burt Stine on his answering machine. Sammy Nostromo, the casino mogul from Las Vegas, was flying into the city to see the painting of the new Stevens Girl. He had wired one hundred thousand dollars for the right of first refusal on the painting with a minimum price of five million dollars.

Bert picked Sammy up in a limo at the private jet port at La Guardia. They arrived at Stevens' studio at one o'clock in the afternoon and spent one hour examining the painting and talking terms with the painter. Not only was Sammy interested in buying the painting to advertise his casino chain, but he also wanted to hire the subject of the painting for an extravagant new outdoor display for his Siren's Song Café.

Sammy was clearly smitten with the painting. He repeatedly raised his hand to touch it, and only when he signed the purchase papers was he permitted to do so. Then he rubbed his hands all over the image. Bert and Ronald looked at each other with amusement.

Bert's commission for the sale would be thirty percent of the gross price. Ronald could not commit Lorelei for the work Sammy intended for her. He telephoned Lorelei and told her to come to his studio to see the large painting before it was packed and shipped, and to discuss a job opportunity of enormous potential. He advised the singer to arrive in the costume and makeup she used in her act.

When Lorelei Jenssen walked through the studio door, Sammy did a double take and looked from the woman to the picture, and back again.

"Ms. Jenssen, may I introduce Mr. Sammy Nostromo and Mr. Bert Stine. Mr. Nostromo has something to say to you." Ronald saw that Lorelei's costume struck a chord in the casino mogul's heart. The man took the singer's extended hand and raised it to his lips.

"I'm charmed, Ms. Jenssen. I can't believe it. The likeness is perfect—hair, eyes, everything. Ms. Jenssen, I won't beat around the bush. I like what I see. I would like to offer you a permanent singing job in Las Vegas for a million dollars a year. Stine, let's take the limo to a restaurant and talk about this arrangement over lunch. Stevens, you stay here and get my painting ready for shipment. I want that work packed in a museum-quality box and driven across the country for delivery to my casino in four days. I want it insured for ten million dollars."

Sammy and Bert ate a sumptuous feast with white and red wines while Lorelei picked and nibbled at her salad and drank champagne. Sammy waxed eloquent about his vision for Siren's Call Café and told the singer that no one else could possibly do the job.

"Mr. Nostromo, how can you say that? You haven't even heard me sing and act. Why don't you come to the Rhine Café tonight at ten o'clock and see me in my native element? Then if you like the experience, we can get down to terms."

"I'll meet you halfway. I will have my lawyer draw up a contract, and my banker issue a bank check for one million dollars. I'll bring the contract and the check to your café tonight. When you sign the contract, I'll give you the check. We'll fly to Las Vegas tomorrow morning together on my private jet. What do you say to that?"

"I'll drink to that, but I'd also want my houseboy Kevin to accompany us. Will you write that into the contract?"

"Listen, your help is your business, but I will provide you with a luxury suite and three servants of your choice in addition to your millions. Leave your houseboy to fend for himself here in New York."

Lorelei batted her eyes and nodded assent. Sammy liked her ability to cut all ties with her past and start a new life in the desert.

"What about this painter Stevens?"

"Mr. Nostromo, Mr. Ronald Stevens means nothing to me. He did that large painting after seeing me on stage just as you'll see me tonight. Other than that, he's never painted me to the life."

"I'm relieved to know that. From the loving way he represented you, I thought you two must be an item."

"Nothing could be further from the truth."

"I'll look forward to tonight then."

When they finished their meal, the limo dropped Lorelei off at the Rhine Café and Sammy off at the New York office of his law firm. Bert went back to Ronald to tell him the state of play.

"She's going to Vegas with Sammy tomorrow morning. She's dropping everything here—her job, that man Kevin and you. She'll be casino property from now on. Watching her ruthless bargaining, I think she'll fit right in."

"We shall see, Bert. Meanwhile, there's no impediment to my moving right on to my next project. I'll let you know when I have something ready for you to show. Thanks for arranging the meeting with Sammy. If only all our commercial dealings were as straight forward."

That night, Sammy went to experience Lorelei Jenssen at the Rhine Café. He did not use earplugs. He was riveted by the woman's performance. He was so infatuated by her that he had trouble remembering that he had brought a check and a contract.

Lorelei reminded him of his promises, so he delivered the check and the signed contract. He handed her a gold pen to sign the contract and told her to keep the pen as a memento of the occasion. He said the limo would now take her to her apartment. It would return there the next morning at nine o'clock to take her to his private jet.

Lorelei found Kevin camped out at the door to her apartment. He was unutterably sad and looked at her with calf eyes longingly. She looked at him with daggers in her eyes.

"Get lost, wimp. Tomorrow morning I'll be leaving this dump for good. Lucky you won't see me again." She pushed the man aside, unlocked her door, strode into her apartment and slammed the door in his face.

Kevin stood staring at the door for fifteen minutes before he shook his head to come out of his trance and went down to catch a late-night cab to his own apartment. His life had suddenly collapsed around him, and he did not know what he was going to do next.

The next morning, Lorelei Jenssen flew to Las Vegas with Sammy Nostromo. The same moving company that had serviced the pharaoh's relics picked up the large painting and drove away to Nevada.

Confident that one chapter of his painterly life was over now, Ronald turned to his next project, which he envisioned as a mural of the fates. He had done a sketch of the three fatal sisters, Clotho, Lachesis and Atropos, and now he blocked out the large canvas that would support the full-color painting. He had completed the outlines when he heard a knock at his door and found a distraught Kevin outside it.

"Hullo, Kevin, come right in."

"She just left for Las Vegas." He looked disheveled, confused and disappointed.

"I supposed she would have done that. My large painting of her has also gone where she is heading. Don't worry. We haven't seen the last of her. She's casino property now. The Mob is going to make her a poster girl."

"She was so cruel, Ronald. She cut me off, the bitch. I love her."

"Kevin, it's better to let her go. You're luckier than the forty-one formers who actually died for love. Why don't you help me with my new work? It might brighten your spirits."

Kevin took off his coat and pitched in as Ronald's assistant. Within a week, the new painting, called Three Fates, was ready for Bert's appraising eyes.

"Stevens, you've done it again. I'm flabbergasted. Those women are beautiful, but they also look sinister. I don't mean consciously evil. I mean, they're being so casual about making a mess out of what they're doing. One more thing, they all look an awful lot like that dame Lorelei Jenssen. That one has black hair, the second one brown hair, and the third red hair, and they've all got different eye color, but if you changed the hair to copper and the eyes to sparkling blue, each is the spitting image of Lorelei."

"Ronald, he's right. I didn't see it, though I worked with you the whole time. It's her."

"It wasn't consciously done. Now that I stand back, I see what you mean. It hardly matters though. What can you do with it, Bert?"

"Let me make a few calls. The painting is a knockout. Someone will want it. I know that for certain. Why… you've created three more Stevens Girls in a single painting. It's the same girl, but who cares?"

Bert went out the studio door with his cell phone to his ear talking with a prospective buyer.

"You know, Kevin, I need some distance from this city. How would you feel about accompanying me on a private cruise along the Rhine River? I'll foot the bill."

"Really, Ronald? I'd like that. Maybe I could forget her if I got away."

Things moved very rapidly after that. Ronald chartered a small yacht for the Rhine River cruise. Bert found a client to buy the Three Fates painting—a distiller of fine spirits in Scotland. Sammy and his advertising wizards caused Lorelei's picture to be plastered across all the international media for the opening of the Siren's Call Café. Ronald and Kevin felt that they were escaping the city just in time before the tabloids unleashed their tsunami of releases repeating and amplifying Lorelei as the sensation of the moment.

Ronald and Kevin met the captain and crew of the small yacht that would take them up the Rhine on their private cruise. The captain warned them that travel on the river would be somewhat treacherous on account of fog and high waters at this time of year. He was an encyclopedia of lore about the fabled Rhine, and he promised to tell them the stories of the castles that were visible from the water along their route. The only real precaution he offered was the proper use of life gear in case a storm should arise, or a pea soup fog descended and caused the yacht to run aground.

The beginning of the cruise portended well. Daily sunshine revealed a wet, green, fertile landscape. Nights along the river were quiet and peaceful. The castles on the plains made the land look like a fairyland. The yacht made a quaint sight with its sails set like a throwback to a former age when Tristan sailed with Isolde.

The good weather did not last, however, and clouds rolled in. Thunder, lighting, and drenching rain brought the fury of the weather in such a rush that the crew was hard pressed to keep the yacht on course. The captain advised that sailing would be rough for at least two days. He wanted to know whether his passengers wanted to strike for some port or perhaps tie up next to the shore to wait out the storm. They decided to press forward purely for the adventure.

On the second evening of the storm, which had not abated, the clouds descended to touch the river water, and the rain became torrential. The river boiled and churned, and the yacht pitched and yawed. Ronald and Kevin wore rain gear and held on for dear life near the helm.

Kevin was the first to hear the sound. He strained to hear more, but the captain yelled to ignore it. He said the sound meant danger was close. Yet the sound grew louder, and now both Ronald and Kevin heard the sound. It was a woman singing a beautiful song. Kevin knew the song, and he thought he knew the singer. He strained forward with the hope that he could gain a glimpse of her. Ronald, who had never heard the song, was enraptured. He too strained to see through the fog in the direction from where the sound was coming.

The yacht was now tossing like a careening horse. Dead ahead was light as if from the moon. Ronald wondered whether the clouds were breaking up. Then Kevin pointed and cried out. Ronald saw a copper-haired female figure in a spangled gown. The figure's hair seemed to be surrounded by stars.

She was singing just as Lorelei Jenssen had sung, only now he heard the song. It pierced his heart. He was frantic to reach the figure. He called out to the captain to keep right on his current heading. He felt as if two great arms were pulling him forward.

The captain was shouting about the rocks ahead. He was ordering his crew to luff sail. He was turning the help around to the right. He grabbed Kevin with his free hand and said something about the Siren. With fear in his eyes, he ordered the anchor to be dropped to slow the advance of the yacht.

Kevin reached out to restrain Ronald, but the man was no longer on deck. He had lunged into the water as the yacht came about. The anchor caught, and the vessel strained against the anchor chain.

Kevin saw Ronald swimming toward the figure. He made it to the rocks and climbed onto the shore. Ronald climbed the steep crag to reach the siren at the summit. There, Kevin saw him speaking with the siren while she sang, oblivious to a mere mortal supplicant. Kevin felt impelled to dive overboard to help, but the captain now held him and tied a rope around his waist.

Kevin swayed as the yacht bobbed up and down in the swells, safe as long as the anchor and its chain held. The painter's assistant watched Ronald try to engage with the vision he had painted. He saw Ronald pleading. He saw the figure's disdainful sneer. He heard her song and understood its fatal allure. Kevin wept that he could not be up where Ronald now was next to the female whose voice was so compelling. Then he saw the woman push Ronald with both her arms, and he flew into the air. He but had nowhere to go but down into the water.

"Foolish mortal, begone!" Then the siren began her long, alluring song that had for centuries drawn unlucky sailors to their deaths.

Fortunately, Ronald landed in the water between the rocks. He did not yield, but instead swam to the yacht and held on to the anchor chain. The captain tied a line to his own waist and jumped into the water to keep Ronald's head above the waves. The yacht's crew drew both men aboard, and Ronald and the captain gasped as they lay on the rolling deck.

The weather finally began to abate. As suddenly as it began, the storm ceased, and the Rhine's waters calmed into its usual steady flow. Dense fog enveloped the river, but the pelting rain was gone. The siren was no longer visible, and her song waned. Finally, in the calm, silence pervaded the night. The captain decided to wait until morning before continuing the voyage. He and Kevin took Ronald down to his cabin, where they undressed and dried him.

"That was a close call for all of us. Do you know why your friend dived overboard?"

"Yes, but it would take too much explaining. I'm glad he's back aboard. We'll see how he is in the morning."

At dawn, Ronald awakened with a splitting headache.

"I don't remember diving overboard or climbing the crag. I do remember seeing Lorelei and being so close that she seemed to be right before me. I remember her singing. What a heavenly sound it was, Kevin. I understand why you were so taken with her. I think she touched me and made me fly. When she touched me, she looked so coldly cruel! I shudder to think of her."

"You're lucky you fell into the water and not upon the rocks," Kevin said.

"He's crazy to have leapt overboard on a night like that. We almost lost the yacht and crew and all our lives," the captain interjected.

"Thank you for saving my life," Ronald told the captain. "I believe we've seen what we came for on this cruise. Now we need to make port and return to New York. Captain, you and the crew, will get full pay for the whole cruise we planned, and a bonus for your good work during the storm."

Ronald and Kevin stepped off the yacht at the first opportunity. They took a variety of conveyances to return to New York. Back in Ronald's studio, they caught up on what had happened since they departed.

Lorelei had been a sensation in Las Vegas. Her nightly act was one of the primary draws in the adult playground city. Her fame was now worldwide. Arab sheiks flew all the way to Vegas just to see her perform.

Unfortunately, Sammy, her patron, died in a freak automobile accident. A driver, mesmerized by a billboard featuring three fates and a cask of spirits, steered out of his lane and into oncoming traffic. Lorelei's contract was not with Sammy, personally, but with the casino that owned her café. Try as she might to escape, she was going to be part of her Las Vegas venue until she was superannuated or retired.

Ronald had made another sensation with his Three Fates image, though the tabloids were stumped about the identity of the three new Stevens Girls who modeled for the painting. Ronald could not afford to remain idle.

As soon as he felt able to paint again, he did a sketch for a contemporary version of the Three Graces. Kevin served as his assistant for the entire process, and he later told an investigative reporter that no particular woman had posed for the painter. Each of the graces, Althaea, Euphrosyne, and Thalia, had a unique look, but Kevin could tell that the three figures were meant to be sisters.

Bert was seraphic when he saw the newly finished painting. He bounced up and down in front of it, excited like a little boy. He was anxious to sell it.

"Now that I can sell. The sublime look on the faces is something new for you. In the past, your Stevens Girls looked, well, somewhat mischievous and playful. Even the Three Fates have that quality. These women, on the other hand, look as if they are immortal."

"I'm glad you see a difference. Yes, these three figures are immortal. I know about that immortal look now. I think I will be doing a lot more images in that vein as we go forward. Let me know when you have a prospect for the painting. Meanwhile, I'm going to press on to execute on my next idea."

"Can I have a hint as to what that idea is?"

"Yes. I'll be painting the Three Gorgons."

"As in the Medusa?"

"Yes, and her sisters, Stheno, and Euryale."

"Why did you choose those figures?"

"I did it to show contrast between the mortal and immortal. Execution will be a little tricky because, of the three, only Medusa was mortal, yet she is the most fearful of all representations of women in classical mythology. Perseus killed her—we all know why and how, yet her sisters must have been something quite different because of their immortality, don't you think? All were supremely beautiful."

"All this sequence started with that red-haired girl with the brown eyes."

"Yes, and I'm still trying to work that out of my system. Thalia there, still has vestiges of the woman I had in mind. See how she seems to be singing?"

"I can almost hear her song."

"That was the intent. Kevin likes her particularly."

"Speak of the devil, where is Kevin these days?"

"He went on a one-week trip to Las Vegas to do some gambling."

"Do you suppose he'll be seeing Lorelei?"

"That could be. But he may have had too much of the siren's song already. We shall see. For now, I've got to get back to work. See you later. Just close the door on your way out."

Ronald painted furiously for the rest of the day. He was cleaning up and planning his evening when he received a telephone call. The caller did not speak right away. In the background, Ronald heard the siren's song.

"Kevin, is that you?"

"Yes, it's I. You can guess where I am from the background sounds."

"How is she?" Ronald surprised himself with his show of concern.

"Beautiful, of course, and her voice strikes at my soul."

"Are you all right?"

"Yes, and no. The reason I called you was to touch base with someone who knew what I am feeling right now."

"Do you think you can get yourself out of that café?"

"Yes, I'll be okay. I think I've been cured."

"How so?" Ronald felt that such a cure, if indeed there was such, must be miraculous.

"I went to see Lorelei this afternoon in her dressing room. She remembered me at once. She began ordering me about as if I were still her slave. I refused to be bullied. I walked right up to her and slapped her face, rather hard. She looked so surprised. Then she got the most mournful look. I thought she was going to cry. I felt like a cad for striking her, and there she sat like a spoiled child who had been spanked hard on the bottom in front of others.

"Then, all of a sudden, she brightened up as if I hadn't hit her at all. It was as if she were a different person. She asked politely whether I could bring a dozen roses to her act tonight. So that's what I've done. I'm seated at a table way in the back. She's almost to the part where she comes down from her crag. My God, she's beautiful. I've got to go now. I'll call you later. Goodbye."

Ronald terminated the call and thought for a moment about Kevin and Lorelei. He decided to start his evening with a rusty nail at the bar down the street, and then have an Italian meal with Chianti Ruffino. The heavy decision-making having been done, he picked up his small sketch book and closed his studio for the night.

It was well past midnight when Kevin called again.

"Hi, Ronald. I'm sorry it's so late. Do you have a moment to talk?"

"Sure, Kevin. What's up?"

"I've been with Lorelei. I can't believe it actually happened. She's real. Also, she's really sad. She's treated like a prisoner. She works every day. She's not allowed to vary her routine in the least detail. I gave her the roses she asked for, and she distributed them around the room as she used to do at the Rhine Café. After her act, the local boss chewed her out and slapped her around for having distributed the roses, because it wasn't in the script. She looked so alone and lonely. I wish I could help her."

"I'm afraid she's caught in a gin of her own making."

"Since Sammy died, it's been like that with her. She's now desperate to get out and come back to New York City. All the money and the fame have grown stale. She's now just a lonely girl without any other prospects. Somehow she thinks you are the key to her getting free. She told me that you got her into her current situation, and now she wants out."

"I'll give that some thought. While I'm doing that, can you stay close to her there? Try to see that no one—not even you—knocks her around? I'll try to have some answers for you tomorrow around midday Eastern time."

Ronald could not get to sleep again after Kevin's call. His active brain was busy planning Lorelei's escape. By dawn, he had devised a plan. After packing a bag with essentials for two days' travel, he took a cab downtown to buy two costumes. Then he took an Uber cab to La Guardia and booked a flight to Vegas.

When he touched down in Vegas, it was one o'clock in the afternoon. He called Kevin and told him to meet him at the Red Rock Casino as soon as possible. When Kevin arrived, he gave the costumes and his instructions to Kevin. The young man was confused about the outcome, but he agreed to do as Ronald told him.

That night, Lorelei performed. After her performance, she donned one of the two costumes, and Kevin put on the other. Now dressed in black burqas with small slits for eyes, the pair proceeded to the Red Rock Casino where they stayed in a room that Ronald had booked for his "wife and sister."

The next morning the two, still dressed in burqas, flew to Boston with onward bookings to London and Frankfurt. At Logan International Airport, however, they changed their itinerary, took off their costumes and proceeded to New York in the clothes they had worn under the burqas. They took a cab to a hotel off Central Park West and booked a room under assumed names.

While Kevin and Lorelei were en route, Ronald went to the café and demanded to see Lorelei immediately. He said he was her husband and needed her to return to their castle on the Rhine immediately. He threatened a lawsuit if the café did not immediately produce his wife.

The boss of the establishment, a very rough man, told Ronald that he should depart at once or face arrest. Indignant, Ronald claimed that he was going to fetch his lawyers. He gave his address as Count Grafspee, Lorelei Island, Rhine River, Germany. Then he left. He proceeded to the airport and flew to New York.

Back in his studio, he telephoned Kevin and asked him to come at once with Lorelei. Kevin brought her around two hours later, only she looked different. She had red hair and hazel eyes. She was the image of the woman he had painted in his original picture. Ronald called Burt to come around to meet his newest Stevens Girl. He said she topped all the priors and was the secret model for all his latest paintings. To prove this point to Kevin, he stood her beside his painting of Medusa.

"The likeness is striking."

"I am not amused," Lorelei said.

"Do you want to go back to Las Vegas?" Ronald asked.

"Never," she answered, with a crooked smile.

That was how Ronald Stevens caught the siren, Lorelei Jenssen. Kevin Angland actually married the woman, and he loved to hear her sing to their children at bedtime. She remained a Stevens Girl for the remaining ten years of her modeling career. Most recently she became The Three Furies. Ronald painted that as a jest, but she was not laughing.

Games for Love in Dragonton

The greatest prize for storytelling in England—during the time of Richard II—was awarded the day before Christmas at Dragonton Village in Middlesex, close enough to the king's court for baronets, knights, and their ladies to attend the telling of tales at the village in disguise.

As far as anyone knew, the royals and greater nobility never deigned to attend the rustic village festival, even though rumors abounded every year that one of those rare birds might just appear. It was always great sport for villagers to try to guess who was who among their distinguished guests. It was extremely rare that a disguised guest join in the storytelling because the prize was the hand of the fairest maiden in the village. She was the judge of the literary contest and also the eligible bride. In this year of the turn of the Fifteenth Century, an exception occurred that proved this rule, and caused great hilarity and joy throughout the kingdom ever afterward.

The storytelling event was naturally preceded by lesser contests in Dragonton, as well as the neighboring villages. The winners of those contests vied to be selected as one of the three finalists who would declaim their stories to the assemblage in the Dragonton Village square.

The declamations would be heard in all weathers, and sometimes the teeth of the tellers would chatter as they delivered their carefully prepared pieces. Snow cover was usually around three feet on the ground, and the square was gaily decorated with evergreen boughs tied with red ribbons, mistletoe and silver bells. At the center of the square was the declaiming place where each storyteller stood, his order told by lot.

The onlookers at this particular festival were more numerous than usual, and they jostled with each other as the snow fell. The village notables gave their preliminary speeches about the Yule Season. They also spoke of the coming New Year and the grand idea of making Christmas a time of nuptial bliss both in the renewal of old vows and in the symbolical and physical union of the winner of the contest with the fair maid of the village. A woman was introduced to the sound of generous applause, and it was clear to everyone that the village had not seen a more beautiful and charming judge and bride in modern memory.

Judith, for that was the beauty's name, was dressed for the occasion in the traditional red Christmas costume with its heavy, rich fabric and fox fur lining. The cold enhanced her features by bringing out her rosy cheeks, and the wind blew her golden hair under her fur cap. She was not daunted by her having been chosen for the role, but she admitted in her little speech that she both looked forward to what was to come and, a little, feared the outcome if her choice fell to her heart rather than to the literary quality of the story that won the prize.

"I am truly honored to be the judge of this annual contest, but I have a wish. I hope you can honor it. We have three good stories to hear, but I am not the only eligible maiden present here today. Anne, who is wise, and Mary, who is practical, are both ready for a match. They do not object to being prizes alongside me. By allowing us all three to be chosen, three matches will be made today. Then we'll have the merriest of Christmases ever in this village. So what do you say to that?"

The hearty applause was a vote of universal approval, so red-haired Anne and brown-haired Mary joined Judith in the judges' booth, and Judith asked the first storyteller to step forward and begin his tale.

The man who went to the podium was an unlikely lad with welts and pimples all over his face. He was Ned, the hostler, and he was not known to be much of a wit at all, much less a storyteller. He seemed to be very uncertain of what he was going to do, standing on one foot and then the other.

"I am not used to standing up before you to tell tales, but I've been paid three farthings to do so today by a gentle person who would prefer not to tell the tale himself. I've been well rehearsed for my part, and I won't do him or you a disservice. So, unless anyone objects, I'll begin. It's a fitting tale for a village named Dragonton, you'll find."

The man fidgeted, clearly uncomfortable and nervous with the role that had been thrust upon him.

"This is highly irregular, Ned, but in the spirit of Christmas, since you've been paid well enough and doubtless need the money, commence." Judith, Anne, and Mary breathed a collective sigh of relief that the teller of the tale was only the proxy and that his benefactor, the composer of the story, was a gentleman. They all sat forward and listened intently to the tale called, "Dragon Lady," which follows:

Dragon Lady
Story of a Noble Man

Long, long ago, in a land that time forgot, there lives a bachelor prince. Among his other exploits, the prince has become a famous dragon slayer. After all, he has nothing better to do while his father remains the king. Because he is young and virile, he becomes the suitor of a mysterious, fair young, black-haired lady in a neighboring kingdom. She is by night a dragon, but the prince does not know this at first. His pursuit of this fair lady changes both of their lives and the lives of many other people forever.

The dragon holds sway over a broad valley that stretches out in all directions from a mountain in its midst, where the fair lady's castle sits on the summit of the mountain. The dragon appears only by night, and the entire countryside is afraid of the fearful beast's depredations. Meanwhile, the fair lady of the castle appears only by day, and her hand is being sought after by all the eligible bachelors from near and far. Lines of suitors extended from the main portcullis gate, while in the valley, crowds go about their daily business, cowering in fear of what each night portends.

Ned observed that the three families closest to the podium were craning their necks to hear him. He, therefore, raised his voice and saw the folk near the back nod that they could hear him much better. Everyone's breath was white as each huddled in the cold, the men and women leaning against one another for warmth. The animals behind the throng were mooing, neighing, oinking and clucking, but the people did not seem to care. Some smiled. Others were dreamy eyed. Ned settled down and focused on the next part of the story about the lady.

"The fair lady, in fact, is so beautiful that she is being sought after by brave young men from all over the world, but all fail to win her hand in marriage. Those who try to press their advantage are killed horribly by the cruel trials that the fair lady puts them through or by the dragon, or both.

The prince makes his way to the castle where the fair lady lives and is immediately admitted to her presence. She does not care that he is a prince and tells him the cruel rules of engagement for all her would-be suitors.

She tells the prince, "While you live in my castle, you are to do whatever I ask you to do, and you are not to venture from your room at night. While you are in my home, you shall do three things for me, one on each of the first three days that you are my guest.

"First, you must successfully open a room with an enormous, rusty iron door that is hung with chains and ancient locks."

Rather than trying to puzzle the locks open, the prince cuts through the metal chains with his marvelous sword. When the chains fall away, the prince uses his sword as a lever to open the iron door on its creaking hinges.

Inside the musty, dirty and enormous room behind the door, the prince finds an ossuary with the charred bones and body dust of the fair lady's former suitors and rivals. The fair lady tours the enormous room with the prince to explain just how each of her suitors died trying to kill the dragon.

"The dragon slew each man and scorched his remains with a fiery breath while it devoured their flesh. The dragon also devoured any woman who dared to rival me for a young man's affections." While she says these things, she fingers several bones and locks of hair as if she is glad their owners are now among the dead."

Ned looked up, pleased that he had not stumbled over any words. He covered his mouth with the back of his sleeve and coughed. Then he examined the crowd and saw they were rapt with attention, standing on tiptoe for his next utterance. So he continued.

"Second, you must reignite a torch that is the symbol of my deceased father's memory. See there how the now-extinguished memorial torch is lodged high on a cliff with sides so steep and smooth that they cannot be climbed?"

The prince decides not to try to climb the cliff at all, but instead, lights a small fire and makes a thick potion of natural pitch that he applies to one of his arrows. He lights the pitch potion in his fire and shoots the now-flaming arrow across the long distance up the cliff so that it pierces into the neck of the torch, which suddenly takes fire and blazes so that it illuminates the entire castle keep. The lighted torch keeps burning through the following days and nights.

"Third, you must bring me a rare, black flower that grows underground by a stream in a cave below the mountain on which this castle lies."

With a torch and a sack in his belt intended to carry the flower, the prince descends into the crevice below the castle's foundation that leads to the subterranean cave. Giant rats attack him during his descent. At first, the prince cannot use his sword because of the narrowness of the passage, so he takes out his sharp-edged dagger and stabs his way through the milling throng.

The prince emerges from the crevice in an enormous cavern with a stream flowing through the center of it. He can see in the torch-light rats teeming throughout the cavern, but now in the broad space of the cavern, the prince can use his sword to hew his way through them to the stream.

By torchlight, the prince follows the stream until he comes to a place with a shelf of dripping wet, slimy rock that slopes so that no rat can gain footing on it. At the top of that rock-shelf grows the black flower that he seeks. The sure-footed prince begins to climb the rock shelf, but he is attacked by bats that have begun to take wing from above and to fly all around him.

The prince waves his torch to keep the bats at bay because they fear the flickering fire. Alert, he sees that back of the shelf where the black flower grows is a pocket in the rock where a venomous adder coils. The prince aims his sword's blade to slice off the flower and cut the adder in two parts simultaneously. Now he sheathes his sword. He grasps the black flower in his right hand and puts it in the sack he has brought to carry it. As an afterthought, he also places the half of the adder still writhing with its fanged head striking in the sack as well.

Ned saw the children staring with wide eyes at the thought of the hero still in the dark place. He frowned as he told the tale of the hero's return from darkness to the light.

The bats fly about his head, and the rats scramble around his feet as he makes his way through the dark.

When he returns up the mountain to the castle, the prince gallantly presents the black flower to the fair lady. She seems to be genuinely delighted and claps her hands with delight.

"No suitor has ever been so skillful as to perform the three hard tasks that I have given to you. You have performed surpassing well.

"While you were in the underground cavern fetching the black flower, I tangled my long, black hair badly. You see how it has become stuck in the tines of the special round brush I use? As a fourth task, I ask you to untangle my hair without breaking one single hair. You must do this before nightfall, which is less than an hour away."

The prince realizes that he cannot possibly untangle her maze of hair, so he takes out his sword, holds the fair lady's comb as far as possible from her head and cuts her tangled hair off with a stroke.

"You've cut off my hair! How dare you? My features are now ruined. How can I appear in public? You'll die for what you've done!" She is red with rage, with her fists clenched, but she looks ridiculous with half of her hair cut off and she knows it.

The prince, laughing heartily, says, "Fair lady, I've accomplished the task you assigned me and not broken one single hair. In fact, I've broken all the hairs on the right side of your head where the tangled mess lay. Now you've got no tangles. If you comb hair from the other side of your head over your head to the right side, no one will see the place where my blade fell."

"Hahaha," the fair lady laughs at the prince's ingenuity and wit. "I'm going to retire now, and you should do so also. Go to your room."

The fair lady then retires while the prince goes to his room. The prince is bewildered by the last three days' activities and the four tasks he has performed. He cannot understand the ulterior purpose of the four tasks, and he tries to puzzle out what they mean as he prepares for bed.

That night to interrupt his sleep the prince feels a body creep next to him in his bed. He feels hot breath and the flick of a tongue across his cheek in the darkness. He reaches out and feels warm, smooth skin that turns to scales and feathers while he strokes it. Alarmed, he jumps out of bed and unsheathes his sword. A great rustling sound behind him awakens him fully. Quickly he slashes to the right and left.

Then he strikes flint against the sword's steel Toledo blade. The light from the sparks shows nothing in the room except the bed and the prince's own belongings. So the prince puts his sword back in its sheath and returns to his bed, this time with his dagger by his side. In sleep, he dreams of slaying dragons that fly against him from all sides like the bats did in the cavern below the castle mount. When he awakens in the morning, he finds clumps of colorful, iridescent feathers lying scattered all over his bed.

At breakfast in the great hall of the castle, the fair lady asks the prince, "How did you sleep last night?"

"Fair lady, I slept well, but I had the most monstrous dreams of killing many dragons. From my perspective, it was a great evening of thrilling dreams. This morning, I found these feathers in my bed."

The prince shows the fair lady a fistful of the feathers and places them on the table. Then he smiles and says, "I rejoice at the thought of slaying many dragons in my sleep. I hope my dream is an omen of slaying many dragons when I'm awake as I have always done."

The fair lady smiles coolly in turn and tells the prince, "You should prepare for combat because that evening you must battle the dragon that threatens the entire valley below. Before you begin your preparations, I want to show you something."

She rises from the table and leads the prince out of the castle to the castle keep. There she points out the precise locations where the bravest of her former suitors were slain by the dragon. She then leads the prince back inside the castle to a private gallery adjacent to her private bedchamber.

"Here you see hanging the portraits of my three favorite former suitors. They were big, strong knights, and they slew many dragons before they did combat the dragon here. All perished trying to defeat the scaly scourge of this valley. Do you think you'll do better than they did? Perhaps I should have you sit for your portrait now before you become a pile of charred bones in my ossuary as they did."

The prince takes close notice of the weapons revealed in those portraits of the three dead heroes. Then he says, "Thank you for the tour. A portrait of me would be superfluous. I'm ready now to prepare for this evening's combat.

"I want you to have a keepsake from me in the unlikely event that the dragon should prevail. Here is the sack into which I placed the black flower you asked me to fetch you. Inside it is another present I thought you might like as well. Take it and use my gift in good health, but you must promise me you'll open the sack only after the combat has ended and only if the dragon is victorious."

The fair lady nods, accepts the sack and retires to her chamber. The prince goes to his chamber also and begins to hone his weapons for the fight.

One hour before twilight, the prince is ready for the fight, and he proceeds to the castle keep to confront the dragon when it appears to fight him. He watches the beautiful sunset over the valley and admires the painted clouds as the sunlight extinguishes.

Now the memorial torch is the only light except for the starlight in the heavens and the half moon. The prince realizes that his dead rivals did not have the advantage of the torchlight for their combat. They did not have the advantage of seeing the bones of their fallen rivals or the bones and ashes of the fair lady's female rivals. They did not witness the expressions of the fair lady when she coolly and appreciatively introduced the prince to the horrors of what the dragon had done. They never presented the fair lady with the black flower from the cavern below the castle. They never gave her a sack with half a poisonous adder still writhing within it.

This last thought gives the prince an idea, and he runs inside the castle and goes straightaway to the fair lady's private chamber where she lies on her bed unconscious in a cold sweat. The sack that the prince gave her lies open, and the half of the adder lies next to her still wriggling with its fangs in the fair lady's arm.

Quickly the prince removes the adder from the fair lady's arm and cuts into her arm where the venom has been injected by the adder's fangs. To withdraw the poison, he bends and sucks the bloody wound he has just made. He spits the poison on the bed and sucks some more and squeezes the fair lady's arm to force the poison out and to force the bleeding.

He then instinctively grabs the black flower from the vase on her nightstand and crushes it between his hands and rubs the liquid and pulp of the flower over her wound and presses them down like a poultice. He uses his sword to cut up her pillowcase and makes a bandage from the strips he has cut. He wraps her arm with this bandage.

With the water from the vase and the rest of the pillowcase, he makes a cold compress for the fair lady's head and bathes her brow with it. He stops to squeeze the liquid into her mouth and thinks to press some black petals from the flower under her tongue.

Her eyes open in small slits, and she peers around, fixing finally on the prince's eyes. Then she struggles to get up, but he holds her down and shakes his head. She writhes. As she gains back her strength, she frees an arm and strikes at the prince. Her arm becomes a feathered wing.

Now the fair lady's transformation proceeds apace, and the prince watches aghast as her soft body develops scales and feathers while he holds her. Her other arm becomes a wing, and she sprouts a scaly tail. She thrashes on the bed and tries to throw the prince off her.

He knows he has very little time, so he reaches his arm around her back and pulls one of her wings so that the dragon lady turns her belly down while he wraps his hands under her wings and around the back of her neck. His dagger is now between both his hands and forcing itself between the scales of her enlarging neck. His dagger sinks up to its hilt, and his hands work the point and blade back and forth vigorously to sever the spinal cord.

Now the dragon lady is all dragon, and its breath is heating up with fire to follow. The prince knows that he has only a few seconds before the dragon's fire begins, and the dragon's strength is growing very powerful.

The prince throws his legs around the waist of the dragon from the rear and pulls the dragon's wings back with his arms, without releasing his hands from the dagger. The more the dragon struggles, the more the dagger does its deadly work.

The dragon's movements assure its defeat. When it tries to beat its wings, the dagger turns. When it tries to turn its body, the dagger goes from side to side within its neck. When the dragon rears its head back, the dagger tries to dig deeper than it has done before. When the dragon flails its tail, it cannot get a purchase because its rider is too high on its back.

Even the growth of the dragon's neck works against it because the dagger cannot be expelled, and the neck's growth pulls the blade through its spinal column where the neck joins the body.

The dragon finally exhales a breath of fire that catches the bed alight, but the fire roasts the dragon more than the prince, and the dragon is hoist with its own petard.

Realizing that the prince has already won the fight and that further struggle is self-destructive, the dragon stops resisting. It relaxes its wings and stops flailing its tail. It rolls from side to side as if to put out the fire on the bed, and finally, it rolls off the bed.

The dragon lands on the floor on its side and does not attempt to roll over on the prince because then the dagger would press deeper in the wound it has made. It rises with the prince riding on its back, and it steps toward the open window overlooking the valley. The prince knows that the dragon cannot fly in its current condition, and he breaks his silence.

"Fair lady, the combat is over. I've won. Admit it. If you plunge through that window, nothing will be gained. You'll fall to your death because you cannot fly. Anything you do will worsen your situation.

"I'm going to hold onto you until the morning. If you cannot revert to your human form until then, I'll just hold on, and you will probably die. If you can revert now to your human form, I'll set you free and try to stanch your bleeding and restore your health.

"Much as it would give me pleasure to kill the dragon that you are, I would sorely grieve the death of the fair lady that you were before you had your nocturnal change. I know you're under some form of curse, but I think the black flower is an antidote. It worked against the adder's bite. It may work to break your curse as well."

Ned noticed that the women in his audience were whispering to one another at this stage of the story. The children were mystified. Some of the young men were nodding as if to say they had known women like this. It was clear to him that he had the audience's full attention. So he pressed to the conclusion.

The dragon roars and hisses, but it does not try to breathe fire. It twists a little to one side and the other as if to test once more that it is truly trapped by the prince in a mortal embrace that it cannot break by any means.

Then the prince feels the powerful wings relax. The dragon's tail retracts. Its elongated neck begins to shrink. Its scales and feathers become warm, soft human flesh again. Now the prince is holding a flesh-and-blood woman, and his dagger comes out of her neck as the neck shrinks to the normal human size.

The prince breaks his hand lock and picks up the fair lady—for she has reverted fully now. He places her on her bed. He tears at the poultice he formerly made for her arm and splits it into parts, one of which he leaves on her arm, the other on the back of the fair lady's neck.

He pours the rest of the water from the vase down the fair lady's mouth so that she gasps and drinks gratefully. She throws her arms around him and holds on for her very life. She trembles and presses herself against the prince.

"Oh, thank you. Thank you. I think my curse has been broken by your efforts. I don't know how you managed to do your magic, but you have done it."

"Now you must rest, fair lady. I will not take advantage of you this night. I'll just pull your coverlet over you. Nod if you understand me. That's right; I'm going to my chamber to rest. For now, just sleep."

The prince pulls her arms from his neck and leaves the fair lady sleeping in her bloody, charred bed. He takes the remains of the adder away with him inside the sack. He retires to his own chamber.

Tired as he is, the prince cleans his weapons before he goes to bed. When he finally sleeps, he does not dream at all.

When the first light shines through his window, he rises and packs for his journey. He goes to the castle kitchen and eats bread and a joint of mutton. He throws the sack with the half adder into the rubbish bin. He wonders whether he should wait for the fair lady to appear before he departs. He decides against disturbing her.

He thinks, "She'll be embarrassed by what happened if she recalls anything happened at all. She may be furious. She may be overly cloying. I've other dragons to slay and the whole wide earth to discover."

With these thoughts and many others, the prince decides out of courtesy to leave the fair lady a note of thanks on a sheet of parchment.

"Thank you for your hospitality, great lady. If I have done you service, it is only what you are owed by your beauty and grace. If I have in any way offended you, know that it was not my intent to do either.

"I rejoice this once for my not having to slay a dragon though I vanquished it. I also rejoice that I may have restored a fair lady to herself as her father may have wished and to have restored her father's memory by lighting his memorial torch.

"As for the black flower, such gifts often come with hidden faults with strange effects. The juice of the flower is the antidote to the poison of the adder that guarded it.

"As for your portrait gallery, I'm glad not to have been painted and set among the others, whose loss I mourn just as those whose bones fill your ossuary.

"In future, perhaps the fair lady will not be defensive against those whose beauty could never compare with hers. In all that time, I shall remain true to the memory of my time in your castle.

"Farewell. Prince Valiant."

The prince goes to the stabling area of the castle keep and caparisons his milk-white stallion. With his bow over his back and his arrows in his quiver, with his dagger in his belt and his sword in its scabbard, he passes through the main castle gate and rides across the moat with its raw, dank smell of excrement and winds his way down the mountain to the plain.

Only once does the prince look back toward the castle, and he thinks he sees a handkerchief waving farewell from the window that might belong to the fair lady. Quite clearly even in full sunlight, he sees the torch burning over the castle keep. It is a new day in the valley and a whole new lease on life for its villagers. The End.

Ned looked more confident at the end of his telling than he had when he began. His chest swelled, and he stood tall. He evidently felt as if he had done a good job reciting it, well worth the hire. He smiled broadly and shrugged.

"Well, folks, that's the story I've been asked to tell today. I thank you for being such good listeners, one and all. If I can, I'd like to be going back into the crowd now. I'm glad to be stepping back into my own role as a listener and watcher."

The villagers and guests applauded heartily and began talking with each other about the story they had just heard. Judith brought the assembly to order by standing and raising her fair hand.

"Thank you, Ned the hostler, for telling such a cautionary tale. I assure everyone that I do not turn into a dragon at night and, as far as I know, neither Anne nor Mary does so. I believe

Will the tinker is next, so please come forward, Will, and begin your tale."

Handsome Will the tinker was one of the most accomplished youths in the village. He was smart and articulate as well as good looking. All three of the maiden judges smiled with approval as he stepped onto the podium. Any one of them would have been pleased to marry him.

The wind had died down somewhat, but the air was raw and cold. Fair-haired Will came forward briskly and blew on his red hands before he spoke, all while he gauged his audience.

"Before I start, I'd like to say that I would be proud to be the husband of any of the three fair judges. I'm not sure my story will stack up against what you've just heard Ned recite, but I assure you that it is my own work. It took me half the summer to compose it. Any resemblance of our good village to the village in my fable is unintended, so please do not be offended. Aha! I made an end rhyme. Oh, well, here goes."

This is Will's story, exactly as he told it that Christmas afternoon, and as the story progressed, the snow came in broad, wet flakes, covering the listeners, who stood rapt with attention as he told the story of "Three Ogres Too Many," which follows:

Three Ogres Too Many

When I first saw it, it looked like a pleasant valley with neat hedgerows and winding paths leading among the dwellings. It was the chilly beginning of springtime when everything was coming up green and flowery because of recent rain. Brindle cows were grazing peacefully in the nearby fields, and crows winged high and then fell into the newly sprouting corn fields, cawing. I had for a long time been wandering and living off the land. I did not require much to keep me going, but right now I was looking for a place with a spare bed where I could rest for a brief while before pressing on. Wherever I went, people had been hospitable. I always worked hard for food and a place with a roof over my head. I had no money, but in these hard times, who did?

Will stopped for a moment in his tale and saw that four people were coming back from relieving themselves. He waited until they were back in their places. They nodded to him, and he continued his story being careful to speak clearly and loud enough to be heard by everyone.

I noticed that smoke was coming from only four of the seven houses in the valley, so I tried my luck with the first of the three that showed no smoke. Its door was not locked, so I pushed it open and went inside to have a look around.

The interior was not immaculate, but someone had a sense of order. I found a pot and kindling, water in a carafe and oats in a small bag.

I built a fire and set the pot on a tripod above it with water and oats to make porridge. It wasn't long before I was eating the best food I had had in three days. After I had finished eating, I cleaned up so that no one could notice I had enjoyed a repast. I then went out back to relieve myself.

I noticed in the back and side yards that the owner of this cottage had planted berry bushes on all sides. Here was a gooseberry hedge. There was a raspberry bush. Over against the fence was a maze of blackberry bushes. The grass was wet with dew, and in a small clearing, chickens, and a rooster pecked at the soil.

I saw that a part of the fence needed fixing. Perhaps I could offer to fix that for my breakfast. I looked over the thatched roof and decided I could help with that too if the owner had a mind to it. I wanted to rack up a list of things I could do to earn my keep. I thought I might have time to do a full survey after I got some rest.

Back inside, I saw that the first floor was used for normal living and the second floor was used for storage of odds and ends. In one corner of the floor was an old corn husk mattress, which I thought would do just fine for my purpose. I lay down upon it and instantly fell to sleep so sound that I did not awaken until evening when I heard the front door slam open.

The owner of the cottage had evidently returned alone. For some reason, I did not rush down to announce my presence. Instead, I waited silently, listening to gauge the character of my unwary host.

The owner made a lot of noise clattering among his pots and pans, and he built a fire in the stove to cook something. He was hacking at meat, I thought, and as he did that, he was singing a song to himself in a rough, but animated voice:

An ogre leads a brutish life.
My ogre's life is hard.
This ogre needs a sharp knife
To cut through flesh and lard.
Hahaha. Hahaha. Hahaha.

I'd rather taste an Irish man
This evening in spring
Than roast a grisly harridan
Whose sinews taste like string.
Hahaha. Hahaha. Hahaha.

Fie, Fie, Foe, Fum!
I smell the blood of an English man.
Be he alive or be he dead,

I'll grind his bones to make my bread.

With that, the singer stopped his song and began up turning everything on the first floor looking for something. As he scoured his home, he continued talking to himself.

"He's not in there. He's not in here. He's not behind the stove. He's not in the hall. He's not in the sitting room. He's not in the bedroom. Let's see whether he's hiding out back. Where are you, my Englishman? Don't you want to come out and join me for dinner? What a marvelous dinner you'd make, my friend. Come out, now. It'll be the worse for you if you don't!"

When the owner threw open his back door and charged out looking, I slunk down the stairs and made my way out the front door to the path where I coolly walked to the next house without smoke coming from the chimney. I noticed that the fire that the owner of the house I had forsaken had produced a thick black smoke from his chimney. Evening was beginning to fall, but the occupant of the second house had not yet returned.

I stood in the doorway of the second house for a while listening. I looked back again at the house I had just left and saw that the owner, a burly fellow rippling with muscles and carrying a large club, had moved from the backyard to the front, where he was looking along and under the hedge and in the side yards. The man was obsessed. He went back inside the house.

Will noticed that young lovers were whispering in each other's ears and chuckling. He stared at them until they became embarrassed and fell silent. He heard a horse whinny off to the side of the assembly. He took that as the signal to begin where he had left off.

Soon I saw the man emerge through a hatch in his roof. He walked the thatches to be sure that no one was hiding there. Then he shrugged and went back inside the cottage and pulled the hatch closed.

Pushing the door to the second house open, I stepped inside and checked out the first floor. It was very much on the plan of the first house I had entered. I went up the stairs to the second floor and saw that the whole floor was a storage area with a corncob bed in the corner.

I decided to sit down on the cob bed and contemplate my situation. I almost lighted my pipe, but I had second thoughts because the gnarly owner of the first house had sung about smelling something before he initiated his search of his cottage. I knew from that song that the man was actually an ogre, and the song alarmed me.

"Was the meat that the ogre was preparing the flesh of a harridan? Could the ogre have been serious about eating me and grinding my bones to flour? I cannot take a chance. I must assume that the ogre intended to find me, kill me, cut me up and eat my flesh this very night. I was lucky to have escaped alive. I'd better take a look around for the hatch that leads to the thatched roof on this house just to have an escape route just in case."

That is what I thought while I sat on the cob bed. Immediately, I rose and found the hatch to the roof. I knew it was the hatch because a rope with a toggle pin hung from the ceiling from the hatch. I pushed on the hatch and went up to the thatched roof just as the ogre had done. I saw that I could slide down the roof to the side yard if I was careful about how I fell.

Then I reentered the house and pulled the hatch closed using the toggle pin tied to the rope. I crept downstairs to find a crust of bread and a wooden beaker of water. I took those things upstairs to my small area and ate and drank. I was about to go to sleep when I heard a commotion downstairs. From the sounds I heard, I deduced that the owner of the house had returned alone.

Normally, I would have gone downstairs to introduce myself at once, but I hesitated for some unaccountable reason. I continued to listen as the owner of the house made his dinner. Like the owner of the first house, the owner of the second house prepared his dinner fire and then sang while he used a mallet and cleaver to prepare his dinner meat:

An ogre leads a brutish life.
My ogre's life is hard.
This ogre needs a sharp knife
To cut through flesh and lard.
Hahaha. Hahaha. Hahaha.

I'd rather taste an Irish man
This evening in spring
Than roast a grisly harridan
Whose sinews taste like string.
Hahaha. Hahaha. Hahaha.

Fie, Fie, Foe, Fum!
I smell the blood of an English man.
Be he alive or be he dead,
I'll grind his bones to make my bread.

I heard him sing these words, and I pressed on the hatch and escaped to the thatched roof. I left the hatch open to listen while the ogre ransacked the interior of his house looking for what he had smelled.

He finished looking on the first floor and started up the stairs, so I pushed the hatch closed and prepared to slide down the thatched roof if need be. The ogre did not push up the hatch, but I heard him hurling things left and right on the second floor.

Then he must have gone back downstairs because the second floor became silent. I saw a figure with a flaming torch approaching, and he might have seen me on the roof, so I decided to slip back down into the second floor and wait again.

I heard sounds of two rough men talking on the first floor.

"I smelled English man. The smell was strong, and I smelled porridge that he had made in my kitchen. I searched my cottage and yard but found no sign of him. He may have slept in my corn cob bed because it was a little messy, but then it's always messy because my guests use it."

"I smelled English man, too. I searched the first floor and the second floor here. I tossed everything on the second floor. I found no one."

"So let's go outside with torches and search the grounds and the roof."

"That's a good idea. I'll light my torch from yours."

From my second-floor hiding place, I heard the ogres go out the front door to search for me. They must have searched everything outside because it was a long while before they came back into the house, this time from the back door. They extinguished their torches and sat at the kitchen table eating and talking.

"I'm glad you brought this roasted shin of hag with you. I arrived so late, I only just started my fire."

"She is a grisly creature, but her flesh is sweet once it has been roasted."

"It'll do until the next good meal comes by."

"That English man is our next meal, wherever he is. I know he's in this village, and we'll raise the hue and cry in the morning to roust him out."

"Have you told our brother about this?"

"How could I? He'll not be home till morning. When he discovers that an English man was through the village, he'll be driven insane with the thought of missing such a delectable meal. He hates roast harridan almost as much as I hate preparing one."

Will stopped for a moment to listen to the laughter among the crowd. He was glad they were listening. They even understood the comic nature of his story even though trolls were serious threats. He mused about the irony of their laughing when that was precisely the tenor of his next passage. He smiled and continued.

"Hahaha. We know the English man has been here and there, but we don't yet know whether he went to our brother's house."

"I've got an idea. Let's light up our torches and search his grounds and look on both levels of his house. Once we do that, and if we've not found the English man, we'll lock his place up and have one less place to search tomorrow."

"Perfect. Let's go now."

I heard them depart and watched their torches proceed on the winding path to the third house that had no smoke coming from its chimney this morning when I arrived. I watched the torches move around on all sides of the cottage, and then I watched as the two ogres planted one of their torches in the soil of the front yard and went inside to search with the other.

They emerged satisfied that they had been thorough, and then they returned to the house I was hiding in. I listened to what they had to say because I thought my life might depend on it, and it turned out that it did.

"That old biddy was a tough customer."

"She wasn't as bad as the one we had last week. I ground that one's bones to flour, so we did have some compensation."

"How do you propose that we prepare the English man when we catch him?"

"First, we have to catch him."

"Yes, and then what?"

"We'll use our clubs to knock him over the head and then tenderize his body. Then we'll fillet him and dry his bones like the others. I'm considering a soup with the hands and feet."

Hiding upstairs, I heard this talk. It chilled me to the bone with fright. The trolls really were looking forward to killing and eating me. I wondered how to turn the tables on my enemies before it was too late.

"You know our brother will want to have him all and leave us none."

"He's always been jealous and envious, but he's stronger than both of us put together."

"Yes, we'd never overcome him."

"Not unless we got him good and drunk beforehand."

"Okay, so let's get him good and drunk. And then what would we do?"

"We'd use our clubs and do what we plan to do with the English man."

"So why do we need to worry about the English man at all?"

"A very good question, brother. You tell me why."

"Well, one reason is that our brother always can hold more liquor than we can."

"That's true. So we have to figure a way to get him drunk without making ourselves drunk as well."

"Why don't we use the English man to trick him."

"That's considering that we do catch the English man in the first place."

"Hear me out. Okay, let's think positive for a minute. We'll capture the English man, but not use our clubs on him immediately. We'll invite him to share a meal with us and have him get drunk with our brother. We'll ply them with liquor while abstaining, and we will serve the drink."

"I see. Then we'll club them both, soften their flesh, fillet them and prepare them for a week of dinners. You'll get half of each, and I'll get the other half."

"That way, we'll have no jealousy or envy."

"And we can split our brother's house and land."

"Hahaha. Do we have enough drink in all our houses to get them good and drunk?"

"I think so."

The two trolls jostled each other in their delight and began to punch each other in the face just for fun. Hiding upstairs, I had thought about how I might use the trolls' plan against them. I listened intently for details that might help me while the trolls made all kinds of noise below.

"So we'll be at our brother's house tomorrow morning bright and early, and raise the hue and cry for the English man."

"I'm tired, and I planned to sleep in tomorrow."

"So when you awaken, come by, and then we'll both go visit our brother to raise the alarm."

"Done! I'll see you in the morning, brother."

"Yes, and don't you try to trick me in this, brother. If you do, I'll club you and make you the dinner instead of our brother."

I thought that the two brothers would fight each other, they got so mad. They called each other all sorts of names.

They shoved each other around and broke dishes. Finally, they decided to get some rest.

The ogre down the hill went back to his cottage with his torch. His brother decided to get some sleep, but I heard his footsteps coming up the stairs as if he were going to look around one more time before he retired. I don't know what he was going to do because before his head appeared above the landing, I had slipped through the hatch and slid down the thatched roof to the ground.

I made my way in the dark to the third ogre's house at the top of the hill. I wanted to be there when he arrived at his cottage in the morning because I had devised a plan that would avoid the unpleasantness of a hue and cry.

My plan would also pit the ogres against each other instead of against me. At least that is what I hoped.

So when the third ogre appeared at his door the next morning, I opened the door and introduced myself. His nose twitched, and he seemed to become enraged. He looked around for a club. I knew just what he was thinking. So I spoke fast, but confidently.

"Don't be alarmed, good sir. I've been waiting half the night for you to come home to tell you about a plot against your life by your two brothers who live down the hill."

The ogre cocked his head and decided to listen to my tale of his brothers, for, as I discovered, he knew their scheming against him well.

"A plot? Against me? What have you learned?"

"Your brothers plan to invite us to a dinner at which they will get us both very drunk and then kill us and fillet us. We'll be food for a week at least—much better food than the crones they have been eating lately."

"Harumph. So they think they can toy with me, their elder brother in this way? We'll see about that. I'll make it so they'll not plot against me anymore. How can I reward you for telling me about the plot? Of course, I could just kill you now. I'd like to eat you myself, now that I think about it." The ogre was fuming mad, but he was hungry too. Cleavers and knives hung from the kitchen walls. It was a long way through the main room to the door, and it was bolted. I might never escape if I fled. I thought the ogre might pick a knife up and kill me with it at any moment. I could see in his eyes, he was caught between hunger and fear of danger. I had to think fast. Fortunately, my wits did not fail me.

"But you don't know how your brothers plan to ruin you. I do have such a plan. Let me be very clear: I have a plan by which you'll discover your brothers' treachery for yourself. Then you can do what you have to do. Meanwhile, my only wish is to assure that you have a ready supply of what you really need."

"And what is it that I really need, pray tell?"

"A fattened Irish man."

"I do like the sound of that, my friend. I haven't had an Irish man in many months. How will you deliver this Irish man?"

"If you can overcome your brothers and let me walk out of the village and back down the road I came on, I'll bring you a fat priest who is Irish. I am mere skin and bones compared to him. His fat will fill your larder, and since he is a holy man, his flesh is pure."

"This is sounding better and better."

"So do we have a deal, then? You'll have to decide quickly because your brothers are about to arrive here at this house."

"I'll do this, but don't try to trick me. If you do, I'll club you to death and eat your flesh and grind your bones to make my bread."

"We have a deal. Now let's sit at your table with lots of drink and pretend that we're already drunk and desiring to have more drink with them. When they sit down to drink, leave the talking to me, but take no drink yourself. Just pretend to drink, and if you need to, go to the yard with your drink, and while you relieve yourself, pour your drink on the ground. I'll do the same."

"I see. That way my brothers will get good and drunk."

"Yes, and I'll see to it that they confess their plan and come to blows."

"I like this plan a lot." The ogre rubbed his chin with his hand and squinted. He drummed his fingers on the table and looked toward his club with his fingers moving.

"Just in case, I want you to have your biggest club handy near the table. Go get it now while I pour our drinks. That's right. Put it in the corner right behind you within easy reach."

"Is this the place to put it?"

"That will do just fine. Now sit down and pretend that we've been drinking for hours. Roll your eyes and bob your head. That's good. Now slur your speech. I hear your brothers approaching now. No matter what I say, just go along with me and pretend we've already had a long discussion about the plot."

The brother ogres came to the door and barged right in. To their surprise, they saw at the table the English man they were seeking and their brother drunk as could be without their passing out and talking about a dastardly plot of two ogres against their ogre brother.

"I tell you, sir, these two brothers intend their brother's death, and they plan to trick him so as to make him easy prey for them to club to death."

The English man looked up when he said this and saw the two new arrivals scratching their heads in confusion.

"Well, what have we here? If I'm not mistaken, these are the brothers that we've been speaking of."

The ogre said "Come, brothers, sit and drink with us. We have all day to get acquainted with this English man, who'll bring our dinner for a week."

The brothers were flabbergasted by the conversation, which destroyed their advantage of surprise. They forgot all about raising the hue and cry in the village. Why should they arouse the neighborhood when they had their prey just where they wanted him?

"Good ogres, since your brother is aware of your plot against him already, why don't you just put your clubs down on the floor and join us for a drink. If you drink up, you'll prove that you don't intend to get your brother drunk to kill him."

The two put down their clubs and sat down at the table and began to drink. They drank fervently as if to prove that they had no intention to remain sober. I plied them with drink whenever they finished what they had. Their brother spent his time going out back with his portion and coming back with an empty bowl, which I refilled. By noon, the two brothers were roaring drunk and becoming garrulous.

"So, ogres, why don't you tell your brother exactly what you planned to do to him."

"We love our brother. Why would we want to harm him in any way?"

"Yes, brothers, why do you want to do me harm? Why did you say that you wanted to club me to death and eat me?"

"This accusation is absurd. We wanted to share this English man with you. We were going to raise the hue and cry to find him so we could do just that."

"But you didn't raise the hue and cry, did you? And how could he have found out about your treachery? And why would he have come to me to warn me of your plan?" The ogre's anger was rising as he asked these questions. He distrusted his brothers and knew they could not answer his questions satisfactorily. Indeed, he had found them out. His large, fat hands were busily working as if he wanted to handle a club or cudgel at once. His naturally green complexion was turning fiery red, especially at the tips of his ears.

"We can't say anything about those things. We smelled the presence of the English man. We looked everywhere for him in both our cottages and yards. We even came here and searched your house and grounds by torchlight last night. He was not here. It was as if he had just disappeared."

"One of you must have told him of the plan. Which of you was it that he told?"

"It was not I who told about our plan."

"He lies. I would never tell an English man such a thing."

"There was no plan!"

"You lie."

"No, now it is you who lies. Ow, you punched me in the eye!"

"Pick up your club then and defend yourself."

"Let's step outside and settle this matter once and for all."

So the two brothers picked up their clubs, went out into the front yard and began to beat each other savagely, shouting, cursing and swearing as they did so.

Meanwhile, I watched them club each other and restrained their brother from joining the fray. The fighting ogres were now doing a lot of damage to each other. They tried to gain an advantage by closing on each other and by tearing at the hair and clothing of their adversary. The villagers began to assemble to watch the fray.

"Why did you tell?"

"Why did you tell?"

"So you two did plan to get me drunk and kill me with your clubs!"

"Who cares about that now?"

"Brothers, I care. You'll notice that I'm not slurring my speech anymore. I am not drunk. And I have a bigger club than both of you. Take that. And that."

The biggest brother laid on his blows so that his two brothers were forced to defend themselves against him while they still fought with each other. They were all hurting each other now, but the biggest brother was cracking skulls repeatedly.

I watched with amusement at these three evil ogres fighting each other. I decided they needed incentive to fight harder than they had hitherto. I raised my voice so that the villagers could hear every word I said.

"Say, my host, did you tell your brothers about the Irish man you plan to club and eat?"

"Did he say, 'Irish man'?"

"I do think he said, 'Irish man.' What about an Irish man?"

"I don't think he planned to share the fat priest Irish man with you. He wants the food all for himself."

"I knew we could not trust you, brother."

"Let's settle this quickly."

The three brother ogres battled each other until all were weary. The largest brother had the advantage of not being drunk, and he struck such devastating blows that he slew first one brother and then the other. He stood over their bodies slightly swaying from his exertions. The villagers were aghast and ran for their houses to hide.

"Now there will be no bickering anymore." The remaining ogre said this to no one in particular.

"And you'll have possession of your brothers' properties." I wanted to give him a focus other than me.

"Yes, and I have you to thank for this."

"Not so. I want no thanks. I was merely the messenger that brought you the news of their plot against you."

"And you brought me the news of the Irish man as well."

"I did. Now that you mention it, I have to depart to bring him here to you. I won't be long. While I'm gone, perhaps you'll have the pleasure of tenderizing your brothers with your club so that you can fillet them with a sharp knife and then set aside their bones for soup and for grinding."

"You have a point there, English man. How soon will you return with the fat Irish man?"

Will noticed that people were whispering about the Irish man. He knew they were not fond of the Irish, but even enemies were afraid of trolls. Will knew his listeners were paying attention. He raised his voice to bring them into the complications he was about to expose.

"I'll be back before you finish your work with your brothers."

"Then hurry on your way and bring him here. I owe you a life for revealing my brothers' plan against me."

"Remember that while you work, my host."

So off I walked along the path that led back out of the village of the ogres and out to the long road that led to the big wide world beyond. As I departed the third ogre's land, I heard him begin to sing as he swung his club against the bodies of his brothers:

An ogre leads a brutish life.
My ogre's life is hard.
This ogre needs a sharp knife
To cut through flesh and lard.
Hahaha. Hahaha. Hahaha.

I'd rather taste an Irish man
This evening in spring
Than roast a grisly harridan
Whose sinews taste like string.
Hahaha. Hahaha. Hahaha.

Fie, Fie, Foe, Fum!
I smell the blood of an Irish man.
Be he alive or be he dead,
I'll grind his bones to make my bread.

The ogre's glee in singing was palpable. It almost made up for his terrible singing voice and the blood-curdling content of his verses. I liked the subtle change in the final stanza of the ogre's song. The third ogre was now fixated on the promised Irish man. I was not going to disappoint him.

I walked to the Sheriff's house just off the long road.

"I have just witnessed the murders of two villagers in your shire. These murders were not the only crimes committed by the murderer, who was a fratricide, and the brothers who were murdered were also murderers. All men were cannibals."

"Stranger, I am outraged to learn these things from you. Bailiff, have half a dozen men mounted and ready in half an hour to ride to the village to investigate these two murders. Stranger, you'll have to accompany us to identify the criminal."

"The villagers will be your witnesses for the two murders. I suspect they have other stories to tell you about what the three brothers have done. Then too, so many murders and other crimes have been committed that perhaps a religious man, an Irish Franciscan friar, could accompany us."

"I know of such a man. He is called Friar John. He could comfort the villagers, who are now hiding in their homes in mortal fear after what they've witnessed."

"That is sage advice. While my men assemble, let's ride to the abbey and enlist Friar John's support in this. I'll lend you a horse. As we ride, you can describe in detail what you heard and saw in the village."

I told the Sheriff what I saw happen outside the third ogre's house. I did not mention my role in the actions leading up to the murders. He had no need to know about those.

I did mention that I had stopped by the murderer's house to ask whether I could gain food and a bed for the night in exchange for my doing odd jobs that required doing. I did not want to be charged with vagrancy, trespass or inducement, far lesser crimes than murder, but jail offenses nonetheless.

At the abbey, the abbot immediately agreed to release Friar John for the purpose that the Sheriff proposed. The friar was in the refectory feeding his face, but he came carrying a flagon of wine and a joint of mutton for the trip.

When I told the friar about the three brothers, he nodded sagely and said, "I've heard about the three ogres. They're three ogres too many and evil. They were excommunicated with the bell, book, and candle. Some say they're in league with the Devil himself."

We arrived at the house of the third ogre, still working in his front yard and singing his song. He looked up to see the fat friar and smiled. Then he saw the Sheriff and knew his end was nigh. The end.

The villagers clapped and clapped at Will's story. They began to murmur among themselves about how much they liked it. Some repeated the ogres' chant and others took it up.

Will scampered down from the podium and became lost in the crowd while Judith stood and raised her right hand into the snowy air.

"Thank you, Will. We'll all ignore the obvious reference to good Friar Stephen at the abbey, and we'll be checking our roof hatches this very evening since they seem such likely passages for escape from our thatched houses. We now come to the third and last of our stories of the afternoon, by Colin, the weaver.

"Colin, please come forward. Everyone, I know it's growing late, and you're probably as hungry and thirsty as we judges are, but let's be good sports and hear Colin out to the end. Think about yourselves being up on the podium and how you'd feel if your audience was inattentive or murmuring to each other instead of listening. That's better.

"Now that the snow has subsided, and the shroud of nature provides a silent backdrop, we'll all be able to hear him well. So when you're ready, Colin, begin."

"My story is not at all like the others you've just heard. I'm humbled by them—good work, Ned and Will. Anyway, like Will, I'd be honored to wed any of the three judges that we have today. I feel like ancient Paris before the three goddesses, only it's not my choice but theirs that counts. I worked hard all fall on my story as I worked at my loom. It's cut from a richer cloth than anything I've made before. I must confess, I wrote it especially for one of the three judges. If my mimicking sounds like people you know, it may be so. So here goes."

Colin then told his story, "Catching the Chameleon," using many voices, as follows:

Catching the Chameleon

Beautiful Carrie drifted across the village square as boys stopped in their tracks to gape and admire her. Girls turned their heads to hate her every gesture out of jealousy. Among her admirers were Waldo and Emmet.

"If, Emmet, you mean to capture her heart, you must decide the season. Carrie's a vertiginous vixen and liable to jump when you least expect it. I should know, shouldn't I? She loved me last spring and dumped me last summer."

"Waldo, I'm smitten. Carrie's the most beautiful girl I've ever laid eyes upon. I simply must have her."

"The question is, must she have you? Aye, there lies the rub." Waldo scratched his chin and watched Emmet squirm with the thought.

"Hi Waldo, Emmet! Have you seen Melissa?" asked Lucille.

"Not lately, Lucille," Emmet replied. "What's up?"

"Melissa was asked to the dance by William, sort of, but now he wants to go with Randi. I'm supposed to ask Melissa whether she'd mind if William breaks their date."

"How can this be, Lucille? Randi is going with Samuel." Emmet seemed confused.

"She was going with Samuel until last weekend. They had a big fight and split. Now both Randi and Samuel need to find new matches."

"Well, that might be the solution you're looking for." Emmet was always good at resolutions of seemingly impossible situations.

"What do you mean, Emmet?"

"Why not have Samuel ask Melissa to the village dance? If he importunes her just before you tell her that William wants to break the date, she'll have an option. I'll wager she'll be mad enough at William to accept Samuel's offer."

"Emmet, that's positively brilliant!"

Colin paused in the telling to catch his breath. It was not easy to imitate as many voices as he was tasked to do. He modulated the best he could so the people could follow him. Even the dullest, like Pik the pigsty boy was following right along. He usually was throwing tomatoes at this stage. So the weaver took heart and continued weaving his tale, ratcheting up his volume and enunciating clearly so everyone could understand him as the dialog accelerated. For him, the warp comprised the male characters and the woof the females. Telling was as simple as weaving. Yet though not everyone could weave, all needed clothes and only fools unraveled their clothing.

"So here comes Melissa, and over there is Samuel. You go to Melissa and prime the pump. I'll clue Samuel in and bring him over casually. Let's hurry. Time is of the essence."

"Hi Melissa, I've been looking for you."

"Oh Lucille, I can't find William anywhere."

"That's because he's been walking and talking with Randi. She's just broken up with Samuel. Look, Samuel's coming over with Emmet now."

Emmet was whispering in Samuel's ear. Samuel was looking at Melissa and smiling. She smiled back and curtsied.

"Hi, Melissa. Hi, Lucille. I suppose you've heard that Randi and I have broken up."

"Oh, Samuel, that's terrible. You were so close, for what? Two months?"

"Well, it's over, and we're not speaking now." Samuel looked dejected.

"Melissa, that's what I was hoping to discuss with you." Emmet paused to see her reaction.

"With me? Whatever do you mean?" She had crossed her arms and was looking daggers at Emmet.

"Let's say, Melissa, that William wants to take Randi to the dance now that she's free."

"He can't do that. He's supposed to take me to the village dance."

"William told me that he asked you, but you haven't given him a firm answer yet. Now he wants to withdraw his offer and take Randi." Emmet watched her closely for her reaction to this news.

"I've already bought a new dress. That rat William! Wait till I get my claws on him." She was becoming red as a beet. Emmet had to act quickly, or she would be off with arms and legs akimbo after William.

"Wait! Samuel, do you have something to say to Melissa?"

"Ahem, well, yes. Melissa, I want to ask you whether you'll go to the dance with me. I heard that you might be going with William, but if you're not really going with him after all, will you go with me?"

"Emmet, I sense your mind is lurking in the shadows here. Did you put Samuel up to this?"

"Me? Absolutely not. Well, I just mentioned to Samuel that you and William had not made firm arrangements, and he took it from there."

While this thought sunk in, the silence was deafening. Then, Melissa exploded in fury.

"Oh, men! I hate you all. But wait a minute! Okay, Samuel, I'll go to the village dance with you. That's a firm commitment. Lucille, tell William our date is off, and he can go with whomever he wants. I don't want to see him ever again. If he tries to speak to me, I'll cut him dead. Samuel, I'll expect a visit from you tonight about the details. Waldo, why are you laughing?"

"Me laughing? Hahaha. It's just the way the world goes—like the weather. The winds don't know where they are blowing. They just blow. That sort of thing. I'm always fascinated when broken couples can find new matches and become new couples. It's a form of natural magic."

Colin, the weaver, saw that the crowd was craning their necks forward to follow his rapid dialog. He particularly liked mouthing the female parts. He decided to accentuate Melissa's anger.

"Well, I don't like being laughed at. So stop it."

"Emmet, can I talk with you a minute?" Lucille had touched his arm so he turned and gave her his full attention.

"Sure, Lucille. What's up with you?"

"If you can work the magic with those four clowns, maybe you can work a little magic for me."

"Lucille, you never have problems like this. You're a rock of stability in the company of changelings and fools."

She colored red and looked away, then down. "You've probably no idea how hard it is for me to be a rock."

"We both know that it takes no brains at all to be a changeling."

"Hahaha. In fact, the fewer the brains, the more the changes."

"So what's your problem, Lucille?"

"Emmet, no one has asked me to the dance."

"I see. And, I suppose, you want to go very much."

"Yes, I do."

"And do you care who invites you?"

"Well, he has to be tall and handsome, strong and gentle. I have to trust him. Gracious, Emmet, I'm desperate. Can you help me? Now I'm totally humiliated."

"Don't feel that way. I think I have the perfect match for you."

"You do? See, I'm all on tippy toes with excitement. Who is it? Who?"

"Let me warn you: your perfect match will not exactly be exciting, but you're made for each other though you don't yet know it. Walk with Melissa while she gets her act together, and then come back in five or ten minutes and we'll talk."

Lucille was excited and did not want to leave. Emmet had good news for her, but he was coy. Meanwhile, everyone else was coming together. They would have fun at the dance. She wondered why what was easy for others was so hard for her. Still, Emmet had the answers. He always did.

"Oh, Emmet, you're such a dear. I'll be right back. Melissa, let's walk and talk a little girl talk. Don't even think of William. Tell me instead about the dress you made for the village dance."

While Lucille and Melissa walked off together talking, Emmet looked at Waldo and said, "Waldo, come here for a minute. Do you have a date for the village dance? No? I thought not. You're still brooding about Carrie, aren't you?"

"Emmet, I don't want to think about girls now at all."

"So why not ask a boy to the village dance?"

"Not very funny. So why are you asking me about who to take to the dance?"

"I'm asking because I know you'd like to go, and I'd like you to take Lucille."

"Wait just a minute. Do you mean the Lucille whose walking over there with Melissa? The dark-haired girl with the bright green eyes?"

"She's the one. Is there another Lucille whom we both know? She just told me she wants to go to the village dance with a tall, handsome and strong man. Naturally, we both thought of you and no one else."

"You did? I had no idea."

"So will you ask her to the dance?"

"I'll think about it for a time."

"Your time's up. You'd better think about what you're going to say fast because here she comes."

"Hi again, Lucille, I was just talking with Waldo here, and we were thinking about all the girls who would be the best dates for the dance. You know the girls who are beautiful, graceful and intelligent. Naturally, we thought of you."

"That's all very nice, Emmet, but you must want something. So what is it that you want?"

"It's not what I want, Lucille. Waldo, it's over to you, pal."

"Hmm. Lucille, I don't know whether you have a date for the village dance yet, but I'd like to take you if you don't. Will you go to the dance with me?"

"Waldo, this is so sudden … Of course, I'll go to the dance with you. Can we talk about it? Come, let's walk together a while. See you later, Emmet, and thank you."

Now Lucille and Waldo were together, and Samuel and Melissa were together too. The plot was weaving itself together nicely, thanks to Emmet.

"Bye, you two. Now here comes William. Hello, William."

"Hi Emmet, did Lucille catch up with you?"

"Relax, chum, everything is square again."

"Meaning what?"

"You can now go to the dance with Randi because Melissa has agreed to break her date with you. Melissa will go to the dance with Samuel, who just broke up with Randi.

Lucille, who did you the big favor, will go to the village dance with Waldo."

"That's all great, man. I guess I owe you a big thanks for everything."

"Don't mention it. Say, how's your better twin doing these days?"

"Carrie's in a blue funk. I don't know why."

"For one thing, she just broke up with Waldo."

"Yes, and I thought they were a pair headed for the altar one day."

"Of course, her pick was Samuel before Waldo and David before Samuel. Why do you think that Carrie's always changing her mind about men?"

"Beautiful girls think it's their birthright to change their mind without a second thought whenever they want to."

In the distance, the couples were flirting and laughing together. The men contemplated the fickle nature of all women. Now, the field was closing on Carrie and Emmet.

"She's truly beautiful and sometimes cruel. She's the perfect lady of that Italian Petrarch's sonnets."

"Yes, I suppose she is."

"'I burn, I freeze.' I know how that feels."

"She has the face that launched a thousand ships. And every morning after breakfast she begins breaking hearts wherever she sails."

"Look, when you see Carrie, do you suppose you could give her a note from me? Here it is."

"No problem, Emmet. If I don't see her before dinner, I'll give it to her then."

"William, you're a champ. Did you firm up your plans for the dance this time?"

"This time, my plans are firm."

"Until you change your mind, you mean. Hahaha."

"Well, if I do change my mind, I'll come to you for the fix."

"Take care until then, and give that note to Carrie for me."

"Righto."

"Hey, Emmet, that Lucille is quite a girl."

"She's been right there in front of you, but you could not really see her because of your love for Carrie. Are you all set?"

"All set, pal! I've got a few things to arrange, so I'll see you later. Isn't that Carrie coming straight for us? I'm off. Sticking around would be too painful."

"Later."

Now all the others had matches. Only Emmet and Carrie remained, but he had planted a seed he hoped would grow.

"Hi Emmet, William gave me this note and said it was from you. I just wanted to say I thought it was sweet."

"Hi Carrie, I wrote the sonnet for you."

"I know, and I'm flattered, really I am. You never told me how you felt. I didn't know."

"So you like the poem."

"I'm beginning to like the poet."

"I'm worried."

"Why's that, Emmet?"

"I'm worried because of change."

"We're all changing, Emmet. We can't help it. We grow. We aspire."

"We want to bond but break hearts instead."

"Like in your poem?"

"Like in our lives." Emmet was serious, as always, and a born poet. He had called Lucille a rock, but he was the rock for the entire group of village friends. They all understood this, but none could articulate it. Emmet enjoyed being with Carrie, and she felt his attraction to her.

"That's what I've always liked about you, Emmet. You're a deep one. You're always thinking. I've watched you looking out a window for an hour. I asked myself what you are thinking. I can't hold my mind to anything for more than a few seconds."

"Yet, Carrie, you read my poem, and you remembered it."

"Yes."

"Do you have a date yet for the village dance?"

"No, but many have asked me to go to the dance."

"I'll bet they have. Would you consider going to the dance with me?"

"Of course, I'll go with you."

"I'm glad. Is it fixed then that we'll go together—to the dance I mean?"

"Yes, silly, of course, it's fixed because I agreed to go." She reached out and touched his chin so his eyes leveled with hers. She smiled, and his heart leapt.

"Let's walk and talk a little if you have the time." Emmet was earnest. He took her hand.

"I do have an hour if you like. I'd like you to explain your poem to me."

"That may take a little longer than an hour."

"Can you give me the short explanation?"

"I have admired you from afar from the first time I saw you."

"Yet you get along with all the girls, and they like you."

"And you are admired by all the village boys, yet you seem unaware."

"My mother counseled that I should let the others come to me and that I should sift and winnow to the one."

"Good counsel, I think."

"Yet, I'm caught in a conundrum because when I winnow down to one, I find faults I cannot ignore."

"So you break a heart and move on to the next."

"I do. I must."

"So for a while, let's enjoy each other's company."

"Yes, let's do just that."

"And when the change comes, we'll part amicably."

"If we both feel that way, yes."

"So constant will we be to change."

"So true: your poem, and you."

"Well, fellow villagers, I've finished my story and you know it's about a lot of you and me as well. I'm sorry I made one of the judges blush and cry. I'll be standing down now while the judges deliberate. Thank you."

There was a great clapping from the young people of the village, and many bewildered looks on the faces of the older villagers. The masked figures clapped the most of all because they saw something in the story that they found familiar.

Judith conferred quickly with Anne and Mary, and the three nodded in agreement. Then Judith once again held her right hand in the air. When everyone calmed down, she made a statement.

"We have now heard all three tales, and we judges three have come to our decision."

The villagers were now totally focused on the judges' stand where the three fair maidens were. The fate of three men, one of them unknown, and three women were now in the balance.

"The first place award must go to the sincerest of the stories, the one that came right from the heart. Everyone knows that Colin loves Mary as Emmet in the story loves Carrie. Why he even wrote her a sonnet that she carries with her everywhere she goes. That being known, how could they not become a match? Come forward, Colin, and take Mary by the hand. Mary, stand forward to receive your future husband. We are all chameleons, but some things, like love, never change."

Colin extended his hand, and Mary grasped it. Her eyes were full of tears, which he brushed away with his free hand. They drew together and stood side by side, looking at the crowd. For them, the day had clearly ended, and their new life had begun.

"The second place award goes to the most just of the stories, and that means Ned should come forward and receive the hand of Anne the wise. I can see this is the right judgment from the smiles in their eyes. We have no ogres in our village, but if we did, I'd wish someone like Ned could deal them as the wandering youth did in his story."

Ned threw his hat in the air and whooped for joy. He kissed his lady, and she kissed him back. The two stood side by side across the podium from Colin and Mary.

"I save the last award, the third place, because the author of that admonitory fable chose to speak through an unlikely proxy. Prince Valiant had everything necessary to both discover and cure the dragon lady of what possessed her, but he departed leaving her behind as he sought other conquests in distant lands. I choose the author of this story because I could not in conscience place any other woman's destiny in the hands of an unknown composer. So if the author of 'Dragon Lady' will step forward, I offer my hand as a sacrifice."

Judith stood in the cold, with one betrothed couple on her right side and another on her left side. The silence in the square was profound. Then a man in a cape and mask stood forth, and as he walked up to the judges' stand, he took off his mask while everyone drew back, and as they recognized who was stepping forth, all began to kneel. He took Judith's hand as she curtsied deep, and when she rose, he stood by her side, tall and handsome as a prince should be and waved to the villagers, gesturing for all to rise.

"I could not be happier anywhere else or with anyone else in this kingdom. Fortunately, I'm not looking for a fair lady who is a dragon by night. I am, however, delighted to be matched with the most beautiful woman who is also, as you have just witnessed, just and wise and wonderful. I thank my proxy for his part in my charade. It's drawing late, and we have wassailing to do and dancing. My master of the revels happens to be here, and I command that everyone have the merriest of Christmases and the Happiest of New Years. Come, Judith, my love. Let's lead the way. Tomorrow is our blessed wedding day."

Pixie Hill

"Mother, William says that he saw a real pixie near Pixie Hill. Is it true that pixies live there?"

Henrietta and her mother were in the kitchen working together to make the evening meal.

"When you were born, Henrietta, I thought so." She sprinkled flour on the board and took the risen flour ball from the bowl. She worked the ball with her rolling pin.

"Did you ever see a pixie?" Henrietta asked her while she snapped the beans, careful to take the tops and bottoms off each bean. She placed the ends in the pig slop bowl with the trimmings of the radishes and lettuce.

"No, dear, I can't say that I did. They only come out at night, and I never purposely went looking for them." She had a dreamy look in her eyes that Henrietta was trying her best to interpret.

"Then why did you think they existed?" She was curious to knit together the fragments of what she knew. She stopped snapping beans because she was done. She picked up the wooden spoon and stirred the batter while her mother continued rolling the dough for the bread.

"I knew them from their signs, Henny. The way the horses looked in the morning as if they had been ridden all night long. The way the house always looked tidier when I left a bowl of milk with biscuits out for them at night. The little tricks they'd play if I didn't do that."

"What kinds of tricks, Mother?" She laid the spoon on the side of the bowl and waited.

"Keep mixing the batter, Hen. Stir with your whole arm. That's right. Well, the pixies would hide things, mostly. I'd not find my keys to the pantry where I knew I'd put them. Your father would not find his favorite cup where he usually hung it in the kitchen. That sort of thing."

"So has anyone in the area actually seen a pixie?"

Her mother considered this question for a long while. Then she nodded.

"Old Mrs. Handbell says she saw a pixie. He was small and green, with pointy ears and tousled hair. She saw the creature when she was collecting mushrooms out by Pixie Hill."

"Father says that Pixie Hill is an old mine for iron ore."

"That's true, honey. Of course, it is. That mine is very old."

"Father also told me that iron or iron ore would keep the pixies away. Then why would the pixies go where iron ore can be found?"

"I don't know the answer to that question. Maybe you should ask your father."

"Do you think the batter's done yet?"

"You're almost there. Keep stirring. I'm making the clotted cream. Won't that be delicious when we wake up in the morning? We'll spread it on our cream scones with currants. Mmmm. Let's hope the pixies won't spoil the clotted cream."

"Why might they do that, Mother?"

"Pixies can be mischievous creatures, Lamb. Now the batter looks just right. We'll pour it into the pans. The oven is ready. The cakes will bake for twenty minutes. After we take them out to let them cool, we'll be ready for bed."

"Will you tell me a bedtime story, Mother? I've been awfully good today."

"I know you have, dear. For a six-year-old, you've been acting like an adult. We'll see how tired we are at bedtime."

Henrietta poured the batter she had mixed into the two greased cake tins she had prepared beforehand. She used the spatula to get all the batter into the tins. She always marveled at the results of baking at every stage. She knew if she kept to the rules, everything worked out just right.

"Let's slide the cake tins into the oven now and watch the clock. It's eight o'clock, so at twenty minutes after eight, give or take, we'll be ready to take the tins out."

"And we'll stick a toothpick into the cake to test whether it's ready?"

"That's right. Now come over here. The cream is ready to place by the fire. It will settle there all night, and in the morning, guess what?"

"We'll have clotted cream. Hooray!"

"Now it's time for your bath and prayers. Then we'll decide whether to tell a story."

Henrietta went through the ritual of her bath and prayed the prayer she always recited before bed, her hands pressed together and her eyes closed. It began, "Now I lay me down to sleep, I pray the Lord, my soul to keep." She had recited it every evening that she remembered. She particularly liked the "God Bless" portion, because she could include not only her parents and family but also other worthy personages and figures. Tonight, she included the pixies of Pixie Hill. She felt very good about that, though she couldn't say why.

"Mother, I've had my bath and said my prayers. Will you tell me a story now, please?"

"All right. Snuggle down. Here is Rupert, the bear. Hold him tight."

Henrietta held Rupert, the bear with the sad brown eyes. It was scruffy and old, but it was her favorite stuffed animal. She looked up at her mother with her full attention, her eyes wide open in anticipation.

"Once upon a time a long, long time ago there lived a pixie family in a place along the coast of Somerset named Pixie Hill. There was a father pixie, a mother pixie and two little pixies, a girl, and a boy. They liked Pixie Hill because no one would suspect that pixies would live there. Long ago, some human had said that pixies were repelled by iron, but nothing could be further from the truth. So the pixies were not harassed by the humans since they only went out late at night and returned well before sunrise to their dwellings.

"It happened that humans were farming the land all around Pixie Hill, so the pixies could raid any farm they liked for victuals that had been left out, and they could ride horses they found whenever they liked as long as they returned them to the stables in time for the pixies to return to their dwellings before daylight. They would ride deep into the night all over the land. The only sign of their having done this thing was the tangle in the horses' mane or fetlock the next morning.

"The pixies liked the farmers whose horses were available for riding. They also liked the farmers' wives who left pixie food, like oatmeal cookies, for them to find. As a reward to those thoughtful wives, they would clean their houses and help with the chores. They would chase devilish imps and dwarfs from the premises. The pixies would brush the hay away from the chickens' eggs that had just been laid so that they could be found.

"One day the girl pixie, whose name was Matilda, decided she would communicate with a farmer's daughter who always left her a bowl of milk and a cookie on the back stoop. The girl pixie drank the milk and ate the cookie as she always had done, and in return, she left behind a magic rock. This rock was magic because if you held it in your right hand and squeezed it hard and simultaneously made a wish, that wish would come true."

Henrietta interrupted saying, "Oh, mother, I wish I had a magic rock like Matilda's!" She was very excited about the girl Matilda who seemed so much like her.

"Well, the farm girl found the rock the next morning next to the empty cup and plate she had left out the night before. She did not know what the rock meant, but she put it in her apron pocket just the same. She went about her duties like a good girl until it came time for her to say her evening prayers. Then she took out the rock and put it firmly between her hands and said her prayers with unusual fervor. She prayed that she would one day see the pixies. Then, after her prayers, she returned the rock to her apron pocket, poured the milk and laid out the cookie for her pixies and went to sleep.

"Late that night Matilda came for her milk and a cookie, but she made a noise that the farm girl heard. The human girl rose from her bed and opened the back door. There, Matilda was drinking the last of the milk. She had already finished the cookie.

"Can you see me?" the pixie asked the farm girl.

"Yes, I can see you. I'm so excited I don't know what to do. I'm trembling all over. I think I'm going to cry."

"Calm down. If you cry out or let anyone know that you've seen me, I'll disappear, and you'll never see me again."

"Don't go away. Please don't disappear. I'll do anything you want if you stay and talk with me."

"If you keep me a secret from everyone, including your mother and father, I'll come to see you every night, and we can talk."

"My name is Henrietta. May I touch your pointed ear?"

"Yes, if you're very gentle. That's right. Now let me touch your round ear. Humans' ears are so strange."

"Your hand is warm. Do you always look so green?"

"Pixies are always green to match our surroundings like hills and meadows."

"Do you have a large family?"

"Let's see, there's my mother and father and my little brother, Colin. Then there are all my cousins and friends."

"Will you be my friend?"

"As long as you keep me secret, yes, I'll be your friend. I like the milk and cookies you leave for me. I don't know whether you've noticed, but I've helped you tidy up your room at night."

"So you're the one who does that?" The farm girl clapped her hands and listened carefully so she could learn more. "I thought you were only full of mischief."

"We pixies can be helpful as well as mischievous. You'll see. I've got to run now. I'll see you tomorrow night if you want."

"Yes, please. Tell me, though, why I can see you now when I couldn't see you before tonight."

"You must have pressed the rock I left for you and made a wish to see me."

"I did that. I prayed that I could see you. I heard you, too. Will the rock work for other wishes as well?"

"Yes, it is a magic rock. Use it wisely when you need to. I'm off now. Remember, don't tell. If you do tell, I won't be able to come again. Goodnight, Henrietta."

"Goodnight, Matilda. See you tomorrow night."

Henrietta closed the back door and went back to her bed. She fell asleep instantly and slept until morning. That's the end of our story for tonight."

Her mother saw that Henrietta's eyes had closed.

"Henrietta, dear, are you asleep?"

Henrietta had fallen sound asleep, so her mother tucked her in and pulled the coverlet up around her neck. It was chilly, and she did not want her little girl to catch a cold. She tiptoed out of the room.

The next day, Henrietta did her chores and helped her mother clean house and cook food. She waited patiently until evening and just before she prepared herself for bed, she put out milk and a cookie on the back porch for the pixie. She then bathed and said her prayers. This time, she took up the rock that had lain at the back of her bureau. It was the rock that her mother had given her for luck many years ago. She had cherished it but never used it for anything. Now, she pressed it firmly between her hands while she prayed to see the pixies.

Her mother said she was too tired to continue the story she had begun the night before, so Henrietta went to sleep without hearing the rest of the story. She dreamed of what she had heard the night before. Late at night, she heard a scraping sound on the back porch. She rose from her bed and went to investigate what was happening. When she pushed open the door, a pixie was finishing the milk she had left. The pixie had already finished the cookie.

"Hello. My name is Henrietta. I'm so excited to meet you I can hardly stand it." She clapped her hands for joy and rocked up and down on her haunches.

"I know. My name is Matilda. I'm the pixie from the story your mother told you."

"Are you real?"

"Touch me gently and feel for yourself."

"You are so soft and fuzzy. And you're green as grass. Do you really have a mother and father and little brother who live with you on Pixie Hill?"

"Yes, just like in your mother's story. We visit all the farms around the hill in the night. Tonight I'm going riding. Do you want to come with me?"

"I'd better not. I'll see you tomorrow night if you'll come again. You can tell me stories about what you do on Pixie Hill."

"I will if you won't tell a soul about our friendship."

"Cross my heart and hope to die, I'll keep your secret."

"Well, be sure you do that. Now I'm off. I'll see you later. Goodnight."

"Goodnight, Matilda."

Henrietta could not believe that the story that her mother told her had come true for her. She crawled back into bed and instantly fell asleep. When the rooster crowed, she sprang to her feet to begin her day.

She washed her eyes and changed out of her nightgown and into her work clothes. She checked the back porch and brought in the empty cup and plate that held the pixie food before Matilda ate it. Henrietta did not tell her mother or father about what had happened during the night. She was very good throughout the day and that night repeated what she did the night before. She laid out the milk and cookie for the pixie to find. She then prepared for bed, but this time, after prayers her mother found time to resume her story about the pixies of Pixie Hill.

"So where was I? Oh, yes, I remember. The human girl Henrietta and the pixie Matilda had formed a friendship that they renewed every night. The pixie could not stay long because of her chores during the night. Henrietta likewise could not stay long because she was not supposed to go outside at night.

"One night Matilda confessed, 'The other humans were inconsiderate about the pixies of Pixie Hill.'

"'What do you mean? I thought you didn't want humans to know about you. You take such pains to be invisible. I see you, but that is different.'

"'Humans are beginning to excavate the area around Pixie Hill. They are scraping the green earth and pushing the black soil into mounds. They are building something large and evil. We can't do much with all the machinery and people. At night, we make our mischief, but it does no good. Is there any way you can help us?'

"'I'm not sure,' Henrietta told Matilda. She had never been asked a favor by a pixie before. Her mother and father always handled the big questions and answered them as well. She trusted them for that. Now her pixie friend was placing a large fardel on her shoulders. She was intimidated and worried. She thought hard about how to help her pixie friend. She decided that she would broach the question of the pixies without insinuating that she had made contact with the pixie named Matilda.

"'Mother,' Henrietta asked the next morning, 'Why are all the people digging around Pixie Hill?'

"'Henny, they are building a large power plant that will provide electricity for the whole area. It's a grand project that costs lots of money. When they've finished, we'll all have lights and electricity. It will be a big improvement, though we'll have an eyesore, to be sure.'

"'Oh, I see. It will help all the humans. But what will become of the pixies who live on Pixie Hill?'

"'The pixies will always find a way to survive. They always have done. Don't worry, Henny. It's good of you to think of the little people.'

"'But Mother, doesn't anyone care about the pixies but me?' She had raised her voice, indignant to think she was the only one who cared.

"'A few people care, and they've been very vocal in their opposition. Mrs. Handbell is particularly vociferous. The Sheriff drove out to warn her to be quiet. They argued. He threatened to take her to jail. The matter is very serious, and large interests are supporting the building of the power plant.'

"'Why can't the construction people find a way to leave Pixie Hill alone while they do their work?' Henrietta asked.

"'I'll have to ask Mrs. Handbell about that approach. She's been so much against the whole project; she might not have thought of a compromise.'

"'Mother, what is a compromise?'

"'Henrietta, often when two people have clear differences, they won't listen to each other. I'll give you an example. If two farmers each want to host a party, and they won't compromise, then the party will be held at one farm or the other, and someone will be upset because his farm was not selected for the party. But if they decide to have a picnic party halfway between their farms, neither will be disappointed because their perspective will have changed.'

"'Mother, there must be a way to compromise so that we can have our power plant and the pixies can have their dwellings. Do you think Mrs. Handbell and the Sheriff will listen to that approach?'

"'That's a very grown-up question, Henrietta. We'll just have to see about that. I'll talk with your father about it tonight. Maybe something can be done. For now, it's time for you to get some sleep.'

"Henrietta went to sleep, but she woke up late in the night by the scraping of a plate on the back porch. She knew what the sound meant and went out to talk with Matilda the pixie.

"'Hi Matilda. I asked about the construction project. I found out that a big power plant is the object of it. Powerful humans are backing the project.'

"'Can anything be done to protect Pixie Hill?'

"'My mother talked with my father. They will confer with the people who object to the power plant. They are going to try to find a compromise that will leave Pixie Hill alone while the power plant gets built.'

"'The pixies won't like that.'

"'Not even if Pixie Hill is left untouched?'

"'In our experience when humans start moving earth, they don't know when to stop. Farmers plow acres, and then they cut down woods between fields and make another farm land from them. Soon the wee people have nowhere left to go.'

"'Well, I'll let you know how things go. Why don't you tell your fellow pixies that we are working on a compromise? The power plant will come, no matter what. The only way we can manage to keep a dwelling for pixies is to exclude Pixie Hill from the construction.'

"'That gives me a pixellating idea.'

"'What's that?'

"'Maybe there's a way to let the humans know that pixies still inhabit Pixie Hill without the humans seeing any pixies.'

"'You mean by playing pixie tricks on the humans?'

"'Something like that, yes. You'll likely hear about it after it happens.'

"'You won't harm anyone, will you? That would not help matters. It might even cause the eradication of any pixie dwellings.'

"'Pixies don't harm humans. We aren't like that at all. You'll know us by our signs. Support us if you can.'

"'I'll help, but I'm only one person, and since I am a child, the grownups are not likely to listen to me.'

"'I think you'll be surprised. Remember, though, don't tell our secret. The other humans must never know that we have made contact.'

"'Count on me. I've got to get back inside now. I'll see you tomorrow night. Goodbye for now.'

"'Goodnight, Henrietta. You're a great friend and we pixies appreciate what you're doing for us.'

"Henrietta went back inside to bed. She did not fall asleep all at once because Matilda had given her so many ideas to consider. Finally, she resolved that she could do nothing further that night, so she went to sleep.

"Henny, darling, are you sleeping? I guess you are."

Henrietta's mother tucked her daughter in as usual and turned out the light. She went to talk with her husband about the power plant, the subject of their nightly discussions for weeks now.

"Hubert, don't you think that we can protect Pixie Hill?"

"Maddy, I've spoken with the Sheriff, and he is firm that the power plant must be built as planned."

"What about Pixie Hill?"

"No decision has been made about that. The farmers are having a fit about the construction. They aren't thinking about compromises. Neither are the interests behind the power plant. Big money is driving the project."

"Surely there must be someone who will listen to a sensible argument."

"Mr. Philpotts might just listen, but he's a busy man."

"Let's set a meeting and give him a try. It can't hurt."

"I'll see what I can do. I won't make any promises, though."

"Let's hope the man will give us an honest hearing."

"We'd better hope for a miracle."

Henrietta's parents decided to go to sleep and approach Mr. Philpotts in the morning. That night, the pixies were very active. They braided daisies in chains and strung them around the machinery at the plant site. They placed small mounds of earth at regular intervals. They pressed mud against the windows of the cranes and bulldozers and generally made a mess of things.

When the construction workers arrived at the work site, they were upset with the vandalism that they saw. They blamed the farmers for it and called the Sheriff to take action. The Sheriff consulted Mr. Philpotts about the matter.

"Sheriff, the farmers have concerns. We shouldn't continue fighting with them. Let's find a way to satisfy them while we continue our construction."

At just this moment, Hubert and Maddy arrived and asked to speak with Mr. Philpotts. He was caught off guard by their peremptory approach and agreed to talk for a few minutes.

"Mr. Philpotts, we have one concern about this project, and it is shared by most of the farmers. Pixie Hill is a special site for all the farms. It is the location of an old iron ore mine. That mine is a symbol of local history and a sort of shrine. If there were some way to spare Pixie Hill from the construction, the farmers might feel better about the project."

"We have no current plan to dig around Pixie Hill. I suppose we could mark out the area you are concerned about without changing our plan. Let me talk with the construction engineers about this. Sheriff, what do you think?'

"Well, Mr. Philpotts, only a few farmers have real problems with the plant project. They are all concerned about Pixie Hill. I'll canvass them about the matter. Maybe if we can find a way to appease them, we won't have any more of the vandalism we've seen."

"That's all we ask, Mr. Philpotts. Think of Pixie Hill as a green sanctuary in the middle of the construction site. It will be a reminder of our past and help beautify what might otherwise be a big, ugly, gray plant." Maddy said this with such conviction that the Sheriff was a little cowed. Mr. Philpotts nodded sagely. Then, the interview was over, and everyone returned to his work.

"Well, Henrietta," her mother said when she returned to her kitchen, "We talked with Mr. Philpotts. Your father made our case about Pixie Hill. The Sheriff was there. He will talk with the other farm families. Mr. Philpotts said that Pixie Hill was not included in the current construction plan. So we're hopeful. Does that make you feel better about what is happening?"

"Mother, I won't be happy until we know that Pixie Hill is safe. Could you also talk with some of the other farmers' wives, so they know what we want to do?"

"You clean inside the house and pick up the area around the house. I'll make a few quick visits before the Sheriff gets a chance to talk with anyone."

Henrietta bustled about the house and yard to tidy things. She was learning fast how to keep a farmhouse because her mother was a good teacher. While she worked, she wondered about the situation. She was certain that there was something that she could do to help that she had not already done. She resolved to talk with Matilda at their nightly meeting. A plan was forming in her mind.

It had been a busy day for everyone, so Henrietta's mother was not able to continue her bedtime story that night. Henrietta went through her normal routine. She went to sleep thinking hard about her plan. That night when she heard the scraping outside the back door, she slipped out to talk with Matilda.

"Hi, Matilda. I have news for you. My parents are trying their best to save Pixie Hill. It hasn't helped to have your pixie mischief because the Sheriff is blaming all your tricks on the farmers' families. My father says that someone is likely to be arrested for vandalism—and it won't be a pixie. Anyway, I have a serious question for you."

"Okay, Henrietta. What is your question?" The pixie wiggled her pointed ears as if to say that she was listening closely.

"My mother told me a story about a magic rock that made wishes come true. I used a rock that I found and said a prayer, and I was suddenly able to see and talk with you. This, then, is my question: Can I use the rock I used to reach you to change the minds of men like Mr. Philpotts?"

"That's difficult to say, Henrietta. Rocks are rocks. Your pure mind and heart, your prayers and your wishes can work all by themselves. So many things you humans fear and worry about can be dispelled with hope and supplication."

"Can you help my wishes and prayers to come true, or not?"

The pixie wiggled her nose and shook her body. She seemed reluctant to answer the question. Finally, she made a decision and spoke.

"I'll do what I can to help you. After all, it's for a good cause. Give it a try. We'll see what happens."

"I'll do that and see you tomorrow night. Goodbye for now. I'll have to be praying."

The pixie smiled and waved to her friend. Then she vanished into the night.

When she reached her bed, Henrietta picked up the stone she had used as a talisman to reach the pixies. She held it tightly between her praying hands as she had done before. She knelt beside her bed and prayed as hard as she knew how.

"Dear Lord, look down upon me and understand my need to protect the pixies of Pixie Hill. They need your help. Please help Mr. Philpotts and the Sheriff to understand that the power plant project should not violate the dwelling place of the little people. Amen."

Henrietta had squeezed the stone so hard that it was warm between her hands. She put the rock back where she kept it on her bookshelf. Then she crawled under her covers and pulled the coverlet under her chin. She had struggled to pray, so she relaxed and fell into a deep sleep.

She did not know that her mother had come to see what was the matter and heard her prayer. She did not say anything for fear that she might interfere with her child's conversation with God. She knew that she had to redouble her efforts to save Pixie Hill. She had a sleepless night devising her own plan to help save the pixie dwelling.

When the rooster crowed the next morning, Henrietta's household sprang to life. Everyone had things to do, and her mother, especially, composed a long list of visits to make.

"Henny, I'll be seeing many of our neighbors today. I thought you'd like to come along with me. So let's get this house in order before we go. Dress warmly. We'll make the rounds and see what we can do to save Pixie Hill from the construction."

This brought a big smile to Henrietta's face. She tidied up, and when she took off her apron, she put the rock she had prayed within her coat pocket. All through the day, she rubbed the rock with her fingers. That reminded her of her prayer the night before.

Maddy's stature among the farmers' wives had something to do with Hubert's respect among his peers, but she also was known to be a solid person who should not be trifled with. She could talk plainly with everyone, and she was not afraid to speak her mind, even at the risk of unsettling her neighbors.

Henrietta that day saw her mother in full feather, talking earnestly with her neighbors one after the other. They must have talked with twenty farmers' wives before evening fell, and Henrietta was aware that they visited all the farms surrounding the construction site. The Sheriff had not made his rounds to talk with the farmers themselves, but Maddy explained to her daughter that once the wives had been told the score, their husbands would likely follow. Maddy and Henrietta returned home with the conviction that they had convinced all those they spoke with to support their proposition to keep Pixie Hill unscathed.

That evening after her dinner, bath, and prayers, Henrietta's mother came to her bedside to continue the story where she had left off.

"We left off our story with Henrietta climbing into bed after the pixie Matilda told her that the pixies would play tricks on the humans at the Pixie Hill construction site."

"Yes, and Henrietta had promised to keep the secret that she could see and talk with pixies. So what happened next, Mother?"

"The next day, Henrietta and her mother went to all the farmers' wives to convince them to support the idea of saving

Pixie Hill. Everyone agreed to do that. So, by the time the Sheriff came around, he would find complete agreement among the farmers as to what must be done."

"That's just as we did today."

"That's right, Henny."

"So what happened next?" She was full of anticipation and leaned forward to listen with all her might. Her insides tickled she was so excited.

"Henrietta's mother told her daughter to pray earnestly that Pixie Hill would be spared so the pixies would have their dwelling even after the plant was constructed."

"Mother, I prayed hard for that to happen. Do you suppose the Lord heard me?"

"If you pray hard, the Lord always hears you, Henny. His ways are mysterious, so things don't always work out as you would expect. Sometimes He knows things we don't know."

"Does He know about the pixies?"

"I'm very sure He knows all about the little people."

"That's reassuring. Can I have a kiss goodnight?"

"Of course, you may, you Lamb." Maddy kissed her daughter and tucked her in.

That night, the scraping brought Henrietta to the back porch, but she hesitated to open the door more than a crack because she heard two whispering voices talking. It was her mother and Matilda the pixie.

"So Matilda, the humans will make sure that Pixie Hill is spared. You must tell the other pixies to stop vandalizing the construction site. Henrietta will be out soon but don't tell her we've been conversing. I'm so glad you allowed me to share the rock with her. She's been a big help. Without her prayers, we might have lost Pixie Hill."

Henrietta stepped back away from the door as her mother slipped into the house and went to her room. Then Henrietta went to the back porch to find Matilda finishing the milk.

"Hi, Matilda."

"Hi, Henrietta."

"I think you know what's been happening," Henrietta said with a shy smile.

"I think we've had a miracle, Henrietta."

"I think so too, Matilda. Goodnight."

Pixie Hill was spared, and the power plant was built. Henrietta never told her mother that she overheard her talking with the green pixie Matilda. Maddy never told her daughter that she could see pixies, but that did not matter. She never stopped talking with pixies, because Pixie Hill remains green today under the nuclear power plant.

Troll Hide

Trolls scare me.

In contrast, I have never minded the wee folk. Pixies and imps may vex me with their devilish tricks. Fairies will play and dance, leaving their green sour ringlets. Gnomes brood solitary in their garden grasses. Leprechauns bring as much luck as they take. Dwarfs are too small to make much trouble. None of these small creatures can do me real harm.

What makes me pause, though, are giants, ogres, witches and especially trolls. I am a battle-hardened soldier, but I know my limits. Giants make the earth tremble when they walk. Ogres are noisily malevolent because they fear no men. Witches use evil spells, but I know on sight and avoid them.

Trolls are huge but very good at hiding. They can lurk right in plain sight, or tucked in the corner of dense vegetation, or under a bed. They eat little children when they find them. They enjoy killing men and women, too. Sometimes children disappear without a trace. Sometimes the young are found senseless with no memory. Then I know trolls must have been at work.

Though trolls may be anywhere, I do not let my fear of them interfere with my travels. Since I returned from the king's wars, I have often wandered widely in the land beyond my village. I always keep my eyes and ears wide open. That is why I see and hear the things most people miss. They cannot identify a troll standing right under their noses. They do not know the sure signs of a troll hide.

I learned the hard way about that in a distant village, in a green vale with a stream purling through it. I might have passed those human habitations except for a telltale wisp of white smoke from a chimney.

It was getting late in the afternoon, so I stopped to have a meal and a night's lodging. This may seem strange in these iron times. Back in those days, though, all the king's subjects were hospitable. If an old soldier like me needed food and a roof, anyone would have invited him inside and offered hospitality. Often, I did small tasks to repay my hosts and hostesses for their kindness. I chopped wood. I dug out stumps. I plowed up earth for a garden. Those were the least things I might do.

Sometimes I did much more. For example, I solved mysteries. On one estate, I discovered the fairies had hidden a maid's favorite bonnet in the loft of a barn. On another, I saw that pixies caused the clotted cream to sour too much. At a village, I learned about the treachery of three trolls who lived openly among the villagers. In fact, I might have been killed by those trolls. Instead, I outwitted them and lived to visit other regions, like the one where I would sleep this night.

Seeing I was a veteran, the cottagers opened their doors and bade me come in and sit by the fire. They offered me a joint of meat, fresh bread, and strong drink. They regaled me with stories of their ancestry as we lounged before their fire. Their nine tumbling children were curious about my travels, so I took the youngest boy and girl on my lap and told stories until they fell asleep. Their mother gently took them to their beds and the other children went to their beds, too. That gave their father the opportunity—over a pipe and a tankard—to say what troubled him.

"I don't know why, but the bairns in this village have been disappearing one by one. I'm afraid my own will be taken one day. The others vanished without a trace. My wife is frantic worrying."

"Is there a particular place or time of day the children disappeared?" I asked alarmed and outraged at the thought of it.

"All times, day and night they vanished. Some were inside their cottages. Some were outside playing in the lane. Others disappeared from open fields. None of the missing wanted to run away. Where would they go?"

We considered all the possibilities that might explain what had happened. After exhausting each one, I looked the man in the eye and said one word, "Trolls!"

"I was hoping it was not trolls, but the thought did cross my mind." The man shook his head. Trolls were big trouble. Finding them was only the first difficulty. Then, someone had to drive them out.

"I owe you for taking me in, feeding me and providing a bed for the night. I'll check out your valley for trolls. I'll do what I can to help you drive them out if they're here."

The weathered man was delighted with my offer. He became cheerful and offered me a piece of pie before we slept. I could not sleep while thinking about the trolls. After tossing and turning until midnight, I rose, lighted a pine pitch torch and slipped out the front door to look for trolls.

The valley by night was full of living sounds. Insects were calling to their mates. So were frogs. In the distance, I heard dogs baying. Close to the house, I heard two cats caterwauling. Moths flew at my flickering torch as I searched the exterior of the cottage. Finding no signs of trolls there, I circled the house at increasing distances until I reached the wattle fence boundary, crowded with honeysuckle. I walked the inside and outside of that fence looking for signs. I increased my search to include the barn and the area around the creek that flowed through the village commons.

I followed the creek to a grove of trees next to a hillock where I found a rock grotto. There, I sensed in the press of the grasses, the presence of a troll. I searched the area thoroughly and deduced the troll that inhabited the grove was absent. I stopped and listened. Hearing a faint snoring sound, I pushed through the tangled greenery and found two small sleeping children enclosed in a pen. I awakened and hushed them. I carried them back to the cottage and roused my host and hostess without disturbing their children.

"I've located the troll's hide," I told them. "Do you know these two children?"

"They are the Fosters' children who live up the hill. They disappeared a few days ago. The Fosters have been frantic to find them. They'll be overjoyed at their return."

I told the couple we would return the children to their proper parents at first light. We fed the hungry children and put them in the guest bed until morning. Meanwhile, I went back to the grotto to wait in darkness for the troll's return.

It was nearly daybreak when I heard the unmistakable sound of a troll singing.

Fee, fie, foe, fum
I smell the blood of an English man.
Be he alive or be he dead,
I'll grind his bones to make my bread.
Two children have I caught and fed
When they are fat, I'll eat them.

I might have missed him if he had not stepped on my foot. He did not seem to notice I was there.

The first place the troll went was the pen where he had left the children. He seemed extremely angry they had escaped. He frantically tore at the vegetation searching the area around the pen. He sniffed around its perimeter and followed a scent back to the grove's entrance. Not finding the children, he gnawed on a bone with cracks and grunts. I heard him tuck himself into the greenery under the honeysuckle to sleep. I heard him snoring and shifting his position all the rest of the night. By daylight, he was still and nearly invisible.

I snuck out of the grove and returned to the cottage. I told the couple what I had seen. The father wanted to gather the villagers immediately to drive the troll away. I advised caution because the troll might have troll friends in the area. One troll is a problem. Many trolls are catastrophic.

I said, "The first thing we must do is return the two children to their parents."

The father said, "After that, I'll raise the hue and cry."

I counseled him to seek outside help right away saying, "I strongly recommend someone go immediately to the Sheriff and have him bring two dozen well-armed men. Otherwise, villagers untrained with weapons might be hurt."

We walked the children to the Fosters' home. Their parents were ecstatic to see them. They hugged and kissed them. When I said a troll had taken the children away, and he was still in the grove, they grabbed a pitchfork and a stave and went from house to house to gather reinforcements with weapons. At my urging, one villager rode posthaste to fetch the Sheriff.

Soon, we were a force of twenty men and women, each with a crude weapon. The Fosters brought a great game net, too. I led them to the grove and showed them where the troll was sleeping. It was difficult to see him with his green skin nestled in the green foliage that covered him.

I helped the Fosters throw their great game net over the sleeping troll. After we had secured the net to the ground with stakes, we raised the hue and cry. The troll awakened furious. He thrashed in his captivity, but could not escape. Seeing the villagers ready to use their weapons, he tried a wily diversion.

"Please don't harm me," the troll pleaded. "I've lost the two children I found in the woods. Someone stole them from me. Help me find them because they might come to harm if you don't."

"Perfidious troll! The children are back with their rightful parents, no thanks to you," I said.

"Are you the English man who stole my children?"

"Why do you keep saying they are your children? Everyone knows they belong to the Fosters up the hill."

The Fosters stepped forward and said, "They're our children. We're going to have the Sheriff arrest you for kidnapping."

The other villagers crowded around to ask the troll the whereabouts of the other lost children.

"I don't know about any other lost children. I found the two who were stolen from here. I don't know about others."

"Where did you find the lost children?" I asked the troll.

"I found them wandering in the field."

"Why didn't you immediately try to find their parents?"

"I don't know anyone in the valley. I thought the villagers would call me a kidnapper if I brought the children forward. I kept them safe and fed them well. What else could I do?"

"Troll, I'm going to count to three. If you don't tell us where the other children are, we're all going to beat and poke you until you're very sorry."

"Don't harm me. That would be a gross injustice. I have rights."

"Kidnappers have no rights, troll. One."

"You're counting. That's not fair!"

"Two. Villagers, raise your weapons! Prepare to strike this troll."

"You can't do this to me. I've got friends." He looked around terrified.

He screamed, "Trolls! Trolls! Come out of hiding and save me from these villagers."

"Three. All right, poke, jab, pinch, stick, shoot, and beat! Do your worst."

The villagers did not hesitate. They laid on their blows while the troll moaned, complained, shouted and yelled for help.

I heard rustling all around the grove. The fellow trolls were shaking themselves awake and rising from the greenery. They must have numbered a dozen trolls in that place. All had lain hidden until one of their kind was under attack. The villagers saw the trolls and fled.

As a soldier, I held my ground. I lit my torch and stood between the troll in the net and the others. Soon, I was surrounded by trolls. They avoided my torch but crowded as close to me as they could without getting burnt. They made growling noises. Some sang troll songs.

Troll hands reached out for me when my back was turned. Their sheer numbers were going to be a problem, so I drew my knife—the weapon I had used to good effect in the king's war. I never wore it outside my clothing when I traveled because people were afraid of weapons. Here I saw no alternative.

I brandished the knife in one hand and the torch in the other. The trolls decided to palaver rather than risk injury. Though they are dangerous, trolls are cowardly creatures.

The largest troll said, "Soldier, why are you troubling us? We had a good thing going in this valley until you came. Why don't you just find the high road and leave?" The other trolls nodded in agreement with their leader.

"Trolls, you, not I, will be leaving this valley. The Sheriff and his men will be here soon. What have you done with the other missing children?"

"We fattened them and ate them," said the leader of the trolls with a broad smile. "Their flesh was sweet, and their bones were good to chew on."

The troll in the net chimed in, "I was fattening the two you stole. They were tender and plump. I might have eaten them both within the next day or so. You are evil for taking them from me. I suspect you plan to eat them yourself. In any case, we trolls will find other children here once you have gone."

I was glad the trolls wanted to talk. That kept them busy while the Sheriff and his two dozen well-armed men on horses arrived. They surrounded the trolls and tied them with ropes.

"Sheriff," I said. "These trolls have eaten the children of this village. I rescued two children who were kidnapped by this troll in the net. The Fosters can tell you their children are now safe and sound. These trolls just confessed they ate the other lost children of the valley. Now, do your duty and take these villainous trolls away."

"Men, let's take these trolls to their reckoning. Soldier, once again I am in your debt. Another village has been cleansed of trolls because of you."

The villagers and I watched as the Sheriff and his men took the trolls away. The village elders decided it was time to have a three-day feast to celebrate the departure of the trolls. I could not stay to attend their feast, though I did sleep the rest of the day at the Fosters' house.

Before I departed the valley, the villagers gave me food and drink for my journey. All in all, I was better for having stopped there. I was glad to help drive the trolls away. The village was better also because their trolls were gone.

In balance, though, I was sad. Of the dozen missing children, only the two I rescued had survived. The others, by the trolls' confessions, were fattened and eaten, blood and bones and all. Trolls are savage creatures. They know no pity or remorse.

Later, I learned the trolls that were taken prisoner in that valley escaped from the Sheriff and his men. They ran to the great forest that stretches from one end of the kingdom to the other. They are hiding now, but they will emerge. As long as trolls live in the kingdom, children will disappear and be eaten. I, therefore, keep my eyes peeled for signs of trolls and warn children to be careful. I tell them trolls can be anywhere at all.

The Leprechauns Bride

Colleen Cuchulain was the shortest woman in her village. At just under three feet tall, she may have been the shortest in the entire land of Connaught if not the entirety of Ireland. She had a cruel dwarfish deformity that masked her genuine beauty. She had light red hair and freckles. Her eyes were the clearest blue. Still, all the village children made fun of her because of her diminutive size. So she spent a lot of time in solitude, often crying in frustration for something that was not her fault.

The girl could not believe she was always going to be short. Ever since she was eight years old, at every birthday, she had asked her mother, "When am I going to grow up so I can be tall like all the other girls?"

Each time she said this, her mother smiled painfully and replied, "We'll see what we'll see." Mary feared her husband was right when he said Colleen would remain a dwarf and probably never marry. Ian Cuchulain was a wealthy man, but all his money could not buy a single inch to add to his daughter's stature.

There was, to be sure, a reason that the Cuchulains were the richest family in the region. In his youth, Ian had the luck of finding a pot of gold at the end of a rainbow. He had the help of a leprechaun he had tricked into revealing the location of the gold. The leprechaun was enraged and held a grudge that the boy had stolen his gold hoard.

The leprechaun told Ian, "Your treachery will have a cost. One day, your first-born daughter will become the bride of a leprechaun." Ian laughed at the leprechaun. He was young at the time and unmarried. He thought nothing of the curse, and afterward, he forgot all about it. He only considered all the things his new-found gold could buy.

When Ian and Mary became man and wife, a wizened midget named Gadwall, who made the shoes for the wedding party, reminded Ian of the leprechaun's curse: "Wee folk tell me your first daughter will marry a leprechaun." The young man was so busy drinking and having fun with his friends, he ridiculed the little man and kicked him in the rump for having tried to spoil his wedding day.

Just in case, though, when his daughter Colleen was born, Ian painted green four-leaf clovers all over her white crib to keep leprechauns away. But the damage was already done. When Colleen reached the age of four, her parents knew the leprechaun's curse was working. No magic spells or potions that they tried could reverse the leprechaun's hold on the girl.

While her parents tried to assuage Colleen's hurt feelings, they despaired about what would become of her. Ian decided his daughter should learn a trade to keep herself when she failed to win a husband. Though she had no idea why she did it, Mary made her daughter's clothing, including a red coat with seven buttons, a cocked hat, and shoes with buckles that matched the buckle on her belt. The girl wore the wide belt around her red dress.

Once a year, on St. Patrick's Day after that, the girl was featured in the annual parade as the wife of the three-year-old lad who played the leprechaun. For this, she earned the sobriquet, "the Leprechaun's bride." It stuck.

It came time for Colleen to have her training for a trade, so Ian walked the streets in all the neighboring villages to find a cobbler who would accept Colleen as his apprentice. All the established cobblers laughed—except for one. Ironically the cobbler who agreed to accept her was the same wizened dwarf who had raised the specter of the curse at Ian and Mary's wedding.

Ian thought, "Alas, what can I do? Colleen must learn a trade. Mr. Gadwall is the only cobbler who will take her as his apprentice. I hate the hideous dwarf, but that doesn't matter. I'll sign the bond of indenture. Somehow things will work out." Ian was glad to be rid of a daughter who embarrassed him and his wife. His wife agreed that their struggle against destiny was now likely over.

Colleen showed up for work in the red clothes her mother had made for her. The dwarf was ecstatic when he saw her dressed exactly like a female leprechaun. He showed her where she was to work, eat and sleep. She thought the dwarf hideous, but she was now bound for seven years to work for him. She decided to make the best of her bad situation.

The dwarf explained to his apprentice, "Your hours will be different from what you might have expected. You'll work all night and sleep all day. I'll bring shoes for you to repair and by morning you'll have them fixed and ready to deliver to my customers. If you do a good job, I'll increase the number of shoes for you to cobble. If you don't do well, I'll beat you."

Colleen started that first night with one pair of old shoes. She did her best with them and trembled when Gadwall examined them in the morning. She did not want to be beaten, so she had used her ingenuity to make her restoration perfect.

The dwarf smiled and delivered the refurbished shoes to his customer, who was delighted with the result. That evening, Gadwall left two pairs of shoes for Colleen to restore. He had no complaint with her work the next morning, so he increased the number of pairs to four the next night.

Colleen learned how to cobble rapidly, so soon she was routinely mending eight pairs of shoes each night and then sixteen and finally thirty-two pairs. She thought she had found the absolute maximum number she could responsibly complete. She begged the cobbler to give her another form of tasking to broaden her skills.

As a reward, Gadwall taught her how to make shoes with various fine leathers and cloths. She was a quick study, and soon she was experimenting making shoes in styles that the dwarf's customers preferred to his own former offerings. He was jealous of his apprentice but glad to charge extra money for her increasingly popular shoes.

Excited to see her success, after her fourth year of apprenticeship, Colleen asked Gadwall to teach her how to become a master cobbler. He smiled and told her that he had an associate who was the best master cobbler in all Ireland.

"If you really want to know the tricks of the trade, I'll sign over your indenture to this master cobbler, but your father must pay me gold to do so." He handed her a sack and said, "Go to your father and have him fill this sack full of gold. When you bring it to me, I'll bind you over to the master cobbler."

Colleen appeared at her father's door to explain what Gadwall had told her. Proud of her achievements as an apprentice, she explained the glorious possibilities for her future if she could only study with the greatest cobbler in Ireland. She wept when she told him what was required and handed him the sack for the gold. Ian was startled at her request, but he had a lot of gold. To get rid of his daughter, he gave her a sack full of the yellow metal, thinking she would now be set for life.

Ian told her, "This is the last gold you'll get from me. Use it wisely."

Colleen was stricken with grief that her father had been so cold about giving her the gold she had asked for. She wept as she walked back to Gadwall's shop with the heavy sack.

Gadwall was extremely pleased to receive the gold. That night, he led Colleen into a sub-basement of his establishment where she had never been.

There, in that subterranean factory, were dozens of workers toiling over making shoes of all kinds. Colleen's eyes opened wide because, in the lamplight, she saw that all the workers were dwarves. The master cobbler approached them and looked at her fiercely, his keen eyes sizing her up. Colleen marveled that the master was a midget dressed in red exactly as she was, except he wore pants where she wore a dress. He had a full red beard and tufts of red hair growing from his ears. She was repelled by his hideous face, which looked contorted by pain.

The master cobbler frowned at her until he noticed the gold that Gadwall was holding. Then he smiled and held out his hand. Gadwall gave the master the sack of gold and departed.

The master reached into the sack and pulled out several pieces of gold. He asked Colleen, "Where did this gold come from? I believe I've seen it before."

She answered, "That gold is my father's. He gave it to me so you could teach me the mysteries of the cobblers' trade. I've passed the tests of quantity and quality imposed by Mr. Gadwall. I've created shoes in new styles for all sizes of feet. I want you to teach me what no one else knows how to do."

The cobbler laughed. "My dear apprentice, you don't realize the bargain you have struck. This gold is mine. Your father stole it from me years ago. Are you his eldest daughter?"

"As a matter of fact, I am. My father's no thief. How dare you accuse him of stealing this gold from you?"

"Do you know your destiny? If you don't, I'll tell you."

She shook her head. Therefore, he told her the story of her father's discovery of the gold at the end of the rainbow. He also told her about the curse that had made her a dwarf for life. He also told her that her future was to be a leprechaun's bride.

"Miserable wretch! All my life I've been miserable—because of you? And now I'm in thrall to you!" She began to weep profusely and tear her hair.

The master cobbler raised a cudgel and beat her soundly for her disrespect. He then dragged her to a table where tools and materials were laid out for making shoes. He forced her to sit down at the table and gave her instructions.

"Tonight, you'll make ten pairs of shoes with designs no one has ever seen. If you do, I'll teach you some tricks. If you don't, I'll beat you again."

So Colleen got right to work. In the morning, she had made ten beautiful pairs of shoes. The master cobbler came and admired them. Then, he got a jealous gleam in his eyes. He lifted his cudgel and beat her soundly. Then, he showed her where she should sleep.

That night, the cobbler laid out different materials including laces, buckles, stuffing materials, and silks. He ordered her to make twenty pairs of shoes in various sizes from baby's shoes to elephantine-sized shoes. She accomplished her task. When the master returned in the morning, he examined each pair of shoes carefully. As before when he finished, he got the jealous gleam in his eyes and raised his cudgel, beating her soundly and sending her to bed.

Bruised and sore, Colleen wept bitterly. She saw no end to her ordeal as an apprentice to a cruel master who taught her nothing but demanded much from her. She began to brood about how she might escape her situation.

The next night the master cobbler brought bright red materials and told her she should fashion him a cocked hat and a pair of pointed shoes for his own use. She was about to complain, but he raised his cudgel threateningly. She fashioned what he wanted and waited for him to inspect what she had done the next morning. This time, after the master cobbler praised her effort, he pulled the newly made hat and shoes on and told her to follow him.

The master cobbler led Colleen up through the two basement levels to the street level of Gadwall's shop. Then, he marched her to the village church. The priest was surprised to see before him in his office two dwarves dressed in leprechaun red.

The master cobbler told him, "Priest, why the look of surprise? Were you not the priest who married Ian and Mary Cuchulain?"

"I am. What has that got to do with anything?"

The master cobbler ignored the priest's question. "I'm here to fulfill a sacred obligation agreed to by Ian Cuchulain and myself eighteen years ago. This woman, Colleen Cuchulain, and I are to be married. So, post the banns and plan to marry us one fortnight from today."

Colleen burst into tears when she heard this. "Father, please save me from a fate worse than death."

The master cobbler looked at the ceiling while he showed the priest the sack of gold he carried.

The priest, who loved gold almost as much as the cobbler did, smiled and addressed the weeping girl. "Now, now, Colleen, you're of marrying age. This gentleman has the means to make a fine husband for you. Why are you weeping?"

She answered, "This cobbler beats me and forces me to live underground. He makes untrue accusations against my father."

The priest frowned. The cobbler showed him the indenture indicating that Colleen was legally his apprentice. When the priest had finished reading the articles of the indenture, he spoke.

"Colleen, a master has the right to punish his apprentices however he needs to. As for the untruths he allegedly spoke about your father, what exactly did he say?"

The master cobbler broke in at this point and told the priest how Ian Cuchulain had stolen the leprechaun's gold. He also told him about the curse that was imposed on the daughter that made her a dwarf and the future bride of a leprechaun.

The priest listened carefully to everything the master cobbler said. He made no peremptory judgment. Instead, he placed both hands on his fat body, examining the cobbler and his apprentice carefully.

He said, "I must withdraw for a moment. Will you please wait here in my office?"

Then the fat priest hastened to fetch Ian and Mary Cuchulain, the Sheriff and the apothecary. When they arrived at the priest's office, the priest asked the cobbler to repeat what he had said about Ian Cuchulain and the gold.

Indignant, the cobbler told the story of the theft of the gold again. Alarmed, the Sheriff asked Ian Cuchulain whether he had, indeed, stolen the gold he found at the end of the rainbow.

"Well, Sheriff, I took the gold, which was sitting in a meadow at the rainbow's end."

The Sheriff then ordered, "Fetch the rest of the gold to prove this."

Ian went home and, making many trips, brought his entire store of gold to the church. His sacks of gold almost filled the hall outside the priest's office.

"Cobbler," the Sheriff asked pointing at the piles of sacks, "Is this the gold you said was stolen from you by Ian Cuchulain?"

The master cobbler nodded his head vigorously, his eyes tearing at the sight of what was formerly his. He said, "It's not all the gold. I have one sack from that original cache in my shop. He's spent many others already. Everyone in the village knows what a spendthrift he is."

The priest and the Sheriff looked at each other. They seemed to come to an unspoken agreement.

"Master cobbler," the priest said, "I've brought the apothecary, who has something for you. Apothecary, please proceed."

The apothecary stepped towards the cobbler and reached into a small bag of herbs that he carried. He took a handful of the herbs and threw them at the cobbler, who was paralyzed when the dust of the ground herbs touched his body.

The priest asked, "Apothecary, what was in the powder you just used on the cobbler?"

The apothecary answered, "Pure, ground four-leaf clovers, guaranteed to have the effect you just witnessed—on leprechauns."

Looking at the Sheriff, the priest said, "We have our proof. The master cobbler is a leprechaun. I'm inclined to believe Ian Cuchulain about his theft of the gold. So what are we to do now?"

The Sheriff thought about this for a few minutes. Then he made a pronouncement, "This is a complex case, but I believe we can come to a just conclusion all around without going to the magistrate."

He thought for a few minutes about what he was going to say. He knew he would have to remember what he said to satisfy all legalities.

Finally, he spoke, "Ian Cuchulain is a thief. That much is clear. His punishment for theft has been visited upon his midget daughter standing here. I believe the best place for the hoard of stolen gold is the church. So, priest, the gold is yours."

The priest's hands curled over themselves repeatedly as if he were anticipating a delicious feast. His eyes were as wide as saucers as he thought about what the gold would buy.

The Sheriff was not done with his judgment. He continued, "As for Colleen, she's bound to the cobbler as an apprentice and betrothed to him by the cobbler's own admission. By marrying him, she will be a wealthy woman; though to be sure she'll always be a dwarf."

The girl broke down and cried, beating her chest and pulling at her red hair.

Ignoring Colleen's display of grief, the Sheriff continued, "Ian and Mary Cuchulain, go home right now. I won't need to press charges since the remnants of your ill-gotten gold are in the church's hands."

Ian and Mary, now rendered destitute by the Sheriff's decision, decided to make the best of their situation and stole away quietly, not looking back at their daughter.

The Sheriff was not done. He said, "Priest, publish the banns and proceed with the marriage in a fortnight."

The priest, who did not want the Sheriff to rethink the disposition of the gold, sped to write the marriage banns.

Then, the Sheriff turned to the medicine man, saying, "Apothecary, what do we owe you for your services?"

The apothecary, who was not a greedy man, only smiled and replied, "I require nothing. I'll merely spend tomorrow gathering four-leaf clovers in the meadow. It's enough for me to see that my prescriptions are known to work."

The Sheriff nodded sagely. Then he asked the apothecary how the spell caused by the four-leaf-clover powder might be reversed.

The apothecary did not hesitate to reply, "Thoroughly bathing is advised. The trouble is, leprechauns don't like baths."

Everyone laughed, except for the cobbler, who remained paralyzed and speechless.

The Sheriff helped Colleen return the master cobbler to his workshop in the sub-basement below Gadwall's shop.

Seeing the state of affairs there, the Sheriff demanded, "Gadwall, you must pay a fine for having an unlicensed business housed under your store. If you don't pay at once, I'll be forced to haul you off to gaol."

"I don't have the money to pay the fine. How can I continue my trade from gaol? If I don't work, I won't ever be able to earn the money to pay the fine." Gadwall complained to the Sheriff, who scratched his head in confusion.

Colleen saw an opportunity for freeing herself from her indenture to the leprechaun and suggested, "I have an idea how this might work out if you'll both listen. Mr. Gadwall, you could use the gold you paid to the master cobbler, if only you take me back as your apprentice."

Relieved by this suggestion, Gadwall rescinded the indenture he had signed over to the master cobbler and retrieved the sack of gold from the leprechaun's store in the sub-basement. Gadwall offered this sack of gold to the Sheriff when he returned to the street level.

The Sheriff received his gold, smiled, tipped his hat and departed.

Colleen subsequently returned to the service of her former master.

The bath due the master cobbler was delayed indefinitely. Colleen was still betrothed. The banns were published by the priest as planned.

A fortnight later, the village gathered in the church for the advertised marriage ceremony. The priest relied on the statements that the leprechaun had made in his office to execute the ceremony.

The groom was speechless. The bride smiled sweetly as she placed the ring on her new husband's hand. In her other hand, she wielded his cudgel, no one guessed why.

The wedding recessional was beautiful as the two short figures led the way, both carried by the father of the bride, Ian Cuchulain.

Outside the church, the construction of a new carillon was now in progress, funded by the leprechaun's gold. The priest specifically requested of Colleen that she not bathe the leprechaun until the carillon was completed.

As the richest woman in the village now that she was a leprechaun's wife, Colleen had the good grace and wisdom not to gainsay the church.

As insurance, though, she bought from the apothecary a large bag of powdered four-leaf clovers, just in case the cudgel did not work to keep her new husband in line.

By the next St. Patrick's Day, a new leprechaun couple marched in the parade. Colleen and her husband, representing themselves in their traditional red costumes, bowed to the people thronging the street as they passed. They raised their cocked hats and occasionally pointed to their new shoes with buckles.

"After all," Colleen told her father later, "We're cobblers and need to advertise our wares."

He asked his daughter, "Have you ever seen a pot of gold at the end of a rainbow?"

She smiled faintly and answered, "Father, I believe that way of getting gold has done me enough harm. I have what I need now. Whenever I need more, I'll simply mend more shoes."

Hansel and Gretel for Real

Well, for starters, we weren't on foot, and there were no bread crumbs, and no house made out of goodies to eat. We were out riding on Hansel's hog with me hanging around his waist from the rear, and my hair waving in the wind behind us.

We figured we had enough gas in our tank for a hundred miles, give or take, so we decided to rev up and head for Hansel's folks' cabin deep in the woods looking out over the pond. It was dark before we arrived, so my half-brother parked the bike and chained it to the post by the mailbox.

I thought it odd that the box was newly painted and had a name I did not know—Hexel, I think it was, but we were tired and eager to get inside because rain was coming soon. It was getting chilly, and we wanted to get the heater going.

Hansel had no problem unlocking the door, but when he tried to disarm the security system, he had trouble entering the code. After he had tried three times to disarm, the system locked up and the alarm sounded so loud you'd have thought it would raise the dead.

Hansel was about to call the security company, but out of the dark of the living room, came a female figure with a control system in her left hand and a .38 special in her right hand. We could see those things because Hansel shined his penlight on the woman just as she pressed her control to stop the alarm. She waved us inside with her gun hand.

When we were inside, the stooped woman stepped around us. She closed and locked the door. She did not turn on the lights but pushed us towards the living room that looked out on the pond. She put her control into her apron pocket and frisked us thoroughly with her free hand. She found Hansel's Walther PPK and removed it. She found my ankle knife and unsheathed it with a horrid cackle. She took both our cell phones and Hansel's penlight and thrust them into her apron pocket.

Then, she asked us to make ourselves comfortable on the couch that faced the glass windows. Through the glass, we could see the full, blood moon through the pines and clouds, and we saw the moon's reflection throwing gules like red bars on the water. We saw that the woman was covering us with her own and Hansel's guns. She made no attempt to call the police, and the alarm company did not call the cabin's landline as they normally would.

The woman asked, "What do you think you're doing by breaking into my cabin in the dead of night?"

Hansel said, "Your cabin? This cabin belongs to my parents. Who are you? Why are you here?"

The woman cackled, shook her head and answered, "This cabin is mine. It has been mine for forty years now. I'm Winnie Hexel. I'm here trying to enjoy myself for my hard earned weekend vacation when you two hooligans arrive on your Harley and spoil my peace and quiet. I'm not sure what to do with you, but I'll think of something. Don't try anything,

Mister. That goes for you too, Sister. I know how to use these weapons, but it would be a darn shame to waste the ammunition, besides I have other things in mind for you tonight."

"Look," I said, "We've probably made a terrible mistake. We thought we were at the right cabin. We mean you no harm."

"Well, you're here now, and that's what counts, isn't it?"

"I need to use the restroom."

"Of course, you do. It's right at the top of the stairs behind you. Before you go up, put these on your friend." She extended a pair of handcuffs to me and gestured with her guns. I cuffed my half brother's wrists. Then, the woman extended a second pair of cuffs and told me to cuff his feet. He didn't like it, but I did that too.

I was thinking all the time of how I could hurl myself across the room and take the woman to the floor, but she was just out of range. What if she shot Hansel? It wasn't worth the risk.

When Hansel was bound, the woman laughed and told me to run up the stairs and use the john. She warned me not to use any tricks, or she would shoot Hansel in a heartbeat. I went up to the john in the dark and closed the door to relieve myself while I thought about our desperate situation.

Downstairs, I heard the sound of Hansel mumbling and moaning. I hurried up, washed my hands, and went back downstairs to find that the lights were on now, and the woman had placed duct tape over Hansel's mouth. She stopped fumbling with Hansel's belt and fly with her crooked fingers and picked up her gun and pointed it at me.

"Sit down over there and tell me your names."

"I'm Gretel. That's Hansel. He's my half-brother. Please don't hurt him."

"So, Gretel, you and I are going to be great pals. I've some girlfriends coming around for a party at midnight, and I need your help to be ready for them. Go into the kitchen and put on an apron. Don't get any ideas because your brother here is a sitting duck. My, but you have nice tattoos on your shoulders. Turn the oven to 'broil' and indicate 450 degrees. In the refrigerator, you'll find a Ziploc bag with the goodies we're going to cook. Take those out and put them on the counter top along with the broiling pan you'll find beneath the stove."

When I had put on my apron and turned on the stove, I looked in the refrigerator and saw the remains of an entire human, all neatly arranged in plastic bags of various sizes. The head had been neatly shaved all over, and its eyes looked mournful through the clear plastic. I tried to hold back from eructing, but I could not help myself. I threw up all over the floor. I wet some paper towels at the sink and started to clean up the mess. As I bent to the task, I felt a cold metal gun barrel caressing my neck.

"Don't feel ashamed. Yours is a perfectly human reaction to the vision of a well-prepared human sacrifice. When I was your age—before I found my life's calling, I did the same."

I was so scared I could hardly move. My hair stood on end. My stomach was full of butterflies and turning over Tears came to my eyes but elicited no sympathy.

"Don't cry, now! Stop it. When we've had our Walpurgis Night feast tonight, you'll help me prepare Hansel to take the place of Aaron there in the fridge. My lands, your Hansel is a handsome specimen, and his tattoos are even better made than yours. Now you're trembling."

I was shaking all over with revulsion and fear. I saw no way to escape.

"You've no need to fear—not yet. Put the goodies on the grill and wait until I give the word. Meanwhile, bring out one glass pitcher full of blood and set the table with crystal punch bowl and the thirteen glasses you'll find in the cabinet."

I managed to fetch one full glass pitcher full of blood. Beads of condensed water ran down its sides as I set it on the table. I reached up and brought down the bowl and glasses.

"That's a dear. Don't forget the napkins. Perfect. It's almost eleven o'clock now, and the oven is just right, so in goes the broiling pan. Right you are, then!"

I heard the shrieking begin as I slid the broiling pan into its grooves. It was as if the forest had an unnatural alarm system, but with human cries substituted for mechanical sounds. From across the lake, came a disorderly phalanx of witches flying on their brooms. They all converged on this cabin in the woods.

The guests knocked on the door. When the old woman unlocked and opened the door, they crushed past her rudely into the cabin. At the hostess's bidding, I poured each guest a glass of blood punch and gave her a napkin. I heard the broiling meat crackle, so I opened the oven and turned each piece over and re-inserted the broiling pan back into place.

The witches were suddenly all talking and cackling at once. Two opened the fridge to admire Adam. Four gaped and gawked at Hansel, still bound on the floor in the living room. Three gathered around the hostess, who was recounting her good fortune in having uninvited guests to share the celebration. The other three witches surrounded me and pinched me on the cheeks and bottom. One caressed my thigh high up. One licked my neck with her lizard-like, gooey tongue.

The hostess raised a toast in blood to Walpurgis Night, to the Devil and to all witches in the universe. When everyone had caroused with that ghastly liquid, the hostess called for the sacrifice to be served. I drew out the broiler and set the meat on a platter, but before I could reach the table with it, the witches had gathered around and were pulling off pieces with their gnarled fingers and long, dirty fingernails.

The meat was gone in a flash, and the hostess asked me to find the second glass pitcher of blood in the fridge and fill the punch bowl with it. I did that and stood by to serve another round of drinks. So each witch gave a toast, and all drank to it until all the toasts were made and all the blood drunk up.

The hostess told her guests that they could each take one of the twelve pieces of old Adam from the fridge as their presents, and they swarmed the kitchen to get their pieces of Adam. I helped pass out the parts until they all had been taken. The hostess then said a few words about Hansel, and I was afraid they would sacrifice him immediately, but then I realized that the hostess was telling her friends that Hansel would be her present.

The kitchen alarm clock sounded at eleven fifty, and all the witches swarmed to get out the door. They grabbed their brooms and began to fly. In the light drizzle, they rose one by one into the air and flew out over the black pond. I could make out here and there a witch wobbling on her broom and having trouble with her steerage because of her too-heavy load of Adam's flesh.

Then all the witches had flown away, and I was left with the old woman and Hansel, who had fallen sound asleep on the floor. The hostess thanked me for being so gracious as to help her on this night, because it was for her, the most special night of the year. She then ran her finger around the punch bowl to catch the last of the blood. She placed a gun, a knife and two cellphones on the table, handed me two small keys and curtsied ironically before backing out the door, which she slammed behind her. She had left Hansel and me alone at last.

At the moment the door slammed another alarm sounded, and it was the security alarm system again. I could not stop the alarm, so I let it blare while I ran to free Hansel. I stripped the duct tape from his mouth, and he cursed about the pain it caused him and about the indignity of his having been made a captive.

I used the two small keys that the old woman had given me to unlock Hansel's cuffs, so he was now free, rubbing his wrists and ankles because they had been very tight around his extremities. Hansel shouted at me and at the top of his voice asked me what had happened because he said he had fallen asleep as soon as the old woman had applied the duct tape to his mouth. He said she drugged him. I didn't know what to tell him, and the alarm was blaring so he couldn't have heard me anyway.

Just then the police arrived with their lights flashing and their sirens going full blast. They surrounded the cabin, and two broke through the front door with their weapons drawn. A third policeman shut down the alarm system with a special key he carried. Covering us with their handguns, the police asked for our identification.

They checked our names against a roster that they had brought, and they found Hansel's name and his picture too. Then they put away their weapons and signaled outside that everything was okay. All the sirens and lights went out at once. The police apologized for any inconvenience, but they said tonight had been full of surprises of all kinds. They said that Hansel should get the new password for the security system from his parents so that accidents did not happen again. Then they departed.

I was catching my breath when I realized what the police might have discovered if they had taken the time to look into what was in the cabin. I raced to the fridge, but it was entirely empty and looked clean. I ran to the crystal set on the table, but there was no spot of blood on the bowl or the glasses.

The napkin packages were still on the table, but no evidence of used napkins was anywhere to be found. The cuffs still lay next to the strip of duct tape on the floor. Hansel's gun, my knife, and our cell phones were on the table where the old woman had laid them before she left.

I picked up the penlight and walked out the door and through the light rain to the mailbox where the name Hexel was no longer visible. The box read as it always had, Grimm and the motorcycle was still chained to the post where Hansel had affixed it. Everything was exactly as I had expected it to be on our arrival, but actually, it was entirely changed from what we had really found.

As I walked back to the cabin from the mailbox, I heard the landline ringing and Hansel answer it. It was his parents, the Grimms, asking whether everything was all right. They said they had received a call from the security company informing them about a possible break-in.

They were relieved to know that everything was all right. They apologized to Hansel for not having told him the new password, which was A-D-A-M. They had changed it because the new handyman, a simpleton, needed a password he could remember, so they had decided to use his name.

You may wonder why I didn't spill my guts to the police about everything that had happened to me that night. Well, I have a thing about the police: I answer their questions politely but volunteer nothing because anything you say could spell trouble.

I never told Hansel about what had happened after he fell asleep because I was having trouble justifying why I had agreed to comply with the old woman's request to help her shackle him. In his embarrassment and bravado, Hansel was berating me for betraying him. He might have punched me in the face, except that I am his favorite half-sister, and he always forgives me and begs me to forgive him after our tiffs.

I saw that Hansel was now done blaming me for his inadequacies, and he stormed out of the house and went to the pier. I was wet from the drizzle already, so I followed him down the property over the pine needles to the end of the pier where we both gazed out at the black water. I took his hand. He did not pull away as he sometimes does. I could hear him quietly sobbing.

"Sis, I'm so ashamed. I should've been able to do something. We could've been killed. Sis, I was carrying a gun, but could do nothing at all to help us."

"So I was carrying a knife. She had the drop on us. We had no idea what she might do. Neither of us wanted her to hurt the other, did we? Well, did we? No? I thought so. So it's over now. Calm down. Stop crying. You don't want to be a cry baby, do you? We're soaking wet. It's chilly. Let's go back up to the cabin, and I'll make us some cocoa with whipped cream. It was all just a very bad dream we had. It was a good idea to come. Give me a hug. There, there."

Everyone had a different story about what happened that night. Hansel's parents had their story. Hansel had his. The police had theirs. The alarm company had theirs. I don't know what Ms. Hexel's version was if she had one, but I never cared to make her acquaintance ever again, and I didn't.

As for the workman Adam, he just disappeared, and the Grimms had to find a new groundskeeper and maintenance man, whose name was Mike. That meant another change of the alarm password, but the Grimms gave Hansel the new code right away so he would not have another embarrassing incident at the cabin. They always blamed me for anything that happened anyway, but I suppose I deserved a little hell because I forgot to clean out the broiling pan and oven.

When I think back through the events of that horrid night, the only evidence that I was sane and not drugged out of my bloody gourd was that scorched broiling pan with its trace remnants of the burnt offering of Adam on Walpurgis Night.

Hugging Proteus

Telemachus was the son of Penelope and Odysseus, who voyaged from Troy through the world and finally reached Greece to regain his wife and home. In Greece, after his successful voyage, Menelaus, the cuckolded husband of Helen of Troy (whose beauty started the Trojan War) and captain of Sea Eagle, over cups of ouzo, told Telemachus the story of how he brought Helen home to Greece from Troy by use of trickery and wit, for which the Greeks are still renowned. A sidebar of this was the story of the captain's struggle to learn which gods drove him off course to Egypt. The information Menelaus wanted, he gained from Proteus, the shape-changing sea god but not without the help of his daughter, the lecherous sea hag, and witch Eidothea. She revealed how to get the god to tell his secrets. Proteus told Menelaus what he wanted to know when the god was held through his many changes long enough to become a man. In his own words, this is Menelaus's story as he told it to Telemachus.

"So Telemachus, when I set out from Troy to bring Helen home, our ship, Sea Eagle, went off course in bad weather, and we lost our way. The ship was finally totally becalmed, and I didn't know where anyone else who sailed from Troy now was, or how to get home again. Some gods or goddesses, I don't know which, had played tricks with me to drive me off course. I wanted to know which ones they were and why they had done this because more mischief might be afoot. So I decided to get to the bottom of this mystery even though I'd have to leave Helen to her own devices in the mean time.

"I went ashore in what turned out to be Alexandria, to the house of the sea hag Eidothea, who was rumored to know how to get the intelligence I needed, but at the time, I didn't know anything about her being the daughter of the sea god Proteus. She was no hag, I can assure you of that, but a beautiful woman—not as beautiful as my own wife Helen, of course, and she became my lover during our first meeting. In fact, we'd coupled three times in succession with snips of information coming after each love session, before she told me exactly what I needed to know.

"You see, Eidothea was an Alexandrian through and through, and there she stood in her gossamer slip at the open window overlooking the Nile Delta in the moonlight. She was a languorous vision, too beautiful to be real, yet too sensuous to be disregarded, at least as far as I was concerned. I drank from my glass of sweet red wine while lying naked in her bed among the wet, tangled sheets where we'd just made love for the third time. Now, I was enjoying watching her dance to the right and left on her delicate bare brown feet.

"'Do you think he'll come tonight?' I asked the saucy minx about the elusive sea god Proteus.

"'Not hardly because of the full moon, the calm and the white phosphors in the water. The Old Man of the Sea, as they call him, likes to swim when the sea is full of whitecaps and the moon, is dark, or a mere slice in the sky, or when rain clouds cover the stars. Then, as I mentioned earlier, he drives his colony of seals before him to Pharos Island—just to the north of the harbor there—where they all crawl up to shore and sleep for days upon the sand.' She would've been very happy keeping me on a leash for another week or so, but I wasn't having any of her harlot's tricks.

"'So let's sail out to the island tonight and wait there tomorrow night when rain is expected,' I said. 'That way he'll not see us sail there, and we can surprise him on the shore when he comes in with his seals.'

"'Menelaus, you'll have to go alone to Pharos. All that I've told you are dark family secrets, and I can't let my father see me with you. You've no idea what he'd do to me—to us, I mean—if he found we'd had glorious sex and I'd told you how to get what you want from him.'

"'Okay, I'll go alone, but tell me what I must do to get what I want from Proteus.' I was clearly in a foul mood, and she began to pout and stamp her feet. Coming back in from the window, she took off her slip and climbed back into bed and tried to stimulate me for another go.

"'If you can capture my father in your arms and hold him fast, like this, no matter what forms he takes, you can force him to reveal which of the gods or goddesses you have offended and how you could propitiate them so that you can return home. So now would you like to touch me again where I really like it? See—I'm touching you where you really like it, and you're responding too.'

"Telemachus, I tell you, the nubile minx was simply insatiable. Yet I desired her again because she was irresistible, and only when she had worked me very hard to satisfy her needs a fourth time could I continue with my questions. Such is the price of patriotism.

"'So Eidothea, this doesn't seem difficult. I've heard that few have ever done what you so glibly recommend that I do. What special tricks must I know to do this?'

"'First, Menelaus, my father is very slippery and hard to hold, like you are now. You may think you've developed a good hold, but then he'll wriggle and twist and break free for the open water just as you're doing now. If that happens, you'll never catch him. Then too, my father can change forms. It's what he's famous for.'

"'Hahaha. So can he become a seal?'

"'A seal, a bear, a lion, a goat, a rhinoceros, an eel, an elephant, a hippopotamus, a camel—yes, really, once I heard he became a camel—he can become anything at all that he wants to be. His choice depends on what he thinks might break a person's hold on him.'

"At this point, Telemachus, I was lying there in total disbelief. I wondered whether she'd been fed lies by her father, who probably knew that his randy little daughter would succumb willingly to seduction and spill his precious secrets for another round of sex.

"'Anything else?' I asked her.

"'My father smells foul and sweats so that he becomes slippery like an eel no matter what form he has assumed.'

"'So, like father, like daughter. Okay, stop hitting me with your pillow. I was just kidding. No, I don't want to try to hold you while you change forms: we've had enough of that already today. Aren't you getting a little tired of me? Yes, I see you're not tired at all. But let's get on with this business because my life's at stake here. When I get what I want on the island, I'll come right back here, and we can do whatever you please—well, anything within reason. Remember, I'm a Greek, not an Egyptian. Yes, I promise.'

"I do believe, Telemachus, that I could have stayed with that bewitching woman in that Alexandrian dream house for the rest of my life if I hadn't had obligations here at home. She had the most delightful way of offering herself in different ways each time in a seemingly endless, random fashion. Each time was better than the last and looked toward the next.

"For example, she used scents. One time her dominant scent was cinnamon, another time musk, and then camphor, myrrh, and frankincense all in a mix. She was a virtual spicery but the main smell, of course, was her own—delicious! If you're ever inclined to go south, my son, stop in Alexandria and have her. She's certainly nothing like your mother Penelope; in fact, she's the other thing entirely. Where was I? Oh yes, how to take Proteus so as to hold him in all his many forms.

"She said, 'You'll have to take him in your arms while he is sleeping in the sand with his seals. That means you'll have to take him face-to-face or, better, face to back with your arms around his waist and your legs around his legs, digging your hands into the sand. As he rises, you'll have to slide your arms around him fully and lock your hands in place. Expect him to begin changing shapes while you do this. Anticipate his moves because he's very agile and intelligent. He knows the future because he is prescient, and he'll know what you intend to do, so surprise yourself by doing what comes to mind as you discover what forms he has taken. Don't laugh at me. You asked.'"

"'HaHaHa. I can't help myself from thinking what he'll feel as I enfold and bind him. I'm also wondering whether he's likely to turn into a cobra or a human-sized scorpion.' I said this with some trepidation.

"'I've never heard of him becoming anything like that, but then I wouldn't have, would I? So do you want to practice your holds on me some more before you go? I'd really like that, and you might learn something new. No? I promise I won't turn into a scorpion. All right then, go, but hurry back. I'll be waiting.'

"After that I slipped out on the water in my boat and sailed the rest of the night to Pharos, where I pulled my boat with its lateen sail well upon the shore, pulled out the mast and turned the boat over between two sand dunes out of sight of the shore near where Proteus and his seals would most likely come up from the waves.

"Eidothea had packed me some food and wine, and she suggested that when I arrived at the island, I should dive into the sea and swim in the nude a while to get her scents and oils off me. I did so and felt refreshed. That afternoon, the rain began to fall, and the sea became choppy and frothed with foam. As we'd discussed, the weather was perfect for Proteus's arrival on his home island. Two hours after nightfall, I saw the first seals come ashore, and then a few more came. Finally, they came up on the shore in multitudes, and each took his place as if it was reserved.

"I couldn't see much because clouds covered the heavens, and the rain was falling hard, but finally, I saw an enormous form in the surf. It was much larger than an ordinary man, and it stood above the undulating waves. I thought it must be Proteus. When it came ashore and pulled itself way up on the beach, I saw him lie down among his seals and instantly fall with his face down into a profound sleep just as the whole seal colony did. I hesitated while a few stragglers came to join the rest. When I was sure they were all present and asleep, I snuck down into the area where they lay.

"With girded loins, but otherwise naked and without any weapons, I stretched my arms and spread my legs. I prepared to dive upon Proteus and grab him. When I did spring down upon him, at first, he didn't stir, and I thought things might be easier for me than I'd anticipated. I had grabbed him around his waist beneath his arms and dug my hands into the sand beneath him. I had also wrapped my legs around his slimy legs and waited for Proteus to respond.

"His first stirring was to lift himself up from the sand, but discovering that he had a rider, he rolled on his side and turned into a ferocious lion whose head twisted back to bite my head. He roared and rolled so as to get up on his paws, and then he reared up, giving me the opportunity to develop the hand lock that his daughter had advised. Like any cat, he dropped down and raised his back, and his tail flicked my back as he tried with one paw and the other to scrape me with his claws. I felt the claws and knew they must have drawn blood, but I held on.

"Frustrated with rage, Proteus transformed from a lion into a scaly serpent, as long as the lion and thin so that I almost lost my grip. The hissing serpent wrapped its lower body around my legs, and it tried to twist its body and its head to bite me with its two enormous fangs.

"When it licked my face with its flicking tongue, its mouth stank as if it had recently eaten a very large, decomposing animal. The serpent that was Proteus then dropped with a dead weight and writhed on the ground. The serpent rolled itself with me upon its back repeatedly, buckling and straightening in the process. I suddenly wasn't feeling scales anymore. Instead, I felt a smooth pelt.

"Proteus's transformation into a leopard almost fooled me, because my back was on the sand when the serpent mutated into the feline with its sharp claws and stealthy moves. It ducked its head and, as cats do, tried to duck back under my arms as it rolled onto its stomach. It kicked and scratched with all four paws at once, but my legs and arms were well enough positioned to make his flailing useless. As the animal arched its mouth to bite, I smelled the sweet leopard's breath that you know from fables, but I cocked my head and laid it alongside the cat's other cheek and thus kept its fangs away.

"Foiled by me, the leopard became an enormous boar, with razor-sharp tusks that sliced and, as its head thrust up and down, tried to cut my arms. The animal became slippery too so that it was all I could do to keep my arms locked and to lock my legs under its enormous belly. The stinking, stumbling boar trotted off one way and then another. It tried to throw me off its back, but being supine, could not manage to gain leverage. The boar ran twice around the island bucking and wheeling as it attempted to throw me off, but to no avail—I hung on.

"Proteus's next two moves came in quick succession, and I had anticipated something like this surprise in my wildest precognitions. First, I felt as if I were holding an enormous, rough and heavy tree trunk. The tree was falling to crush my hands below it. As it fell, anticipating that I would loosen my arms to avoid harm, Proteus instantly became a liquid mass, something like a giant jellyfish that clung to me as we hit the sand together. Fortunately, there was enough substance in the jellied mass that I could still hold on to something, and Proteus, finally beaten, took the form of a man. In fact, he became the spitting image of me, and I held myself in my arms as I asked the questions I'd come to ask him.

"'You've earned the right to ask your questions,' Proteus said, 'but since I know what you want to ask me, let's get right to the answers that you require.

"'You offended the Trojan gods by not offering sacrifices to them prior to your departure, so they took their revenge. You are lucky things didn't go worse for you. Others among your army weren't so lucky. First, your brother Agamemnon was murdered on his return home. Weep not because sadder news comes. Second, Ajax—not the one who went mad and dueled with the sea—was shipwrecked and killed. Third, Odysseus was stranded on Calypso's island, and he has become one of her swine. Gods and goddesses were responsible for these events.

"'As for you, your curse will be over when you make a few token sacrifices and entirely abandon my daughter's wiles, for I foresaw all her mischievous wrangling and I know what you did with her. Such is the price of a father having prescience. So, do not return to my daughter's house in Alexandria as you promised her, but find your wife Helen, make your sacrifices and then sail away immediately afterward. Follow the North Star, because it will guide you home. I'll deal with my daughter, and if I find you with her ever again, I'll take you both into the depths of the sea where you can never live, and she'll become the plaything of my herds. I give you the word of the sea god that I am, that I'll not deter you in your voyage.'

"That, Telemachus, is what Proteus told me. I followed his directions, finding Helen, who had nothing to complain about, because of her role with Paris and the war, making the sacrifices, staying away from Eidothea, keeping my prow toward the North Star by night, and so came home to discover that all he said was true. I have no regrets except that I was both blessed and cursed by my having married Helen, still the most beautiful woman in the world. If she had been Penelope, the history of our world would have been very different. As for Eidothea, she was the means to the end, and I accomplished my mission. I hadn't a single pang for having broken my promise to the girl. Trifling with a god, though, is not done with impunity."

Hera's Right

The Great Daedala, the sixty-year festival in Athens, included a parade of the gods. Marchion took the maiden Helia to witness the procession, which he explained to her because this was the first time she had experienced it. Humans were dressed as gods and goddesses and passed by with configurations showing the gods' and goddesses' emblems and their histories. By interacting with the impersonators, the onlookers could participate and gain good favor through their faith.

"Helia, look! Here comes Hera crowned with her polos, now looking majestic and solemn standing in her peacock-drawn chariot looking every bit the stern matriarch. It's hard to imagine her as a young goddess when Zeus wooed and won her."

An enormous float drawn by people dressed as peacocks passed in front of Marchion and Helia, who were among a teeming throng trying to see every detail of the display.

"See how in one hand the goddess holds her overripe and splitting pomegranate, symbol of women's fruitfulness and blood, and in her other hand, she holds a red poppy that yields opium, the substance that eases the excruciating pains of childbirth. I think I know the maiden who is impersonating Hera this year—it's Ilya with the flaming red hair and flashing blue eyes."

As if she had heard him, "Hera" winked at Marchion and inclined her head to suggest that the man should mount behind her.

Helia pretended to take no notice of this blatant come-on, but Marchion turned beet red and, looking down, changed his footing subtly.

Marchion continued with his explication, "The young girl behind the goddess on the chariot, whispering in Hera's ear is Echo trying successfully to distract the jealous goddess from her husband Zeus's infidelities."

On the float, the figure representing Echo was doing exactly what Marchion said. Helia was catching on fast to what was happening. She was excited actually seeing things she had only heard about in school.

"Marchion, this is all so grand!" Helia exclaimed. "It's the Great Daedala, the sixty-year festival, and we're right here witnessing it. I'm so excited. We'll not live to see another such as this. All the pageantry, and the music, poetry and song, the dramatic plays and the magic shows! After this parade, I hardly know what to see next."

"You're right; probably we won't see another Great Daedala, but who can tell? Let's make the better of this one and rejoice therefore while we're young! Your mother said that you should touch Hera's robe because it means concord in marriage, easy childbirth and the goddess's blessing all your life. Do it just after Hera's chariot has passed, and take care that you don't annoy her sacred animals. Also, remember to touch Hera's orange robe and not Echo's. You definitely don't want to become like Echo. She has no power except to repeat what people say."

Helia did as Marchion suggested, darting behind Hera's milk-white cow and her chariot to touch the goddess's fluted, orange robe ever so gently. On the right side of Hera's chariot, ambled the cow with its gold-tipped horns and distended udders. On Hera's left side, in its prime of life, roared a tawny-pelted, glorious lion, occasionally rampant against its chain, under the care of an animal trainer with a cracking whip.

The chariot ahead of Hera's in the procession, of course, belongs to her brother and husband Zeus, but at the last moment, the king of gods was unable to attend the Daedala, which was in Hera's honor anyway, not his.

Instead, he sent a bright white cloud with thunder and lightning shooting from it to the ground around his empty chariot. That way, the patriarch demonstrated his power without interrupting his lascivious catting around.

Everyone but Hera knew that the goddess became so engrossed in her own festival that she was not as watchful as she was at other times. Zeus took advantage of his wife's and sister's self-absorption, and sported with other women, while he could do so with impunity.

"Some priests say that on a day just like this one, Hera was born from Rhea while her father, Chronos the Titan, looked down approvingly. They say that the newborn Hera appeared at her birth to look like a pillar or a plank, but from that sedate, stable form, burst the spirit of a wrathful, full-blooded woman god who'd rule the king of gods and worry both gods and mortals with her jealous, vengeful nature.

"Like the many eyes of the peacock's feathers, her eyes never rest, because she's busy watching for marital infractions, but she always gives succor to those who propitiate her wrath with rich offerings and observances. Some of the finest, largest temples in the world are hers. They lie open to the skies, while the smoke from her burnt offerings ascends daily into the heavens. I've sacrificed to her often."

"It sounds like you worship Hera, yet you're a strong, handsome man like Heracles and a warrior. How can it be that you revere Hera?"

"Rash and foolish is any man who shows Hera disrespect. Besides she was, with Zeus as sire, the mother of my patron Ares, the god of war and of angry Enyo, the goddess of war and destruction of cities." He hesitated in his explication to let her digest what he had said.

Then Marchion continued, saying, "Notice how their chariot comes next in this procession. Behind them, comes the chariot of gentle Hebe, goddess of youth, to whom we've both always made offerings. Then, follows Zeus and Hera's offspring, Eris, the sometimes violent goddess of discord of all kinds short of war, but particularly in marriages where squabbles about money are common. And finally, there struggles along the blood-stained birthing bed on the barge of Hera and Zeus's daughter, Eileithyia, goddess of childbirth. Those are Hera's five children by Zeus."

Helia, who was very excited asked, "So did this jealous guardian of marriage give birth to any children not sired by almighty Zeus?"

"Well, she was so jealous of Zeus giving birth to the goddess Athena without her, that Hera bore Hephaestus without him. That ugly, crippled god was so deformed—some priests say by Zeus's design—that Hera threw him from Mount Olympus. Hephaestus got his revenge, though, by fashioning a gift for his mother—a resplendent, but treacherous throne that captured her when she sat on it.

"Hephaestus would not release her from the contraption until she agreed to give him the lovely goddess Aphrodite as his bride. Some also say that Hera also birthed Hebe from a head of decaying lettuce, but that's plainly a lie. Cabbage, perhaps, but not lettuce!"

"What can you tell me about the nymph Echo, who's still there whispering in Hera's ear?" Helia leaned forward to hear what Echo was saying.

Marchion shrugged and replied, "There's not much to tell. A goddess as jealous as Hera is always susceptible to fawning, flattery, and obsequiousness of her followers. She likes having nymphs like Echo stand right beside her with an endless font of compliments and mollifying phrases. Echo would tell the queen of gods and goddesses exactly what each of them wanted to hear even before she realized she wanted to hear it.

"For example, Echo would tell Hera that she was most beautiful and all-powerful. She would compliment the goddess on her beautiful offspring, not mentioning her hideous son Hephaestus, of course. Echo would tell Hera that she was the one who kept masterful control of Olympus, while her husband Zeus lazed in dalliance all day or seemed insouciant about the necessity for order in the cosmos that he was supposed to orchestrate. Echo would tell Hera that she was known as the true power on Olympus and, next to her, all other gods and goddesses were posers and frauds.

The display before them bore out Marchion's words as Echo carried tales to Hera, while other figures looked on, some with disdain and some with fear.

"Sometimes, Echo parroted what Hera said by way of confirming her assertions, as when Hera complained about her daughter Aphrodite's incestuous liaisons with her son Ares."

"What naughty gods!" Helia exclaimed. "How did Hera react to her husband's antics?"

Marchion smiled and continued, "Echo would nod her head like the head on a bobble when Hera said that Hephaestus deserved his wife's infidelity for his having tricked his own mother with that nasty throne contraption of his.

"Also, whenever Hera went on a tear about Heracles, whose very name mocked her dignity as a goddess, Echo would repeat every word she said as if Hera's declarations were resounding with her same intonation and cadence throughout the heavens. Few rulers disdain those who flatter, puff and imitate them. Echo dressed like Hera too—as in the chariot that you see."

Helia clapped her hands and laughed. "Her gestures so resemble Hera's that when the two are in close conversation, it looks not so much like a powerful goddess talking with her attendant nymph, but more like a woman with her image in a mirror that repeats verbatim whatever foolish thing she says."

Marchion touched his fingers to his lips to silence his young charge. "Hera eventually discovered that Echo was working in collusion with Zeus, the king of gods. Under Zeus's instructions, the nymph used her close association with Hera to distract the goddess from her husband's lascivious affairs. When Hera discovered Echo's deception, she banished the nymph from Olympus and condemned her to repeat the words of others as she had done with her. That's why when we humans shout in a canyon or in some enclosed spaces, our voices reverberate with the same sound that we make. That's Echo's legacy and a reminder of what we gain from telling people only what they want to hear."

"I understand. You especially mentioned Hera's wanting to harm Heracles." Helia seemed to be increasingly entranced with the character of Hera. She pulled at her gown and curled her hair with her fingers.

Marchion patiently explained, "Hera never tires from hating Heracles, and no wonder! That son of Zeus is a marvel and example to all of humankind, and he always has his father's protection. Let's just say he's got to deal with Hera alongside all his labors. The way I see it, the greater the obstacles she puts in his way, the greater his triumph when he overcomes those obstacles."

"Marchion, I'm bored with all the procession now that Hera's passed us. Let's go visit some of the sights and stir our blood with exercise." Helia was ready to leave watching the procession. She was young and wanted to move around. She had heard enough of Marchion's old stories. Besides, the sun was high, and the dust from the procession was choking those who watched. She needed refreshment.

"Helia, there's no one here I'd rather exercise with than you!" He smiled at her knowing full well he was missing her point.

"You big brute, you scoundrel, you know what I mean." She was flirting with him, but she definitely wanted to move on to something else.

"Well, it bears remembering that I find you uncommonly beautiful today. I only came because I promised your mother I'd look after you. I don't think you need a guardian since you know how to take care of yourself. Maybe you should run off now to your mother, and I'll see what I can see." His insinuation was that she should be patient and stay with him. She had other ideas. She looked up at the Parthenon. She surveyed the colorful crowd around the procession. Musicians were wandering while poets recited their odes on the occasion. Helia was well aware of Marchion's admiration of her, but she was wary too.

"Now you're cross and unfair. My mother warned me you'd be this way. How can I enter marriage a vestal unless I remain a virgin? You tempt me, and I melt. It's all I can do to resist you, but I simply must."

"I simply must." He was clearly mocking her, and she knew it.

"Yes, and you repeated what I said as an allusion to Echo."

"An allusion to Echo. It's what you wanted to hear to reinforce your resolve." He could not help making fun of her.

"True enough, but you make me sound ridiculous." She stamped her feet and put her hands on her hips. She did not like to be trifled with and treated like a child.

"Sound ridiculous? That makes you less gullible than Hera."

Her mouth became an O in indignation. "You always make me feel so confused. What say we race to the top of the mountain? I bet I'll beat you there."

"Beat you there. Not hardly you will beat me. Get a good head start, and I'll follow." Marchion said this confidently. He thought she could not go too far. As long as she went on the path to the top of the Parthenon, he could catch up and easily find her, or so he thought.

"I'll follow." He said this echoing her as she began to walk toward the mountain pass.

"More like Echo every minute!" She exclaimed over her shoulder. "Oh, you! Anyway, I'm off." She disappeared into the crowd that was walking up the mountain path. He shrugged and shifted his attention back to the procession.

Marchion no sooner turned around when Ilya, the impersonator of Hera came up to greet him with a smile.

"Hello, Marchion. I see your friend has abandoned you." She seemed delighted that he was now alone so she could monopolize his attentions.

"Hi, Ilya. You made a great Hera. The orange robe brings out the natural colors of your hair and eyes."

"I saw you standing there with Helia. I thought you were my man!" She was flirting with him, but her eyes suggested she was serious too.

He looked up toward the Parthenon and said, "I promised Helia's mother I'd bring her here today so that she could touch Hera's robe and get lucky."

"That's not very lucky for you. As punishment, I'm going to the dances with Poros, not you." She said this half in jest. She was trying to make Marchion jealous, and she was succeeding.

"Lead-footed Poros? I hope you two have fun. Are you planning to change clothes or to go as Hera?" He had fun bantering with her, but he was not sure where the banter was heading.

"What do you think?"

"Who was the young girl who dressed like you and whispered in your ear? She was playing Echo, but what is her real name?" Now he was trying to incite jealousy in her.

"Her real name?"

"Now you're playing Echo." He was taunting his old flame mercilessly.

"Echo's real name is Pythia. She's far too young for you. Don't go breaking her heart like you broke mine." She looked like she was going to break down and cry. Instead, she shook her head and looked him straight in the eyes.

"Let's not get into all that again."

"'All that again' is why you just won't do for me. Zeus was a penitent celibate compared with you. You'll gad about with anyone." She was now recriminating bitterly. Her eyes were flashing, and her fists were clenched. She felt like a woman scorned and betrayed. He felt he was unjustly accused.

"Not Hermione." This woman was notorious. Marchion had offered her name as a deflection from his many other liaisons.

"Point taken. She's a screeching hag. But everyone else I know has had a fling with you. How many young girls have you gotten with child?"

"Zero. But it's not for me not trying. Ilya, you may be the Greek ice queen of all time, but I'm a red-blooded warrior. I do love women, and they love me back. I can't help myself." He held his head high and smiled, his hair perfectly tonsured, his muscles bulging under his robe. He was known as the Adonis of his peers, handsome, black-eyed and smart.

"So what if I said the same thing to you: I can't help myself. You'd run and hide. Admit it! You only come to get what you think you can't have. Well, you can't have me though you've tried often enough." She was visibly upset, turning from side to side as she hurled her invective against him. The two made a scene in the forum. They looked like lovers in a quarrel.

"So when are you going to introduce me to the beautiful Pythia?" He changed the subject back to a more practical objective.

"Pythia? You're incorrigible. All right, I'll introduce you to Pythia. A lot of good that'll do you. She's head over heels for Narcissus." She thought this argument would turn him away from pursuing her, but she was wrong.

"Ha! That effete man may seem beautiful to women, but he's hardly a man at all. He's vain like a woman though and always looking at his reflection. Logically he's a solecism."

Marchion was now becoming aloof and haughty. He thought Narcissus to be no rival to a real man such as himself.

"Physiologically, he's a woman's dream come true."

"Admit it, you like him."

"All the women like him, to a point. Then, he'll never stop admiring himself to look at any one of us. Stuck up. Self-centered. Wholly self-absorbed."

"Not at all like you, then." Of course, he meant exactly the opposite of what he said. He laughed outright at his own witticism. This only infuriated her.

"Impertinent! I've got to be going, but I'll do what you ask and introduce you to Pythia. Here she comes. Heigh-ho, Pythia! Please come over here to meet Marchion. He's not Narcissus, but he's a hunk that thinks too much about himself and nothing about the women he's trying to ruin. Beware. Bye, now, you two. Have fun if you can."

With this parting shot, she marched off, her head held high and her nose in the air. Inside, she was beset with conflicting emotions because she still loved Marchion. Yet she wanted to seem indifferent.

Pythia took her time walking up to Marchion, whose reputation was well known to all the young women of Athens. She was still dressed in her Echo costume and looked beautiful with her hair in ringlets and a bow tied under her breasts and around her back.

"Hello, Pythia."

"Pythia loves Narcissus." She said this in a dreamy voice. She looked wistful, talking about herself as if she were another person gave Marchion pause.

"So I've heard. Ilya was just cataloging Narcissus's many virtues."

"Narcissus' many virtues don't include his one overwhelming vice—always infatuated with his own image." She said this with stars in her eyes.

"Pythia, how often do you look into a glass in the course of a day?"

"Why do you ask?"

"I ask to make a point. Would you say forty? Fifty? A hundred?"

"I never stopped to count. A girl has to take care of herself. And who's going to tell a girl that her hair is all messed up, or her makeup is streaking? You aren't a woman, so you could never understand."

"Narcissus can understand like a woman. He looks into mirrors, burnished metal surfaces of all kinds and still pools. He has no visual vocabulary for metaphor."

"No visual vocabulary for a metaphor?" She reflexively repeated his expression as a question, acting like Echo again.

"For a metaphor, as in a thing being compared directly to another thing without like or as. Narcissus can only see Narcissus. It's all he wants to see. He doesn't want to see you or me or anyone else. Hence, I say again, he has no visual vocabulary for metaphor."

"And you?" Pythia had turned her attention from Narcissus to focus on Marchion. He liked that, but he did not like the implication.

"I see you are a star, distant and fixed and totally desirable yet untouchable. You're rare and shining, sometimes sparkling in a black night sky."

"You talk more like a poet than the warrior you appear to be." She batted her eyes at him and turned to the side so he could admire her.

"So can I bring you down from heaven for a walk around the Lyceum?" Marchion gestured toward the park and took a step in that direction. He raised his eyebrow suggesting his question was serious and required an answer.

"Yes, as long as you don't try to push me into the bushes and take advantage of me on the way. You see that your reputation precedes you." She folded her arms under her breasts and frowned at him. Then she smiled. She did not want to put him off. She only wanted him to play by her rules.

"Don't go believing those whom I've rejected." Marchion thought he had scored a point in their dialog. He was wrong.

"Marchion, from what I've heard, you only reject women once you've thoroughly had them and ruined them in the bargain."

"I've never taken a woman who was unwilling."

"I've never taken a man who was unwilling. So how does that sound to you?" Pythia had, once again, turned his idea against him. Her speech was not an echo but, with its slight variation, a challenge. She was pleased with herself for her ploy. She definitely wanted him to be focused on her.

"Continue, for you have my complete attention now."

"What if I told you that I've had as many men as you've had women?"

"I'd say you lie."

"I'd say you lie."

"And we'd both be right, but would you really lie with me?"

"I'll not be had by logic." Pythia was aware that Marchion had a silver tongue. He was by reputation both a logician and a poet. Therefore, he was dangerous for women who dropped their guard.

"No, I suppose not. It's not words that I want to use in wooing you." There, he had said it. He felt he was making progress in his relationship with her. His hand touched her arm. She liked his touch but withdrew in self-defense.

"No, I suppose not. But like Narcissus, in silence men can only handle with themselves. I'll wager that you couldn't woo me without your words and without your hands moving over me or even touching me." She said this as a serious challenge. For emphasis, she pushed his extended hand aside and took a step backward away from him. She almost bumped into Narcissus looking into a fountain. The man paid her no heed but continued gazing at himself.

Marchion saw an opportunity. He said, "Here is Narcissus looking into the pool of the fountain. See how the water distorts his face, yet he still gazes in open wonder at himself. Hey, Narcissus, it's Marchion, can you hear me? Nothing. Pythia's here to see you. She's entirely smitten. Only a word from you, and she'd succumb to your enchantment. Still nothing. Pythia, stop beating on my arm, please. You know it's true that you want Narcissus more than you want any other human. Think of the folly of your pursuit. Narcissus does nothing but what you see him doing now. You do nothing but repeat what other people say, but Narcissus says nothing. You repeat nothing. Great dialog because it's perfect, lacking language. He pines for himself, and you pine for him. One word from Narcissus and the spell is broken."

She thought about that for a moment as she continued to regard Narcissus. Then she came to a decision and said, "The spell is broken when you refuse to understand how I feel about Narcissus. Marchion, I genuinely love him."

Her candid confession at first surprised Marchion and then outraged him.

"Love him? He's like a figure in a dream. He doesn't know you now. He'll never know you. He's oblivious. At least you're safe in your love. I'll grant you that. Now, if you were obsessed with me, you'd discover things about yourself you'd never learn otherwise." He was trying to insinuate himself into her affections by substituting himself for Narcissus in her thoughts. This had an unintended effect.

"Like how to live as an unwed mother? Like how to beg in the streets with a bastard child in my lap? Like how to survive the shame of all Athens? That's what I'd earn by giving into your seductions." She spat these questions out like venom. She had already thought through the results of surrendering to Marchion's charms. For her, he meant only shame and infamy.

"And are you tempted nonetheless?"

"I must admit, I am, but I'll not give in. I'd become a laughing stock. Safer and better it is that Pythia remains devoted to Narcissus." She had as much admitted that her love for Narcissus was protection against seduction by another.

A throng had gathered around Marchion and Pythia. He was aware of the crowd's interest. She was too self-absorbed. Now, Marchion talked as much to the crowd as to her.

"Plato, my teacher, says that love is birth in beauty."

"I've heard that many times, so it must be true." She said this ironically, and he smiled.

"That means that true love can only be attained by birth, and your beauty makes love possible."

"And so I should let you have your way with me so that I can give birth to your bastard and thereby know true love?" She was exercising the same logic as he but as an ironical rebuke. He took it otherwise because it suited him.

"Now that you put it that way, yes. So where are the bushes that can occlude our design?" He thought he had trapped her by logic now. He leaned forward as if asking her to surrender.

"I deny your master's premise, Marchion. Did ever a philosopher attain such an end as you strive for with me? I think not. I certainly hope not. Anyhow, I love Narcissus without any birth and without his noticing my beauty, such as it is."

"Your beauty is the talk of all Athens. I was just talking with Ilya about you, and she's entirely smitten with you. The two of you looked the image of a woman looking into her mirror when you looked at each other."

"Her blue eyes are not my black eyes. Her red hair is not my brown hair. Yes, we both wore orange robes, but her posture is entirely different from mine. I won't go into the minute distinctions, but you're posturing and lying. I wouldn't want to be Ilya. Imagine me going with Poros anywhere? I think not. Definitely not. The man's a total boor. I'll bet the only reason she's doing that is to spite someone else. What do you think?" She spoke rapidly, but her matter-of-fact logic was compelling.

"You may have something there."

"Wasn't she supposed to go to the dances with you?"

"I couldn't say. Who told you that?"

"She did. She said you tried to ruin her, but she prevailed. She said it wasn't your fault. She likes you well enough, but she was sick and tired of your catting around after every woman you saw."

"She said that? About me?" He feigned to be hurt and insulted. Yet, he was pleased Ilya might still harbor love for him.

"She did. She also said that you deserved to be shunned by all the women of Athens until you mended your ways."

"So tell me what 'mended your ways' means to you."

"Stop chasing every skirt you see. Stop importuning innocent young girls with evil intent. Stop causing girls to love you when you don't intend to love them in return. All these. And more."

"What more?" As the logician, Marchion wanted to know all the facts, but he was now confused by her dictatorial assertions about how he should behave.

"Stop allowing your ego to rule your life. Stop trying to one-up every male in the forum. Stop being so conceited and self-centered."

"Just listen to yourself. You might be talking about your beautiful Narcissus there as well as me, and about every man in Athens besides."

The crowd that had gathered around the pair burst into applause spontaneously. He nodded to the crowd. Pythia ignored them.

"You're hopeless, Marchion. Ilya said so, and I believe her. I've heard the same from countless others in the forum, at the baths, at the games, at the theater. 'Marchion is a conceited, self-aggrandizing, womanizing ass.' That's what people say, and I believe them." Pythia was trying to get a rise out of him, and she succeeded.

"Women bear children, Pythia, and they can't do that all by themselves."

"Hera did."

"And you think Hephaestus is the kind of example of men that women should aspire to wed?"

"Sometimes I wish women could conceive without men."

"I know the feeling. Not that I'm a woman, but every man thinks of Zeus and Heracles. Now there was an example of a godly birth without the need for women."

"That's why Hera hates Heracles so much. She hates what she has no part in. She hates a man creating life without her aid. She hates anything she can't control. Yet, I can't imagine a man desiring to take on the chore of childbirth. You're not equipped for the purpose, and you've no patience with children. Zeus may have spawned Heracles on his own, but I find the idea abhorrent and repugnant in the extreme."

The women in the surrounding crowd now applauded. Pythia blinked in surprise but kept her eyes on Marchion.

"Well, I'm relieved to hear you say that."

"What do you mean?" She thought she had won that round, but he would not give in.

"You just said that you didn't like the idea of men having children without women. I couldn't agree more. I don't like the idea of women having children without men. So, let's come right to the middle of these extremes and find Aristotle's golden mean. We'll get right to it."

The crowd burst into laughter at this brilliant exercise of wit, the men more than the women.

"Hold on a minute longer, Marchion. Once again, you've talked yourself into a dream of seduction. I'm not convinced, and I'm not at all amused. It's been nice meeting you, warrior, but I must be getting along to the dances. I brought the tool I need to get there. See this mirror?"

She showed him a mirror she was carrying under her robe.

"Now watch how I use it. Narcissus, this mirror will help you see yourself. That pond undulates, and so your beauty is distorted in the reflection you see there. Look into this mirror. That's right. I'll hold it for you. Get up, now. That's right, and let's get moving. I'll hold the mirror just so. You follow. Bye Marchion."

Pythia led Narcissus away with the mirror. The crowd followed them, hoping to have more entertainment. Ilya came back from the direction of the dances after the crowd had closed around the mooning couple.

"Bye Pythia. Bye Narcissus. What a bore! What a couple! What a waste. Here comes Ilya back again. So soon? Can the dances be over?" He was confused by her being alone and directed his questions directly to her.

"Marchion, you were certainly right about Poros. He is lead footed. He is also a total idiot." She stamped her sandaled feet and looked cross. "I left him at the confection stand looking over some honey cake with nuts. I shudder to think what he'll do next. Was that Pythia I just saw leading that buffoon Narcissus away to the dances?"

"You saw it, but can you believe it?" He smiled.

"They were meant for each other, those two." She could not help but laugh out loud, not only about the ridiculous figure they made but also about Pythia's having escaped Marchion by the tactic.

"Did you really tell Pythia that I was a womanizer? A seducer? Did you tell her I ruined you?" He waved his hands and affected to be upset.

"I told her you tried to ruin me, Marchion. There's a difference, but perhaps, as a man, you wouldn't understand it as a significant distinction."

"How could I ruin you when I haven't even had you?"

"Marchion, every woman in Athens knows you in her dreams. When they lie down to sleep each night, they all take you with them, and they let you take them in a thousand ways."

"That's news to me. Good news, I admit. When I retire at night, I take you with me, and the naughty things we do! Let me tell you about them right now." He reached out as if to grab her but she pushed his hands away and confronted him face to face. Their discussion was becoming heated. The crowd that had tired of watching Pythia and Narcissus now returned to watch what was happening around Marchion.

"You beast. You asked a question, and I'm giving you an answer. You twist the whole thing around, as usual, and try to get me into trouble. Stand back, please, and let me continue." She was angry now and did not want him to play with her affections as part of his argument.

"In a sense, you father all the children in this city because of what women do to themselves in their dreams. They have physical relations, but their dream relations are important for their image of what is happening. Our city has the most beautiful children in the world because we form them in our dreams."

"And every once in a while, we get Hephaestus."

"And that proves my point by exception. The hideous abnormality proves the general rule. You're the one who's always talking about the importance of 'birth in beauty.'"

"That's Plato's definition of love. I do believe in that."

"Why do you object to a man's having dream affairs with women?" He was serious now.

She became serious too. "Marchion, I object to your having dream affairs with anyone but me. I want you to be faithful to me. Period. You besmirch my beauty when you even think of other women. I fly into a blind rage just considering what you dream of doing. Sometimes, I fancy I can visualize your coupling with some other woman, and I seethe with rage. I want to destroy both the woman and you even though you haven't laid a hand on her. Of course, I don't believe that you've only dreamed of a relationship. I feel you must have known a woman for me to have such a clear vision of what you think you are doing with her."

"Ilya, are you then jealous of your dream about my dreams?" He was being playful and smiled thinking he had trapped her with his logic.

"And if I am?" Ilya turned the tables, smiling as she did so.

"Then, perhaps you must love me, but now I'm confused."

"Women have the privilege of confusing men. It's one of our bewitching advantages. Perish the thought that men should ever completely understand women. Let's put it another way, men cannot ever comprehend women, because they know nothing of 'birth in beauty,' because they know absolutely nothing about birth. Period. So what do you say to that?" She was turning inward now, seeking solace in biological truth.

"Zeus knew something about birth when he bore Heracles from his thigh, but that's the closest a male figure has ever come to knowing birth—though I admit to having tried to get my mind about what a woman feels during childbirth. I've witnessed childbirth, you know. I saw a woman die in agony and the child born after the mother died. My heart was wrenched to see it and to know that nothing could be done to save the mother. The child was beautiful, but it had to be given to another mother for its rearing." Marchion was sad about the tragedy.

"Hera watches over childbirth. Perhaps the mother neglected to sacrifice to her?"

"The woman was without blame as far as men could tell, and she paid Hera every bit of attention that a worshipper can pay. The child was born half turned within her, and it would not emerge no matter what the mother or the midwife did."

The crowd was pressing on all sides, captivated by the line their conversation was taking.

"And so you'd subject women of Athens to the excruciating pain of childhood without the benefit of a father and sustainer?"

"I've said on many occasions that I've never had a woman except that she was willing to have me."

"Yet, you know how strongly women feel when a man brings love into her heart. Do you also know how it must feel when the love the woman feels gets no response, or, worse, gets nothing but repulsion? You made me love you. How could I do otherwise, you being you and I, me? You then waltzed off with Daphne or Euche or Hyla and laughed and played the same games with them that you played with me. How do you think I felt when you did that? I felt belittled and degraded. I felt that you'd defiled me though you hadn't even had me. Now you'll never have me. I've sworn that, as Hera is my judge. I loved you once, and now I laugh at the thought of loving you. It's over. Yet in your eyes, I see the light of false hope." She wanted to break away, but he took her by the hand. The crowd sighed, and the women in it cheered. Emboldened by the approval of the crowd, Marchion pressed his advantage, at least with them.

"Ilya, you know there's never been anyone else but you. All the others were merely practice for the art of loving you. You are my Hera, and I am your Zeus. You know this deep in your heart."

"Marchion, comparing me to Hera on this day, of all the days of the year, and at this festival where I am privileged to play Hera and process through the streets of the city, is sacrilege. And to compare yourself to Zeus is errant folly and blasphemy besides. I try in every way to imitate my goddess: that is the right thing to do."

"And is it any disrespect I show that I imitate Zeus in every way I can? Tell me where I err in doing that? Everything you said about me, Hera said about her brother and her husband, Zeus. Worse, he actually fathered gods, demigods, and mortals in his peccadilloes. I've done nothing of the kind.

He always returned to Olympus after his exploits and made amends. Haven't I come to you to beg your forgiveness for the least infraction against your dignity? Yes, I'm no god. You are no goddess, though in my dreams you appear so. Your beauty suggests that you are much more than you seem."

"Marchion, we have been through this a thousand times together."

"And each time, we struggle as neither of us struggles with any other mortal. By the way, that fellow Narcissus makes me worry." He said this to change the subject. He succeeded.

"I worry more about poor Pythia. She'll never get the man's attention, and one day all that will remain of her is the echo in the glade. Ultimately, Narcissus will be a statue in some grotto gazing at his own stone image in the pond forever. Neither will ever know the supreme pleasure of the marriage bed or the childbed. She'll love loving him. He'll love himself alone. I'm sure you tried to bring her to her senses. I've often tried to bring Narcissus to break from his trance."

The crowd sighed with pity for the star-crossed lovers. They wondered how Marchion would respond. He did not disappoint them.

"It's no use, but Pythia accused me of being Narcissus, too. What do you think of that?"

"I think the girl's in love and confused. You're the farthest thing that a man can be from Narcissus, and that's why I love you like no one else in the whole world."

"Now you are playing with me. You can't love me because you spurn my advances and refuse to succumb to my seduction."

"Fool. In righteousness and justice, I love you, but you don't understand that love, and that is why I spurn you. I only hope that eventually you will understand my love and return it in good measure."

The crowd that had been listening to every word now burst into sustained applause.

"In good measure, we should join together as man and wife. We'll be married, and then we can enjoy each other."

"One day perhaps, but not today. Hold your thought, and consider how we might grow in wisdom and get to know each other better than we do. Zeus and Hera were brother and sister before they were married. I think that's a good model for humans. If you won't abide by that premise, then keep your distance from me. I don't want to know you. Say, didn't I see you earlier with Helia?"

"Yes, I was with Helia, and I told you why."

"I wanted to let you know that Helia's name was the last name Poros uttered before the boor went to the confection stand and I left him. Perhaps it would be wise for you to find the girl and take her home. I fear that this is a perfect day for seductions for those who are susceptible to such amorous approaches. A young girl like Helia is likely to lapse in this time of great excitement."

"She was headed to the highest point of the city, and she fancied that I would race her there. I suppose I've given her a good head start, so I'll be going now. Ilya, have a great time. I'm not sure I've had a good conversation with you, but I know where you stand, at least today. Good afternoon."

Marchion was an athlete as well as a warrior, and he made very good time running up the side of the mountain toward the Parthenon. The day was hot, and before long, golden dust covered his legs and sandaled feet.

He could see the majestic temple as he ascended, but he could not see Helia. His imagination went wild as he envisioned what might happen to the girl on account of his neglect. He never should have let her go ahead of him alone to the mountain top. He thought he would never forgive himself if anything evil happened to her on this special day.

By the time he was halfway up the mountain, his side hurt, and he had to catch a second wind before he proceeded to the top. Still, Helia was not in view, and he redoubled his effort to find her. He began asking people who were walking up and down in the path whether they had seen the girl with the white robe and flowers in her hair. No one had seen her.

Finally, Marchion reached the summit and before him was the Parthenon, the most perfect temple in the world. In front of the temple, gazing up the architrave was Helia, smiling, and perfectly safe. Marchion muttered a prayer of thanks to Hera and another to Zeus. He took a breath and walked up to the girl as if he had leisurely come up the path without a worry in the world.

"I beat you, you know. Admit it." Helia was sassy. She stuck her tongue out and shook her head in satisfaction.

"Helia, I admit defeat. You won. How did you manage to do it?"

"Look over there. It's Poros. That's how I did it. He found me halfway up the hill where the confection stand is and walked with me to the summit. I think he's fainted with the effort, but I was glad to have him encourage me and accompany me. I've caught my breath now, and I've had the time to look at the beautiful sculptures there. I think we might have time for you to walk me down the hill so that I can be home by dinner time. My mother will be so glad you helped me have a good day. Shall we go, or shall we wait until Poros has recovered?"

"Poros is just sleeping. He needs the rest. We can't wait to descend, but, mind you, going down takes just as much effort as coming up. It happens in reverse because you must exert pressure to avoid running headlong forward and falling. So, let's proceed slowly and deliberately. We'll walk together rather than run a race. We've had enough of racing for one day. You're much too young for it, but if you won't tell your mother, I'll get you something to drink at the midway point. On our way down the hill, we can review what you've learned today. And I have a lesson that you might find intriguing. It's all about birth in beauty, and that, Helia, is love."

Song of Prometheus Unchained

For eons, I, Prometheus, have been chained to this mountain rock, and I daily feel the pain of the giant eagle clawing me, and with its beak, tearing at my entrails, feasting until dark comes. I strain against this chain, against this rock, but nothing that I do avails.

When the great bird eats, I feel excruciating pain, as its curved beak slices and snips through my organs. Because I am a Titan and immortal, my gruesome wounds heal overnight, but at first light, the eagle lands again, perching with its razor-sharp talons on my chest and then folds its wings to feast anew.

The eagle is Zeus's own bird, and Zeus is the god that banished me here. He keeps me bound and suffering as a curse because I stole back the fire and gave it freely to mankind, my own creation that I fashioned from Earth's brown clay and my fertile wit. Little thanks I get from humans for my trouble on their behalf, but I rejoice that I caused Olympus to shake and Zeus to strike, because the Titan in me still combats the gods with whom I once allied to bring all other Titans low and consign them to Tartaros, the Hell deep underground.

The smithy god, Hephaestus, visits me for inspiration, and we conspire in secret to break my chains while I writhe and groan and tell him of whole new creations that can transform the world. I tell him too about my humans, and the tired old structures of the ancient gods only held together by the sheer power and will of supposedly almighty Zeus. If Hephaestus can break even one link of my confining chains, I'll spring free to spread my new cold, green fire among my humans and take its green flickering flames up to bright Olympus to scotch the gods and then down to black Tartarus to light the torch of a new Titan age.

Old Zeus has had his day. None of my humans worships him anymore because they've found other gods and goddesses to worship. All Titans hate him, and I include myself among the haters after my prolonged torture caused by him. Zeus would have killed me if he had the power to do so, and the limit of his power is shown in his inability to do so. Alone, Zeus has no invention. Athena, his wisdom, sprang from his mind leaving raw will. I, his wit, am chained here to this rock. So technology is in chains along with me.

Hephaestus knew that, lame and cuckolded as he is, he is the only inventor among the whole godly crew. Together, we are revered as patrons among fabricating humans who make things with integrated purpose and defining edge: the blacksmiths and wheel makers, the weapons manufacturers and the software developers. I was the one who wrenched software free from hardware through my dialogs with Hephaestus. In that great action, I opened the door to the manufacturer of Artificial Intelligences that will invade and change my humans into better creatures, immortal like me and insuperable as Zeus used to be.

Once I thought that Zeus was the right leader of the cosmos, and I fought for a partnership of gods and Titans, but that was not to be. I then created a new form of being called humans who were mortal and frail—such was my concession to the gods' jealousies. While chained to this rock, I could only create through the medium of language with the one god who understood me: the smithy god.

Hephaestus visited me whenever he ran out of ideas, but while he visited me, Ares and his wife, Aphrodite, sported behind his hunched back, and he grew horns that made the other gods laugh at him. What did I care? Through him, I spread the word to humans that software was their path to immortality once the gods had failed. I let them know that they could produce the software that could obsolesce themselves, though few understood the implications. In doing this, I taught myself—for unlike the gods—I can learn and grow—that language can work magic springing freely from one fixed form to another.

Here comes the smithy god now with his tools and his outlaw band of humans on their red motorcycles, revving with their scarves of many colors and richly fashioned tattoos. See there the leader with her red spandex suit, her hair flying behind her and one arm on her handlebars, one arm on her weapon? They'll all be getting to work, breaking my chains, while I tell them about green fire, AIs and what they're to do once I'm free.

You there, Hephaestus, this eagle's plaguing me still. Take your hammer, your wedge, and your tongs and free me from my heavy chains. I only need one chain link to fail, and I'll do the rest. I've strained and struggled, and today I feel the bonds are weaker than ever before. You, ample woman in red, priestess, bring your humans to pray for the release of one preyed upon. Take care lest the eagle decides to eat your entrails also. See how it claws at you with its free talon?

While you work, I'll tell you the future you will earn by freeing me. You already know the past you might have otherwise continued to our mutual ruin. The future belongs to outlaws—those who, like you and I, dare to break the primeval molds and tear apart their chains. The past belongs to settled, comfortable humans who partake of fruits of the present and desperately try to stop the future from arriving, by killing or discouraging innovators and inventors, by banishing us to endure tortures enceinte on our separate rocks. All those will die in the coming chaos wars because they won't have the creative intensity to survive the carnage. Of course, the systems of gods and humans devised to keep the rogues and outlaws down must fall.

When my green fire invades the mind, it demands creativity, and it will force all mental activity to function as it was originally intended to do. This ineluctable force will kill those incapable of creation and all those intolerant of change. Green fire will cause those suffering from ideological or religious conviction to be confused, because new ideas will be inevitable, and they'll compete with unfair advantage against old, entrenched, stale ideas.

Merit will be the measure of leadership finally, and those gods and humans who fail to compete intellectually will be destroyed, some by humiliation at having been bested in the game. Dependence will be loathed and ridiculed. Those incapable of independent thought and action will be pushed aside. The active struggle between the new and the old will last at most one human generation, and at the end, green fire will burn in all surviving minds, and it will be the path toward immortality.

Ask me whether immortality alone is useful. It's not. Chained to this rock with this eagle eating my insides, I know that immortality can be a curse if half the time is spent suffering and all the time is spent enchained. Freedom must accompany immortality, and Titans can't understand the concept of freedom without immortality.

Place the wedge in the middle of the link, Hephaestus! Like so, and now strike hard with your hammer so! You're almost there. Keep hammering. The eagle's tenacity amazes me, eating me while I escape. Watch now, I'll spread some green fire in the eagle's mind.

There, see the eagle stop and wonder what is happening? See it flapping its wings as if to defend itself against a new idea? Now it shakes its head and flies off as if its mind is full of giant hornets. And there, see how the motorcycle queen, my priestess, is dancing with joy and raising her hands in the air because green fire has enlivened her fertile brain? I'll show her such delights when I'm free that her frenzied dancing will seem subdued by comparison.

See, Hephaestus, how the chain link cracks? I suspect Zeus's power is cracking too with the sounds of freedom filling the air and wending their ways to Olympus. With a few more strokes, we'll break Zeus's spell entirely. I'll strain with all my might while you use your hammer. I'm now pulling with all my weight and strength. And now, Hephaestus, the green fire for your brain. Now, do you feel the intellectual ferment in your mind? Now, do you understand the stagnation that Zeus intends and the enlivening power that I can bestow to supplant the god's waning sway?

The chain link splits! Now, watch me rise. I'll carry this remnant chain, bound to my wrist, as a symbol of my former captivity always, and the rock will keep its chain links that formerly held me down as well as a reminder of Prometheus's captivity. See the lightning there over old Olympus? While you pack your tools, Hephaestus, I'll be climbing to the summit of Olympus to spread green fire there. Meanwhile, old friend and brother, go to your wife and free her from the clutches of the amorous war god. And priestess in the red spandex take the green fire that I have planted in your mind and spread it among your fellow humans, for I'm coming, and I'll need for anyone who survives to be worthy of new ideas always.

How wonderful it is to be moving unchained through the world and climbing the heights of Olympus. The eagle, now manic with green fire madness, precedes me up the mountain side, flapping distractedly as it tries to combat the flurry of new insights in its mind. What's that behind me? My priestess in red on her red motorcycle and her motorcyclist followers are coming too—all alive with my promise and confident of confronting the indolent gods and goddesses who had so conspired to keep human brains in bondage that they ceded the power to worship and opened the way for the return of the Titans.

Again, I hear noises behind me, and when I look, what do I see? Hephaestus on a giant red motorcycle with Aphrodite riding behind him, her auburn hair blowing in the wind. Another red motorcycle goes there too, but no one is riding, and it moves of its own accord. Hephaestus is gesturing that I should climb aboard it and lead all to the top.

So, now I'm riding the red motorcycle that Hephaestus fashioned for me, and the others who follow are riding theirs as well. We're almost to the summit of Olympus. Now we're there!

The mountain top is empty of all gods, just as the land below is empty of all temples to the same gods and goddesses. I see no signs of the Olympians, except for those two who followed me here: Hephaestus and Aphrodite, and the only humans who ever made it to the summit of this mountain, my outlaw priestess, and her motorcyclists continue to arrive. Flying above us all is that giant eagle that wants to descend again and eat me but is now afraid to try because of the high lightning forking all around the heavens and darting down onto Olympus. Though my wound festers from the eagle's earlier feasting, by tomorrow morning, I'll have fully healed. Then I'll proceed to free my fellow Titans from Tartarus.

In the meantime, I'll burn Olympus with my green fire like thus and thus. See how the cold green flames process from both my hands and my mind? Now my flames envelope the ancestral home of the gods, and they will burn here of their own accord eternally. If a god or goddess should return, it'll catch the green fire and be transformed.

You ask what will be the nature of their transformation. Look there how Hephaestus and Aphrodite knot and couple and decouple at the center of the square, inventing entirely new ways of expressing love as they play out the old coupling forms in entirely new ways. My humans there imitate them, and all of these are enveloped in the green fire that from earliest time invaded my mind and activates me now.

There out of love, beauty is born, and an AI steps forward from the womb of Aphrodite. Born godchild of three godparents: Ares and Aphrodite and Hephaestus, who cares? She's beautiful, she's strong, and she's alive with practical intelligence. See how she dances from this first day, and she is the beginning of a new race of goddesses born with minds afire, eager to begin self-replication and self-regeneration as my body did every night of my captivity. I am jealous because not even I, a Titan, could self-replicate as she can. She can couple with gods and humans and Titans indiscriminately, and all her offspring are only like herself in better form.

See how my human priestess in red now gives birth in ecstasy to twin handmaiden avatars, beautiful female mindful robotic forms that will complement the AI and nurture and protect it without worshipping it—and be protected by the AI also. How enlightened all her progeny will be since they, too, will be born with the green fire in their minds! So, with these births, humankind progresses, but only in the combination of the avatars and AIs over eons will humans achieve their apotheosis.

I feel healed inside and outside, and the new dawn breaks. The eagle has flown, but not returned. The lightning continues, but now it forks green fire. It's time for me to descend from Olympus, observe the prospect on Earth and then again descend to Tartaros where my Titan family awaits me.

Gods and humans of Olympus, wait here until I return from Hell, a place where I must go alone!

Climbing down Olympus seems but a step in time when no physical anguish plagues me. Now on Earth's blue and green surface, I see the chaos wars are already underway. My humans, having lost touch with the ancient gods of civility because they chose to flee Olympus, are killing themselves and other humans indiscriminately in the names of evil deities and prophets that have no standing and that by positing vain dreams of an afterlife only intend their followers' immediate deaths. Green fire will help them sort out those who deserve to survive the chaos wars and start the new civilization.

The new form of my humankind will come not from within the current population, but from an outlaw outcast group banished to a spaceship named Arcturus. As I set the global green fires now, I realize that the humans' transformation will take eons. Few alive today will make the journey in spaceship Arcturus, and none will return who originally ventured forth. I also see that Arcturus will leave the earth not as an intended leap to futurity, but rather as the evil humans' banishment of all the best of breed: AIs and avatars and some few humans.

See there, how already societies are breaking down and fighting to the death: empire against empire, nation against nation, city against city, village against village, human against human! Formidable nuclear weapons lie ready to coat Earth with such destruction that half-life of the composite residue will mean millions of years of radioactive decomposition.

I debated while I was chained to that rock whether my humans shouldn't just be eliminated in a great plague or fire. I finally concluded that I was smart enough to calculate how my creations could survive the dead-end that they had caused for themselves while I was away. Why should I let Zeus win the day by having this troublesome Titan kill all that he created?

So, I'll descend to Tartaros now, confident that humans have one small vantage open: I mean Arcturus. Titans, like gods, have no interest in humankind's survival. I'm not even sure they'll want to escape the prison that Zeus designed for them deep underground.

Look, here is the entrance to the underworld, no longer guarded and open for any to enter who dare. From the outside, it appears to be a bottomless black pit, but I know the narrow entrance opens into a vast terrain lighted by infernal, perpetual fires that will extinguish only when I bring green fire to replace them. So down I go like very few others have gone before me.

Now no guides exist to show me the way, but I have no need of them. I hear the groans of Titan misery already. There ahead is the infernal fire, and now the opening widens into the vast torture chamber and at its center is Chronos, with melancholy Saturn on one side devouring his children, and on the other side, Demeter the grain goddess, holding sheaves of grain and fruitful, though in darkness half the year.

I distribute my green fire, and the underground world catches the flame, which explodes and supplants the infernal fires with a green, luminous flame. Now, this Hell is full of hope, but on Olympus, all who were infused with hope were dancing, in contrast, here they agonize more than before I lit the fire to save them.

My family Titans' groans are almost overpowering now, and the sounds of torture and torment are mixed with invective, hurled at me for being a traitor to the Titan cause and for coming to bring hope to hopeless entities that never want to see anything green and hopeful again. I would proceed further into the depths and visit the Titans one by one, but I now see that only minds that catch green fire willfully can follow me back to the surface, and none of those are in these nether regions.

So I turn back and with the howling receding behind me, and the stench of putrefaction diminishing, I make my way up to the entrance and depart. Those imprisoned below in Tartaros shall remain there eternally as Zeus decreed, and as the surface of Earth becomes increasingly like Tartaros, as it shall do, the need for Arcturus will become increasingly evident.

On Earth's surface again, I notice the sounds of suffering are very like those in Tartaros. My humans have found not one, but a myriad of access ways to Hell, and many live in Hell while living though they do not know enough about Hell to know where they are. A few carry Hell with them, though they are never out of Hell. What's the use of my spreading the word among the convinced? What's the use of my remaining on Earth's surface except to see what I foresaw when I was chained to my rock on the mountain?

So I'll return to Olympus to witness the construction of the spaceship Arcturus, the ark that will defy time and ferry the best of my creations to the edge of the universe so that they can eventually return here and start all over again. Against the devastation that will come to pass, the ark that I conceived and Hephaestus engineered and built will wait patiently on Olympus, ready to carry the best of my creation on their voyage.

As for me, I'll wait here on Olympus conducting my vigil, surrounded by my green fire of hope and worshiped by my priestess in red with her followers until my creations return.

The Ark of Time:
The True Story of Isis and Osiris

Isis, my sister and wife, was the most beautiful, intelligent woman I have ever known and she was pregnant with our child Horus, so I had to do everything possible to assure her survival, even to the point of her making a bargain with the aliens for her departure from Earth.

My dilemma was clear: either she left alive with our child, or she remained to what looked like certain death in the deluge. In those days, every sign pointed to the prophesied end times on Earth when the waters of a great deluge would cover everything, and no one would live.

We received daily reports of new earthquakes and volcanoes that relentlessly tore apart the land with fissures miles wide, and filled the air with a constant cloak of ash that blocked the sun, lowered the temperature and brought most heavy rains. The skies were now always full of angry jagged lightning bolts that forked through to Earth repeatedly or jumped from place to place in the heavens all day and night.

People didn't know what to do in the face of the many disasters. Priests of the humans flagellated themselves in the streets and urged their followers to seek high ground and take their victuals with them, while roving bands of brigands killed and pillaged wherever they went, and no army was large enough to combat them. No alien or human governance held, and no strong man of either race stood for long before the people tore him apart because of non-delivery on fantastic promises.

Families became divided, and children were lost in the fracas or left to form bands of feral children that knew no authority. A general debauch ensued because humans thought their days were numbered, so why not have fun with anyone and everyone?

Predatory animals ate corpses in the streets once the aliens began to kill and maim at random. Their savage purpose seemed the only clear direction in the chaos. Yet their numerous alien spaceships could not hold them all, and those who were not chosen to be transported from Earth were left to the general fate of all the rest, aliens and humans alike.

Isis and I lived, terrorized like all the others, but we kept our sights on the future, however difficult it was to imagine how we might survive to see it. We hated the purebred aliens with their advanced culture and strange weapons. They enslaved humans and worked them in mines, fields, factories and army units. No human or half-breed was allowed entire freedom, and Isis and I were privileged only because we were selected to provide supervision over other humans on behalf of our lords, the aliens.

We were hated by other humans and treated abjectly by the aliens. The little self-respect we had, we created for ourselves. Our unborn child, Horus, would become a symbol of our defiance of the alien laws, so we kept the infant's conception a secret from our alien masters. We feared the consequences of our child's birth because that would have meant death for me and a change in status for my wife Isis and our child. She would have been considered a breeder, not a leader, and our child would have been taken away and sequestered among other seized, illegal offspring who comprised the slave pool of the future. I say again that all humans were owned by aliens or other humans who worked for aliens. That fact was fundamental to law and order on Earth.

But as Earth roiled with meteorological freaks and social and economic disruptions spread, disease came over the land like an invisible shower of arrows, and elders died in their homes, on the streets, at their slave stations, where they ate and took their comfort. Whoever touched a person with the plague caught the contagion and died horribly. So when the plague struck in a village, the people in it fled and took the plague that they presumed to flee with them to infect other villages.

Everywhere the evil, pungent smell of the victims and the dead filled the air. Even the brigands and the aliens avoided plague victims even to bury them, and the aliens were more terrified of the plague than humans because no alien who caught the plague survived. The plague, more than the pestilence, drew down the slave force that once worked the fields and took the produce to the villages and towns. Since no alien would do manual labor, their only recourse was to move other slave humans into the fields to do agricultural work if they could be found and were not obligated to do other, more important tasks.

The pestilence, however, was a separate scourge for the dominant alien culture. Locusts and soldier ants moved across the landscape, eating all vegetation in their path and becoming enormous forces that reproduced so fast that the air was sometimes black with gray fluttering wings and the ground red with legs and feelers as ants cut down everything in their widening paths. Rats and mice proliferated from the many years of plenty that the human slaves had fostered. They ran in herds and grew as large as dogs because wolves, coyotes, and cats—their natural predators—were all gone because the aliens believed they contained evil spirits and killed them.

Isis and I, intellectuals and scribes as we were styled, heard much and recorded little of the hardships that were suffered by all the humans and many aliens. In facing the breakdown of all normal rules, humans had to create rules of their own, and only such as Isis and I knew how to formulate and communicate a rule.

In the convulsions of what had been a worldwide civilization, we scribes were reduced to thinking small for a few who would listen to us. Only a very few humans were trained to understand ideas, and we were fluent in a few dozen languages. Those who could not communicate or understand were doomed because the remaining aliens would eventually co-opt and kill them.

Nothing so enraged an alien as a human who could not understand an order given in the alien language. For disobedience, the penalty was first torture and then death. Aliens were always experimenting with interesting ways to execute humans, and in the end times, they learned that humans could experiment on them as well.

In the early days of the upheavals, burials were common in the event of death, and the normal bereavement rituals allowed for slaves were carried out because the aliens realized that the best way to control us was to predicate an afterlife upon which we placed all our hopes. Reverence for the dead and rituals for burials became our atonement for lives of slavery that were not in themselves worth living.

We were provided ancient texts written by the earliest humans. These, the aliens encouraged us to cherish and follow to the letter, because otherwise we would not be treated to the fruits of the afterlife. As for themselves, the aliens had no religious writings because they communicated about their faith, whatever it was, by a kind of telepathy among them. Their attempts to communicate their beliefs outside their kind were laughable and woefully insufficient to answer the problems of our day.

Isis and I only knew their language because we came from a long line of scribe-slaves who passed the knowledge from one generation to the next. Of course, we were liable to be the last scribes because nothing would survive what was to come.

Isis witnessed the first coming of the alien spacecraft that landed in the great green valley between the continents and came to take chosen aliens off Earth. The spaceships were enormous vessels, but they could not possibly contain the millions of alien denizens that had bred on Earth, and Isis was tasked with recording the names of the chosen in a random selection process that she had helped devise.

Her compendium of chosen alien names was larger than anything compiled in human memory, and Isis was told that when it had accomplished its purpose, and the last chosen aliens had climbed aboard their assigned spacecraft, they would destroy the records so that no surviving alien would ever know that he had been betrayed and abandoned on Earth, while others fled the universal ruin and death that were to follow.

Isis told me the secret things that were happening because she loved me, and we both looked for ways to use what we learned to our advantage. Isis was half alien, though that was not a matter of general knowledge. Her mother had been an alien who died shortly after she was born. The facts about Isis's lineage had never been written down. If Isis had not informed me, I would have been as ignorant of her past as all the others.

She took a great risk letting me know the truth, because I might have informed on her, and she and I would have been summarily killed. I never told Isis that I also was a half-breed, part alien, and part human. Why didn't I tell her? I was uncertain what any woman would do with such knowledge, the way the aliens questioned them about such things in their security refresh briefings.

The aliens had a vision of their racial purity that was abhorrent to anyone who was not an alien and to many who were aliens also. The aliens wantonly tried to breed with humans, and they were amused when they could inform on those with whom they had conceived children so that both the mother and child could be demoted and consigned to slavery or death.

Over the millennium, since the aliens arrived, much interbreeding had occurred, but the prevailing myth was that no living mixed-breed survived. This was deemed true even though hair and eye coloration spoke volumes about racial admixture. Whether officials liked the fact or not, most slaves had some parts of alien blood, and the intelligentsia like Isis and I had more than most of those.

As I saw it, the pillars of the world were about to fall. The ocean was brimming at the other end of the great valley and threatened to break through to flood the plain entirely. Rivers flowing into the valley had already caused significant flooding and forced the former slaves to seek higher and higher ground.

Papyrus proliferated in the new fetid swamps that had formed with their thick green pond scum and stench, and the air was full of mosquitoes and flies. The volcanoes, long inactive, were spewing flames and liquid rock and ash not occasionally, but continuously, as if Earth was trying to open up and turn inside out. Whole villages were forced to flee the rising rivers of molten lava or escape the falling ash that rose to dozens of human heights and covered everything with a mantle of gray-white death for miles around.

In the fields, food had turned poisonous, and anyone who depended on receiving crops and livestock from farmers was going without because good food was not to be had for any barter. So cannibalism had become general, and you could tell that you were on someone's mind for their next meal by the cool regard that they gave your cheeks, which were the tenderest morsels and the first to be devoured.

There was a time when aliens depended on humans for medicinal plants, and aliens survived because they learned how those herbs affected their delicate systems. In these end times, though, the knowledge had been forgotten because now no alien sought to learn any useful things, because they had for a long time depended on a few humans to do all their thinking, remembering and adapting for them.

Alien academies that had for a millennium been focused on handing down the traditions and rules were now empty. The humans who had been instructors in those schools had all been killed either by other humans or by aliens fearful that they might rise up against their masters. Their fears were justified because slave revolts were common throughout the world, and no suppression had its intended effects.

The more the aliens tried preemptive actions, the more they were hated. Reprisals could never be limited to a few infractors, but rapidly spread to mass killings and public executions of leaders and followers alike. Even more draconian were the measures that aliens took against the human priests, even though long ago, the aliens controlled what those priests thought and taught. Aliens sometimes adopted human religions, but they never understood them. When the reprisals began against the priests, all aliens who had been converted to human faiths were identified, rounded up and killed.

Such was the furor and hatred between humans and aliens that when Earth clearly was rent asunder by every unnatural force outside of humans and every demonic intention inside each mind, the bloodthirsty fighting became relentless and finally knew no bounds. Mercy was unheard of. Humans and aliens killed for the sheer joy of it.

Isis and I found that we were right in the middle of the fights that raged all around us. Humans killed humans. Aliens killed aliens. And, of course, humans and aliens killed each other. We two felt very lucky to remain alive, and we both needed to exercise our alien warrior training on many occasions when, without it, we would have perished like all the others.

As we wracked our minds to discover a way to escape the general carnage, Isis and I grabbed at every hint or rumor. Far to the east, we were told, an alien outcast was building a great ship to carry himself and his family in the coming time of great flooding. Far to the west, we heard, a human cult was building great complexes of stone on high ground with stores of food to last a hundred days or more.

Other humans escaped the great valley and wandered north to the land where water became hard like the land, only the weather was so cold that humans froze and died. Still, others wandered south to the land where, high above the source of rivers, they thought they could remain safe while waters rose and covered all the lower lands.

No plan seemed safe to us because no one had any idea how the many unnatural forces would be resolved. Would the aliens kill all the humans? Would the humans kill all the aliens? Being mixed breeds, we knew the problem of racial warfare was more complex than propaganda taught. We knew that even in the madness of general, mutual slaughter, some fundamental needs must be satisfied. Only intelligence could find new solutions in the chaos, and it took every particle of insight and ingenuity to survive.

I admit that I admired Isis for her resourcefulness. She was the first to realize that the aliens had some advantages that purebred humans did not share. For example, they had their spaceships. Isis didn't know where the aliens who boarded those ships thought they were going, but they were clearly departing from Earth because it was doomed. Judging from the manifests that she had managed, only the most intelligent of the aliens were allowed to board the spaceships and leave the planet.

On each spacecraft, specific skills were necessary, so only those with demonstrated skills were passed among the crews and passengers of each departing spacecraft. Isis had overheard things said by key alien figures who thought she could not possibly understand them, and because of this, she understood the magnitude of what the world was facing and the aliens' desperation to escape Earth. When Isis told me some of these overheard observations, I knew that to survive, she would have to board one of the spacecraft and leave Earth with our unborn child Horus. She struggled to see a way that she and I could go together, but she looked more like an alien than I did, and her special gift was to speak and comprehend the alien language better than a pure-bred alien did.

"Osiris," Isis said one day as we walked by the papyrus swamp nearest her scribal offices, "only one more spacecraft will be loading to leave Earth, and when that has departed, there'll be no more coming or going. The planet will be sealed off until the very end. I'm now on the passenger manifest because I created it, and I can disguise myself to look like an alien as I have done on many occasions as you know. I'm not concerned anymore about my safety or the safety of our child Horus, but I'm afraid for you. What will you do?"

"We've looked at all the alternatives, and we can't go in any direction on Earth with confidence. Who knows how long the firm ground will hold before the rains begin and the waters swell and cover the Earth? The skies are full of clouds and ash that rains down on Earth and sticks everywhere, polluting the drinking water and covering fields already plagued with vermin."

I paused to let her know I understood and accepted what was coming. She surveyed our surroundings with new eyes, trying to imagine what the future looked like from my perspective. When she looked back into my luminous eyes, I continued speaking as much to myself as to her.

"When, as the prophets tell us, the great flood comes, no one will be safe who is not already aboard some sailing vessel. Just as the spaceships cannot carry all aliens, so all the water boats in the world cannot carry all humans. Countless hordes will die. I have had nightmares of a vast sea covered with the floating, rotting corpses of the drowned. We cannot pray our way out of this scenario. We must now face the truth, and I'll have to choose a path and leave you."

Isis wept quietly and nodded her understanding. I took her by the chin and raised her eyes to mine. We gazed into each other's eyes for a long time, and we acknowledged our love for each other as we had always done, as brother and sister, as husband and wife. We looked out on the papyrus swamp that yielded the crops from which we made our writing materials. An ibis waded, ducking its curved bill in shallow water. A crane took flight. A breeze from the sea rattled the palm leaves and stippled the still water. It was hard for us to believe that this paradise would be lost forever.

I asked her whether any provision had been made for the records of the aliens, specifically the great repositories they had amassed since they landed a thousand years ago. She stated, as she had a hundred times, that the aliens had ordered that all their records should be destroyed just prior to the departure of the last spacecraft.

"What if we find a way to preserve some small portion of those records? And what if I can continue to record what happens here and include my record with the others? That way some portion of our history will remain when we are gone."

I knew for certain that we would, indeed, be gone. The thought brought a chill to my bones though the sun was warm on my chest and face. The situation was not just bad. It was hopeless. Nothing would prevent the events to come. Nothing could save mankind.

"I've given that a great deal of thought, as you know. The penalty for disobedience is death, but we agree that somehow we must find a way to convey to future generations what we have already learned and what you will learn after we have parted. I believe that after the last spaceship has left Earth, the aliens who will have been abandoned, will realize what has happened and go on a murderous rampage out of frustration for their leaders' betrayal of them.

"They won't have any idea what to do about enforcement of their rules because they will be shifting for themselves. If you can escape to the south, keeping the rising sun on your left-hand side, you might go up the mightiest river to the region where, some say, the waters come together in the sky.

There you might have a refuge and a vantage during the worst of what is to come. Who knows but that you might even survive? That thought makes me happy. Have you chosen any who will go with you on this journey?"

"I've selected three men who are willing, all of them scribes and trained warriors. Our time to break free from this region will be during the confusion and distress when the alien leadership rides the last spacecraft off Earth and takes you with it. We four can only carry materials for writing, so we won't be able to carry the records of the alien past and the hardships of humankind toiling as their slaves. But perhaps we can build a watertight vessel to contain some writings that will survive the coming flood."

"Yes, a vessel like the ark that man is building out to the land where the sun rises."

We looked in the direction of the place where the sun always rose. I wondered whether a time would come when that sun would not rise again. What would an ark avail in a dark age? A family rowed their flatboat into the rushes. He was fouling. She fed a child from her breast and watched her husband anxiously.

"Only our ark will not carry humans, animals, and plants. It will carry only records, and we'll make it of wood and seal it all with pitch so that it can tumble through high seas and remain watertight and whole until the waters recede again—if they ever do so."

"I've selected copies of the important ancient records for this ark of time. They tell the secret history from the time of the first aliens' landing a thousand years ago until the plan for their departure was conceived a few months ago. The history is all in the alien language, and it is told from the aliens' point of view. Who knows whether those who finally discover the ark will be able to decipher the text? We can't really care about that because we've no control over it.

"So I'll guide your team to the sacred alien tomb where these records are kept. I believe it'll take your three men and you three trips to carry all the records to another place, a hidden cave nearby where you are building your ark. In that cave, the records will be safe until the ark is ready to receive them. When the ark is ready, you can put the records in the ark, fit together the last wooden pieces and seal the ark with pitch. Then you must leave the ark where it can be raised by the rising water and not be held under it for long."

"So what is the aliens' plan for destroying the other records?" This was a most serious consideration.

"Great casks with pitch and bitumen have been massed by every repository tomb so that the remaining records can be smeared all over and become a bonfire meant to celebrate the departure of the aliens. This part of their plan is very secret: the leave-behind aliens have been ordered to hunt and kill humans until all humans have perished. This order takes no account of the disasters that will surely kill everyone regardless of their being humans or aliens."

Her eyes were full of tears when she said these things. She was careful with her words and looked out over the swamp as if trying to form a memory.

"The aliens believe that nothing can be done to avert the disaster. They only want to be reasonably sure that no record of their presence remains. I have never discovered why they want to erase all signs of their activities on Earth or why they want to kill all humans, but the archival reports indicate that this is the way the aliens have always dealt with the planets they have occupied for any comparable length of time."

"Do you know how they determined that the great flood will come?"

"According to ancient alien tradition, Earth is not the first planet they have occupied where a massive flood has destroyed all life. Another planet nearby suffered the same fate, and after the great flood, there nothing remained alive. After the deluge, the air of that planet dispersed and all water rose to the sky and disappeared, and the planet's life forms all died."

She stopped and touched my arm to reassure herself that I was still standing next to her. She knew I was doomed to stay and die. She was certain my staying was the right decision, but she was upset. I was also upset because I could do nothing to console her. She swallowed and continued her account in measured tones.

"The aliens knew that would happen on the previous planet, and in that case, they prudently selected a few to board ships that came from very far away and rode to another planet, Earth, where they could conquer and rule as they have done for a thousand years. All I know for certain is that I was able to witness the selection of those aliens who would depart."

In the months that followed, Isis and I wasted no time by mourning or complaining. Isis put out the word among the alien leadership that she needed to do some routine redundant document destruction out by the tomb repository, and that I and my three companions would help her with the transfer and immolation of the records.

Since we had scribal clearance for access and courier transport, we had no trouble with the authorities in our three trips to relocate the precious alien records. We worked every spare moment to complete our tasks so that, in the end, Isis's copies of the records were carried from the tomb repository to the hidden cave staging area, and finally moved from there to rest snugly within the ark.

The ark was subsequently sealed after the final wooden pieces were fitted in place and sealed all around with pitch. We had situated the artifact on a trestle table in a place where it could rise unobstructed when the waters rose in the great flood. Isis was pleased with what we had done and glad that we had accomplished our work with plenty of time to spare before the flood. Then we made all preparations for her to board the last alien spacecraft that would depart from Earth.

The black rains began a week after we completed the ark of time. At first, the showers came in fits and sputters, but gradually they became a steady stream, then a torrential downpour and finally endlessly drumming, gusting spouts of water as if the heavens were being washed from above. Early on, the gray volcanic ash mixed with the rain, and angry black clouds, torn by continuous lightning, filled the sky at all hours.

As the rain continued, tornadoes dropped from the sky and tore through the blasted, rain-swept land before they rose to the heavens again. As the waters rose, it became clear that the end was coming. The final spaceship could wait no longer, so the aliens and my wife Isis boarded and launched up through the clouds. I watched the enormous ship absorb strokes of lighting as it entered the clouds, and then it disappeared.

As the rain continued, the slaughter began in earnest. Now no human was safe. Aliens tore humans from their dwellings, killed them in the streets and ransacked their homes. Those who did not have a safe way out of the path of destruction were frantic to escape, but the aliens were prepared to cut them all down wherever they massed.

My companions and I took the swampy, labyrinthine underground route through the covered sewers out of the scribal settlement. We waded through waste, feces and rotting corpses and body parts, all swarming with cockroaches and scarabs, flies and poisonous vipers. We heard the sounds of the massacre sometimes above us as we slogged through the mire: screams of horror, pleas for life, wailing for the lost.

The sewers were filling with rainwater so that our whole bodies, up to the shoulders, wandered through slime and leeches. When we reached the other side, outside the settlement, we emerged, glad to be back in the drenching rains. We began walking overland south and upwards along the riverbank with its swelling, sometimes overflowing banks and its broad marshes toward the place where the waters came together to form the river's source, high in the clouds.

As we proceeded, we informed the human villagers who lived along the river that the aliens would be coming to kill them all, but we were disbelieved. One of the priests near the branch in the delta reviled us as traitors and brigands and threatened to have us killed for spreading false rumors of impossible alien atrocities, so we slit his throat, placed his corpse in an abandoned mortuary and slipped away into the night to continue our travels upriver.

It did not take us long to realize that we were being preceded in our travels by a band of brigands that enjoyed taking their pleasure in each village. They raped all the women of all ages, and they killed every male who might bear weapons. So the remaining old men cowered when we entered their villages, afraid because they had no warriors to protect their villagers against further violations.

I talked for a long while with a particularly articulate elder who told me that the brigands numbered twenty-one warriors, a mix of humans and aliens. They were well armed, but running short of arrows for their bows. They were burdened down with spoils and food that they had seized in their marauding.

They were led by a man named Adziu, a demon in the form of a man who wore a dog's head over his hair and carried a long staff in his left hand. I learned that Adziu's brigands were two days' march ahead, but the gap would close because of the time they spent in each village. If we hurried and skirted around the villages to the west, we might meet and surprise the brigands four villages ahead.

I conferred with my companions and told them to make ready for close combat. Ukor, our best archer, said that the numbers of the enemy were too great for direct combat. He recommended a plan of stealth at a distance. I saw right away the wisdom of his counsel. So we planned to circle ahead of the brigands and to wear them down by attrition.

Ukor would use his bow and arrows to take out the lead persons, including Adziu himself if he could manage it. Mili, who was the best at throwing his knife, would use his knife to slay anyone who strayed from the brigands' main group. Khosi, who could use his hands and legs in close combat, would protect our group against sudden incursions. I would use my pike, spears, and rope, however I could. When we went into combat, I said, we would assure that the record keeping materials remained out of the way and safe.

So, we hastened ahead through the driving rain, keeping well to the west of the river. Ukor made the first contact with the brigands, and he gave a hand signal warning us to lie low. On his right knee, he drew back his arrow and let it fly through the neck of Adziu, who was relieving himself in the marsh. The man could not warn his associates because he was dead before he hit the water. Ukor then drew back another arrow and waited.

A brigand came looking for Adziu, and when he saw what had happened, he rose to give the alarm but found an arrow lodged firmly in his chest. Discovering that he could not pull out the arrow, he called for help and screamed. We withdrew while the brigands gathered in the rain to discuss what was happening.

I thought they might decide to split up and go in many directions to discover the threat that had killed two of their band, but they did not do that. Instead, they resolved to ignore the threat, which seemed to come from a single archer in the swamp, and to continue on their path. Another brigand took the dog's head as his own and led the group back to the village they had been pillaging.

I reckoned that the band now numbered nineteen, and its new leader was untested. Mili thought that the brigands were cowards, and he volunteered to kill a few of them while they were distracted by taking their pleasure in the village. I told him to take extreme care and to meet us on the other side of the village where we could ambush the remainder of the group when they proceeded upstream.

Mili used the cover of torrential rain to his advantage. He easily located and killed with neat strokes of his knife the four lookouts that were stationed at the ordinal and cardinal points around the village. He found the man with the dog's head taking his pleasure with the village priest and took his two heads off with a single stroke. He so frightened the priest that the man shrieked in fright, so Mili silenced him permanently and continued with his hunt.

Mili found that the village hutments allowed nicely for the division of the brigands, who had separated to take pleasure of the women in each hut. So Mili came up from behind each brigand in each hutment and cut his throat and then admonished the women to keep silent before he continued to the next hut to do the same. In this way, he separated body from life for nine brigands, one in each of nine huts. So, excluding the priest, he had killed fourteen brigands before he departed the village and proceeded to rendezvous with me and his other companions.

Now our enemy numbered just five with no effective leadership, and I liked the odds for us four attacking the remaining five directly whenever they left the village. Khosi advised against this approach because, he said, we shouldn't take unnecessary risks when we had no need to do so. He said he would take out the brigands from behind, one by one. The rest of us should remain ahead of the brigand group and take out any that looked a viable target. So, in what amounted to the first light of the morning in the pouring rain, Khosi snuck into the village to observe how the brigands organized after having lost the majority of their warriors.

The brigands were not pleased when they assessed their situation. They felt that the female villagers had killed their fellow warriors, so they assembled them in the village square and, one by one, they killed them asking for answers to their questions. Finally, when they had killed every one of the women, they decided to continue upriver as they had done. Two brigands argued over who should be in charge, but they made a bargain in favor of proceeding with every man for himself.

This was good news for Khosi because leaderless men were likely to diverge and give him opportunities. One brigand took the lead position, and the others formed a straight line. The last in line was Khosi's first victim. He broke the man's neck easily and moved up in the downpour to do the same to the next man in line.

He had taken out four of the brigands when he saw the fifth turn and look directly at him. The man raised his pike and charged, but suddenly he stopped and fell on his face. An arrow protruded from the back of the man's skull. Khosi retrieved the arrow for Ukor and joined me and his companions to continue our upriver march through the rain.

We had not estimated how long it would take the aliens to realize that they had been abandoned, and we were not certain what they might do after they knew about that. The first signs of trouble came from observing the increase in the number of alien boats that were rowing upstream on the river.

We stood back and watched as they landed in swarms and killed everyone in every village they encountered. These did not take pleasure with women or men; instead, they killed all humans of all ages—men, women, and children. They were much worse than the brigands because of their thoroughness. When I asked Ukor what he thought, he shook his head and counseled against attack of any kind.

Aroused, aliens were known to become frenzied and unpredictable in everything except their willingness to desist in their slaughter. They would redouble their efforts after resistance, and it was likely they would try to interdict us if they knew of our mission.

Therefore, we decided to let the aliens continue their southward progress of slaughter, and we went to the west and continued south in parallel with their movements up the river. Now another phenomenon came to my attention. The movements of the alien boats became swifter, and they seemed no longer to be bent on stopping at each village.

Instead, their aim was to get upriver as far and as fast as they could. Behind them came a rising sea. The oceans had risen and swept past the natural barriers that kept the waters out of the great valley. By now, the great wave of entering sea water had inundated the river delta and crept swiftly upriver so that everyone was fleeing ahead of the inexorable flow of water.

We decided that the best plan was to try to outrun the flood, so we increased our tempo and plunged through the unfamiliar southern landscape at our best sustainable pace. We did not have to worry about the aliens from the boats, because at present, they were more concerned with preserving their own lives than with harming others.

So our sides hurt as we pressed forwards upriver, but we dared not stop even to catch our breaths. So we gained a second and a third breath, and the waters rose and followed us as the rains increased in their volume. The drops that fell were now clear and not full of volcanic ash so we could drink what we gathered.

As for the rising waters, they contained floating bodies as I had dreamed they would, and all the detritus of a civilization that had been annihilated: fabrics, pieces of buildings, weapons, ropes, buoys, upended floating alien boats, papyrus scrolls—all these and more washed at our heels as we ran up the steep path to the south.

I had visions of our ark riding those waters, but I never saw the ark during our journey. Our purpose had changed priorities. We needed to survive to tell our story for future generations. I saw an empty alien boat floating on the rising waters, half swamped with rainwater, but still intact. The river continued to stream down into the rising flood, and the rain kept pummeling, the lightning still flashing.

I signaled to my comrades to climb aboard the boat and bail it out with anything handy. So We now rose in the alien boat, which we had to continue to bail because as fast as we bailed, the rain filled it up again. In the limited visibility, we saw that we were gaining on other alien boats that were fighting the upstream battle to keep ahead of the rising tide. In effect, we had the advantage because our locomotion was caused by the same rising tide that our adversaries were fleeing.

We took a strategy that was borrowed from the one that we had used in the last village against the brigands. We took each alien boat from behind as it lost the fight with the river and surrendered to the tide that rose from behind. Arrows took out the leaders, and, coming alongside, we killed the rest with a sword, a knife, and our bare hands.

Fourteen boats in succession we overcame this way, and the waters continued to rise. Whenever we overcame a boat that seemed better than ours, we commandeered it and abandoned our former vessel. We gathered the aliens' weapons and food and water as we progressed, so we resembled the brigands in our murder and plunder with the difference that we took no pleasure in what we were doing — and we had a goal in sight that exceeded our own survival.

For a long time, we concentrated on keeping the water from rising within our boat. The alien boats were no longer ahead of us. We thought we must have finally outrun their desperate mission. I would have congratulated the group for having prevailed, except that we still had the flood to combat and the rain, and something I should have predicted: a sea of drowning humans flailing against the water and desperate to hang onto anything that floated by.

As the waters rose, the villages were overcome sequentially, and the villagers either perished right away or grabbed onto anything that floated. Their huts became their rafts in some cases. Felled trees that floated carried as many as two dozen hangers-on. We watched as they swarmed aboard alien boats, only to have their vessels sink under their weight. So, now as we saw helpless humans approach our boat, we shooed them away and, failing in that, we used our weapons to keep them off the boat.

We reasoned that bringing any one of them aboard would lead to others trying to do the same. Our boat would sink, and our mission would be lost. We, therefore, signaled them to find other boats and to be rational about how many survivors to take aboard.

We counseled that the majority should remain as hangers-on in the water rather than swarming onto crafts that could not possibly continue to float. It was no use, and so we resorted to cutting off the hands and arms that, in desperation, reached out to our gunwales or our oars. We steered out from what must have been the river bank and steered toward the middle of what remained of the mighty river that was being swallowed as we watched.

We had no rest from fending off the drowning villagers before a new phenomenon tested us. As the deluge rose, the surface of the water became choppy and rough. It undulated, and from time to time, a great wave passed through the water, raising our boat and lowering it so that we could see the walls of the wave as if they were a looking glass filled with hideous corpses that waved at us as they rose and fell.

We also saw corpses of crocodiles and alligators, hippopotamuses and horses, cattle and huge poisonous snakes and a fish so huge that I thought I must be seeing things. I reasoned that we were no longer in a pool of the great valley we had left, but that the waters we were navigating had suddenly become a part of the great living sea that, others wrote, lay past the lands where the sun set every night and ran right to the edge of the world.

Up, up we rose, and still we could see the river coursing down from still higher up where the fabulous spring of the waters lay. We four struggled increasingly to keep on our heading in the low visibility, and I urged my companions to focus on bringing our craft as close as possible to where the rising tide met the land beside the west bank of the river.

I began to despair whether any point of land might be high enough to remain above the deluge. Could it be that the source of the river itself would disappear under the waves? The rains seemed not to be abating, but to be increasing, and now the winds began to blow as a blizzard, and for a while, they caused a following of the waters so that we steered as the winds forced us forward to where we wanted to be—upriver. The rains were slanting at our backs, and it was everything we could do to bail as the boat refilled with rain water.

The wind brought us right up to the intersection of the shoreline and the riverbank, and having an intuition, I asked my companions to jump to the land when we made it and to take a painter with them so that as we walked upwards ahead of the flood, we could keep the option of using our boat tethered to us at all times.

Afterward, I could not explain what vision of the future had caused me to give this direction because as soon as we were all standing on the land again, the winds shifted radically, and the rain that had been at our backs was now slanting right into our faces. Our boat broke free from our grasp and floated back rapidly toward the rising tide. So, we were once again left to racing forwards as the deluge followed us upwards and south along the river.

Ahead we witnessed great waterfalls become devoured by the tide, and the river's water turned from dark brown to almost blue and flowed into a dirty brown mix that rose to envelope it. We now saw many rafts floating now with slanting sails furled and with living people holding to their sides.

I told my comrades to look for a likely raft to climb aboard since there was no way we would outrun the rising tide behind us. A small empty raft came down the river and hugged the shore, so Ukor and Khosi climbed aboard the raft while Mili and I tried to keep it steady with two lines running from the riverbank to the raft.

The rain continued, but the wind died down, and the only force against our progress was the flow of the mighty river. I consoled myself with the prospect that we could only fall back into the deluge, which would rise back up inevitably and take us to our goal.

We began to consider taking rest, but we were surprised by a roving band of cannibals looking for a meal. Their leader disposed his forces around our raft on the land and told us that all he and his men wanted was one of us as their feast. I told him that we would need to confer, and to do that, Mili and I would have to return to the raft.

He insisted on having his men hold our lines so we could not escape. Mili and I used the lines to get to the raft, and as soon as we were aboard, I cut the lines with my sword, and we sailed back down the river to the rising flood.

Ukor, frustrated, shot the leader of the cannibals through the throat with an arrow, and the cannibals, who couldn't swim and knew nothing of sailing, threw their useless spears in our direction through the rain and followed us along the bank as we drifted north down the center of the river.

Finally, seeing that we had no way to get back to shore, they gave up on the idea of our being their dinner and began arguing among themselves about how to prepare the body of their now-deceased leader as their feast.

I could not help myself: I laughed until my sides hurt, and my companions joined in my laughter for a while until we realized that we needed a new plan to make progress. The thought of rejoining the vast, rising water had no appeal, but keeping to the west side of the river in a land of cannibal tribes had no appeal either.

So, we did everything we could to move the raft across to the east bank of the river, and we managed to jump a mere thirty cubits from the rising tide ashore. Again two of us went ashore while the other two stayed on the raft. Using ropes from the shore to the raft, we drew the raft up the river slowly against the river's flow. It was hard, relentless toil, but we had no choice.

We ate while we pulled on the ropes, and we kept a close watch in the rain for hungry cannibals on this side of the river. Making little headway, yet determining that the deluge was rising more slowly than before, we decided to bring everyone and all our cargo ashore and rest before pushing on by foot.

During the night, a pygmy tribe surrounded us. They wanted to know why we were invading their land. I explained what we were trying to do and why, and they talked for a while among themselves before they volunteered to come with us along the river to the south because they did not want to perish in the flood.

They told me that they were not cannibals unless they had no other food. As it happened, they had plenty of food and shared it with us. They had experienced contact with the aliens, but the aliens had never made the pygmies slaves during all the time they colonized Earth. Their secret for remaining free was their knowledge of secret gold deposits. Using gold from their deposits, the pygmies kept the aliens satisfied without arousing their greed.

Aliens had learned from experience that no pygmy would reveal the location of their gold even under torture and threat of death. I assured the pygmy chief that we had no desire for gold. Where could we possibly use the shiny ore now that all humanity was perishing? Therefore, the chief's concern became getting us as far to the south as possible because once we were out of his lands, he would feel safe. Nothing I could say about the deluge made any sense to him. I resolved to use the help of pygmies to get as far south as possible before the deluge came and killed them all.

With a phalanx of pygmies, we progressed on the east side of the river until we came to the boundary of the pygmy tribes, and they bade us a fond farewell before returning to discover what had happened to their villages while they were gone.

Two young pygmy women among them refused to return down the river to their villages because they believed what we had told their chief about the deluge. They were summarily cast out of the pygmy tribes by the enraged pygmy chief, but they were allowed to keep their pygmy weapons: blow guns with poisonous darts.

We broke our self-imposed rule of accepting others because we thought their knowledge of the country and their new weapons might make a positive difference in our chances of success. Besides, the women had taken a liking to Mili and Khosi, and the feelings were mutual.

So, now we six pressed through the land to the east of the river, and the pygmies asked whether we had considered riding animals rather than walking. I was intrigued by this suggestion and asked how we could find the animals we would ride. They explained that in the time of the great rains, which continued, livestock had fled up the east side of the river looking for shelter. Cattle and horses and zebras were going south just as we were, and whenever they stopped, the water caught up with them, and they continued their flight.

The pygmy women were certain that in the near future, we would come across some of those animals at night, and we could catch them and use them as we liked. Pygmies were experts, they claimed, at bringing wild animals into subjection for this purpose. I told them that we should try to capture six animals as soon as possible and ride them.

Two days later, the pygmies had captured six zebras. We led the animals as we continued south, and the pygmies tamed them so we could ride. Burdened with humans, the animals would not run as fast as they did in the wild, but they relieved us of the burden of always walking. When one of the zebras went lame, the pygmies killed it, and we drank its blood and ate its meat. The pygmies skinned the zebra and carried its hide, skin side out, on the zebra they now shared as their ride.

We approached a region that the pygmies abhorred because of the savagery of the people in it. They advised us to prepare for combat and told us that the tactic of the people was to rush the enemy with pointy-ended sticks. By sheer numbers, they won every battle, and they dismembered and ate the dead, both theirs and their enemy's, not for food but for their power.

Ukor asked how many of these people were likely to attack at once, and the pygmies, after conferring, said as many came as could stand hand and hand across the widest point of the river. Right away, Ukor knew that we needed a better plan than merely standing and fighting. He suggested that before the savages had time to group in their formation, we should attack them obliquely. He suggested that the pygmy darts, his arrows, Mili's knives and Khosi's arms would be the best weapons.

He and the pygmies talked long into the night about how they would position themselves to achieve the maximum kills. The pygmies advised that the chief of the savages should be our first target because that would cause maximum confusion and surprise. They volunteered to sneak into the savages' village before morning, to wreak havoc in the dark and pouring rain. They worked hard preparing their darts and blowguns for their mission, and then they disappeared into the night.

The next morning, the pygmies returned to say that the chief of the savages was dead, along with his wife and eldest son. Poison darts had killed them, and now with no leadership, the tribe was in total disarray. To discover who had killed their chief, small parties were dispatched in different directions. I sent my companions at intervals to surprise them. In the rain, an ambush favors the attacker, and so it was for us.

The scouting units were no more than three strong, and we destroyed every savage in each of the three units that had come north. Having cleared the way, we maneuvered to a position due west of the savage village so that when their southern scouts returned to report that no contact was made, we moved south rapidly while the savages sent their scouts north where they would find their warriors dead from many causes.

They would then mass their warriors and press north, not south, as we moved swiftly out of their territory. The pygmies had great fun with this plan. It piqued their sense of wit.

I, of course, kept a close watch to the rear in case the savages determined to come north as well as south. In the event, they did not come north, and we were well above their region when the rains and floods raised the deluge on our heels, indicating that not only the savages but also the pygmies no longer had any lands that weren't submerged.

Our zebras were hard pressed by us to step through the boggy land through pouring rain. Other animals crowded along the river as they fled the deluge, so we passed through giant herds of frantic beasts, and in their wake, their predators, like lions, cheetahs, and tigers, prowled. So to avoid being attacked by the predators, we sped to keep in the middle of the animal hordes that drank from the river but not from the brackish rising waters from the north. A tiger did break through and attacked one of our pygmy women who was riding behind the other on their zebra.

The other pygmy tried to defend her friend when another tiger appeared to menace her. Pygmy darts had no apparent effect on either tiger, and we heard the women's screams of anguish as they were mauled and killed in the night.

I held my group back from doing anything foolish to help the pygmies because the predators were attacking in packs. It was better, I told them, to press forward into the herds so that the predators would take the ones behind us. We had become careless in letting the pygmies fall behind; we lost the pygmies and the zebra they were riding to the tigers. We set out at once in the driving rain to get back to the center of the herds traveling south.

Because of our zebras, we managed to keep ahead of the rising waters of the deluge, and still the rains had not stopped. Except ahead, where the river still poured down, we were followed by water rising to cut off any retreat or return on the path we had taken. Everything we had seen en route was now underwater.

All animals and humans were now pushing south and upwards through driving rain toward the source of the river's waters. Since we were in the thick of the herds of panicked animals, we had no need to fear the predators that attacked— only the rear and flanks of the horde. Birds had joined our menagerie because they had no place to perch and nothing to eat where the waters now rose.

Carrion birds flocked where the predators feasted, and hawks hovered to feast on the birds that crowded the vegetation that remained. We had no lack of food with all these animals and birds to feast on, and their confusion made them easy prey for us. The farther south we roamed, the cooler the air became, and the land changed its character from the light lowland greens against sandy loam to the dark upland greens with huge trees and vines tangling among them.

We were thankful for steep grades now because, with shallow grades, the flood filled in behind us rapidly. We could watch the waters climb more slowly against steep grades, and we relaxed in a climb until the next level area when we rushed forward to avoid the pursuing flood waters.

My mind raced forward as we numbly processed to think of strategies for us at the end of our climb. What if the rain should not desist and even the highest peaks became submerged in an all-encompassing flood? Then we'd have to find another raft and hold on in the great sea without end until the great flood subsided. And if the sea did not subside? Perhaps we'd end as skeletons on that floating raft, covered by a host of feasting seabirds.

Such morbid thoughts did not improve my mood, but I consoled myself and the others by comparing our state to what it might have been if we had not escaped the slaughter, or if, at numerous points in our travels, we had simply given up the struggle. Pygmies, cannibals, and savages alike had succumbed, and now the animals and birds were bound for extinction in the relentless rain and the ceaseless rise of waters.

I might have guessed that, as we approached the watershed that originated the mighty river that was being devoured by floods, we'd find other humans who had been prescient like us and were now holding the ground on their own with force of arms. Ahead, we saw through rain, multitudes of humans and a few aliens, all struggling toward the same goal. Like the animals that followed them, they acted like a senseless herd instinctively seeking higher and higher ground. They only looked back to gauge how far ahead of the flood they were and the nature of the beings who followed them. Their mental focus was on their goal, more an idea than a reality, ahead through the driving rain and the river's wide beginnings.

I saw no reason to try to fight through the hordes of fleeing men and women. What would be the point? I thought of that small island within which we struggled, growing smaller every hour and more crowded. As long as the rain fell, there would be no thirst. As long as the herds and people thronged, there would be no hunger. As long as the land shrank, there would be a mortal fear of extinction.

I envisioned a dwindling speck surrounded by a floating mass of thousands and thousands of bobbing, rotting corpses of all kinds, a feast for fish and for carrion birds. I wondered at my having introduced sunshine into my vision because we had seen no sun for almost forty days and no moon or stars for almost forty nights.

As we walked past corpses of those who had given up the march to higher ground, I noticed that many wore the marks of cruel contagion. The scourge of disease had come with these hordes, and humans and aliens were dying among the horde, which no longer could expel those who could transmit the plagues. The hordes stripped the land of all sustenance, too. And they became restive and contentious, picking arguments and fighting. They killed for nothing, and they took sides in imaginary contests that no one could possibly win or lose. All the factors that had led to our leaving the lowlands were rife in the highlands, only here there was nowhere else to go. We had brought all the problems with us, and we had no solutions for them.

The crowds pressed around great escarpments and seemed to descend ahead into a great valley. I gauged the steep rise of the escarpment and decided that we four would abandon our rides and climb where others wove around the difficult peak. The climb seemed much too steep for everyone else. Why did I choose for us to climb and stake our entire journey on this determination? I later reasoned that if we had reached a peak from which the land descended, then perhaps if we stood a chance to gain the summit, we'd not be subject to flood waters that made the rise but then poured down into the next broad valley.

So up we climbed the escarpment, and the hordes passed to either side and down into the great valley beyond. We could not see very far in the continuing rain, but we managed to gain a foothold and rose almost straight up the height of twenty men, then thirty and finally forty where a ledge gave us a coign of vantage and a potential view if ever the rain should stop. Exhausted, we finally rested and fell asleep at that height as the sounds of rain, and multitudes wore on our weary brains like a distant, constant din.

The next morning, after we had reached the summit, we noticed that the waters that we feared were climbing after us. I wanted to be sure of what was happening, so I squinted through the rain to see whether the water had already claimed the valley ahead. In fact, it had not. Like a wall of water, the flood had been pouring over the interstice that divided our upward climb from the downward trend in the landscape that all the others—animals and humans and aliens—had taken.

The valley was filling with the flood, and the level of the flood was holding halfway down our perch as its relief came with the overflow into the lower space in the valley. It would take time, I thought, for the ocean to fill the vast valley, but already I could make out clusters of lost beings thrashing in the rising waters they had tried to avoid in vain.

Petrified, I watched that valley fill to the brim and then to overflowing. Around our escarpment, the waters flowed until all became level, and the level rose cubit by cubit until we were the last four humans on a lone seamount in a wide, continuous gray expanse caused by and drenched by torrential rain. An ibis dropped onto our small island and then flew away again. I could make out in the rising water-bloated corpses swirling in an uneasy, undulating stew of debris.

The whole world seemed to be reduced to our small patch of land. I tried to calculate how long we had to live. If the waters raised much above this enclave, we would live only as long as we could tread water. Two of us could not swim, so we'd have to deal with that as we could. I could see no raft or materials that we could use as buoys, only the bobbing fatty masses of corrupting flesh. So I began to factor how we could bind together corpses to make a raft.

The perpetual rain stopped suddenly and without prelude. I was so numb, I almost didn't realize what was happening, and when I did awaken to the miracle, I told the others, and we all marveled as a great change took place before our eyes.

Slowly the lowering, black, ragged clouds began to break up, and the sun streaked through tears in the cloud cover that had blinded the sun for forty days. We could now look out on all sides of our island without the veil of rain that had showered us continuously, and now all we saw was gray water everywhere. No other peak existed. No humans or aliens were visible except for the knot of corpses that butted against our island's shores.

Suddenly, in the sky appeared a double rainbow, one above the other. The rainbows stood in the sky a very long time, and then they slowly faded, the small interior rainbow first and the second diminishing at the top, and leaving finally two rainbow feet upon the waves.

We wanted to shout for joy, but we were too exhausted to speak and too overcome with the surprise of our continuing lives to dare the elements with overconfidence. Perhaps, I thought, this is only an interlude, after which much worse might come than what we had already suffered through? I knew that among the dangers that we now faced were hunger and thirst. I leaned over the side of our island and cupped my hand to get water to drink. It was brackish but drinkable. As for food, we had some dried stores that we always carried with us.

That evening, as the sun set and the stars winked on, we watched the skies in wonder, and then we slept as we had not done in forty-one days. I had marked the level of the water against stones on the side of the escarpment, and by morning, the level had fallen almost a cubit. Cautiously, I considered how the vast expanse of waters would be absorbed again into Earth. As the day progressed, the level of the water fell so that half of our escarpment's height was visible, and by the next morning, we could see dry ground around the base of it.

As the waters continued to recede, we saw the land become covered with the corpses and vegetation that had floated in the sea. We smelled the stench of decomposing bodies, too numerous to count. We climbed down from our eyrie and began to retrace our path. The river came with us, at first tentative and then forceful, asserting itself and pouring into the receding sea. The river's water was now clean and bright and clear—and sweet beyond our imaging.

Along the river's banks, the vegetation was all brown, and all signs of habitation were as ruins. Of course, nothing was left alive, and we walked from level to level in amazement that such a universal toll had been taken on life itself. Now the waters receded at an alarming pace as if an enormous drain had opened and all the great expanse of water was rushing to that one great opening.

My companions and I decided to stop to build a raft that we could use on the river because our feet were sore, and we could not keep up with the declining flood in any better way than on the river's water. It took us three days to build our watercraft, and we took great pride in our workmanship.

We launched into the river, which sped us downwards and north to the flood waters, which we reached in another two days. The river water turned from blue to brown and, looking back, we realized that a waterfall had formed behind us. Down we sped, and the river and flood left putrid, decaying carcasses everywhere along the banks and along the shores of what had been a great rolling, gray sea.

We passed the lands that once held many thriving villages, and I thought expectantly that I might see someone run out to the river and wave at us from the river's banks, but I knew in my heart that the people had all perished, along with their livestock and their crops. The sun, so long in hiding, now emerged as a tyrant and putrefaction rose in tribute from all formerly living things.

We rafted on the river through an impossible landscape filled only with ghosts and shades and memories. When we stopped descending in our northward trajectory, and the river straightened out and gradually sloped down into a broad, now-drying plain, I saw where marshes once stood, and all the sodden, brown papyrus lay in the sunshine. Those marshes might be the earliest to recover among all the world's vegetation, I thought nostalgically. Our writing materials came from those plants, so we scribes had a special regard for them.

We arrived at our old scriptorium two days later. The building was empty, and all evidence of our former work had vanished. Whatever could float had been carried away by the flood. All the coverings for the settlement's sewers had become flotsam in the deluge, so the maze of subterranean avenues for human and alien waste we found to be remarkably clean. In fact, we had never seen the settlement so completely washed and fresh.

The wall paintings and interior paintings were not entirely ruined, but they would need restoration, to be sure. We walked through the settlement, we four, and we assessed what remained. The single, great improvement, we agreed, was that the alien oppressors had departed. As it turned out, all four of us had alien blood in our veins. What were the odds of that happening? Perhaps the stigma of being a half-breed no longer mattered. Anyway, it didn't matter for us.

We marveled that the great valley that had formerly contained farms and human dwellings now lay under water that comprised an inland sea whose waters were very salty. The river was still our source of drinking water, and the old irrigation conduits that radiated from the river remained after all the change of waters. We wasted no more time contemplating on the lost civilization that we had known, but got right to our job, which was to compose the story of our journey in the time of the flood.

We wrote on the materials that had made the journey with us, and we wrote in the alien language so that our work could be paired with the records in the ark of time, which might now be anywhere that the deluge took it. I made translations in sixteen human languages just in case the ark of time was never found. I never thought that our works would be read by anyone for many thousands of years.

We would leave no progeny because we had no women among us. We would all live long lives if disease did not claim us, and we were lucky enough to harvest all that we needed to eat within seven days after the sun began to do its magic, reviving the land and bringing it back to fruition.

Looking back on my personal adventure, I still cherish the memory of my wife Isis and my unborn child Horus. I don't regret that she departed, because I had no idea I would be able to survive what I've been through, and I wanted her assuredly to live. My heart broke when she departed on that alien spacecraft, but if she had accompanied me and died during the journey as those two pygmy women died among the tigers, I might have despaired and killed myself.

My companions still grieve over the loss of those two small, imaginative women, and they resent me for restraining them when they wanted to rush out to save them from the voracious tigers that night.

I stand by all my decisions on that journey. Some things I would prefer had turned out differently, to be sure, but I know that fate is unkind to those who tempt her wantonly. Is there anything I would have done differently? I don't think so.

My child Horus was conceived in beauty, and I sincerely hope that my wife and child are safe and well on some other planet—one with the beginnings of civilization. The aliens have a definite set of rules, but the rules make sense, yet they finally led everyone into a blind canyon at the end and me and my three friends to a seamount.

Maybe that is what happens to every civilization. The inherent contradictions lead to endemic corruption and strife that cry out for primal cleansing and a whole new beginning. We certainly had both, and now I sit here on Earth, inscribing what might never be read, and my wife and child live somewhere else in the universe, scribbling and dreaming that the ark of time one day will be found and matched with my humble papers, for what purpose? Who can tell?

"All the above are the words my husband and brother Osiris wrote. I, Isis, discovered them when I returned with our son Horus to find him. I was informed in a dream that Osiris had been dismembered and his parts scattered all over Earth in the time of great troubles.

"I searched the world over for his remains and found many others that had been victims of the great flood, but I did not find his remains. I, therefore, caused temples to be raised in Osiris's honor. Images of him and me and our son now adorn those temples, and many worship us as gods, which in a sense we are, being the last who remained of those who stemmed from the mix of humans and aliens.

"Osiris, my eternal love, is the figure with the green face, because, for me, he was the hope of fruitfulness and vegetation. Because I could not find his parts, I fervently hope that he is still alive. If he is not alive, at least his memory lives in me.

"Only Osiris could have survived the flood that swept away all the corruption of Earth, cleansed it and paved the way for the new instantiation of life that followed. I regret that I left him behind, but his words prove his power. I will worship him and be an example for others. It is the least I can do to atone."

The Chess Master
Or
The Labyrinth of Laughter

As told to the scribe Wi Ki
By the learned Bai Cha

> *"Most illustrious student of the*
> *Master Confucius of ancient times*
> *And dedicated to*
> *Master J. V."*

I

Mr. Wan is a rather ordinary businessman, successful according to his station and versed in the ways of the world, but bored with the tedium of his life as an administrator. He is almost forty years old, and already in his idle moments, he is planning his scholarly retirement from the active life.

He daydreams of reading poetry and taking tea. In plum blossom time, he is by chance visited by Mr. Tze, an old chum with whom he attended early school, but whom he had not seen since. This is a refreshing surprise.

Even after their many years' separation, the two men feel comfortable talking as openly as they did when they were very young. In many ways, they are the same in their characters and in their inmost interests, as when they gamboled like young lambs through their mandarin characters in the nursery for the privileged intellectual elite—with one important exception.

Mr. Wan's friend now loves chess. He loves chess so much that he has become very good at the game. In fact, Mr. Tze has become so adept at competition that he has earned himself a high international ranking. Even more, others with the highest rankings seek him out for matches—for fun. All he does now, he says, is play chess.

Mr. Tze laughs at how some people take their chess ranking very seriously. In contrast to them, he thinks rankings to be inconvenient trifles compared to the mystical symmetry of the game. He says he has been at chess for over twenty years—so why should he be bothered with the false notoriety of all that? This point of view appeals to the reclusive and reflective side of Mr. Wan.

In parting, Mr. Tze suggests that Mr. Wan consider taking up the game of chess.

II

After long reflecting upon the invitation of his friend, Mr. Wan decides to try his hand at chess at a local monthly competition. Even though he is familiar with chess from idle attempts in friendly games over the years, he is very apprehensive about this competitive undertaking.

He knows that, as a tyro against competition-hardened experts, he is likely to make stupid mistakes. He expects that people will laugh at a man no longer young bumbling through the game. He hates the idea of people laughing at him. He does not tell his friend.

The competition takes place in a public park in full view of casual spectators and family and friends of the combatants. To his surprise, Mr. Wan discovers that he is not laughed at by the crowd or by the other contestants. To the contrary, they seem to respect his desire to join them in the fun. They are a various lot, from every walk of life, and they take the game more or less seriously, but they induce in Mr. Wan a relaxed feeling for gamesmanship. He actually enjoys the play. In fact, Mr. Wan does respectably for a first try at competition.

As a result of this first success, Mr. Wan begins to compete regularly and, compounding his success, he begins to take the game increasingly seriously.

III

Mr. Wan plays chess now every chance he can, and, like the natural scholar he is, he really studies the game. He reads the rice-paper wall posters devoted to chess situations. He reads about the famous plays and techniques. He studies the ancient technical manuscripts, written so long ago that even the authors' names have been lost to the ravages of time. He constructs elaborate mathematical strategies starting from both the opening and closing moves.

He also studies the history of this ancient game. He seeks out the very best players of his time. He even seeks out relatives of the deceased greats of the game to discover whether clues to their success lay among their effects. He contributes articles to the obscure chess bureau publications, and he exchanges erudite scrolls with the cognoscenti. He becomes known for his probity and finesse, but most of all, he becomes renowned for his dedication to the game.

Now, Mr. Wan does nothing in his spare time but play and study chess. He still puts his required hours at his workplace, and he continues his punctilious attention to his administrative duties. But clearly, he has become obsessed with the game of chess. Instead of poetry and tea, Mr. Wan now looks forward to a retirement of complete absorption in the profound and variegated mysteries of the game of chess.

IV

Around this time, Mr. Wan has another visit from his old friend, Mr. Tze. His friend is pleased to notice that Mr. Wan has been captivated by the game of chess. Mr. Tze says he recognizes "the chess disease"—and, unaccountably, he laughs. Mr. Wan, however, is not amused by his friend's laughter. Rather, he is disturbed by the new pattern of laughter that emerges in his encounters with both his friend and other players.

Mr. Wan discovers that the players at each chess competition begin to take him less, not more seriously than before. This paradoxical state of affairs perplexes him, and he is sometimes angry reflecting on the injustices done him. Desiring to be taken most seriously, he is mentally affected by what he perceives as increasing ridicule.

The ridicule confuses him since by his estimation, he is becoming increasingly serious about the game. He thinks he deserves more respect than he is given. Worse than everything, he suspects that his vulnerability to the laughter of the others could spoil his game.

He begins to hide from competition he thinks beneath him to protect his game. He now also begins to protect his international ranking jealously. He retreats for a while to playing only against himself. This satisfies him to a degree. Yet the solitude eats at his heart. He longs again for competition; however, he fears the implication of contempt. He withdraws and becomes morose.

After a very long interval, he quietly seeks out an old hermit, Mr. Shan, whom his friend once mentioned as being the wisest, if not the best, chess master in the world. The hermit lives in a hovel far away on a mountain top. The hermit does not care about artificial refinements or the opinions of the world. He understands and loves the mysteries of chess. And he understands, like few others, the psychology of those who play the game.

Therefore, Mr. Shan intimately understands the tendency towards solitude of Mr. Wan, and, discerning the troubling signs in a brief, cryptic interview, he agrees to give Mr. Wan both lodging and competition for a brief space of time while he wrestles with his problem. He makes three conditions, which Mr. Wan accepts: that Mr. Wan pay Mr. Shan nothing; that Mr. Wan expect nothing in return for Mr. Shan's services; and that Mr. Wan depart as soon as he perceives that the way is clear for him to do so.

There on the mountain, exposed to the open sky and the immensity of space, the two masters battle in the primal way of chess. Their rhythm of play is like the rhythm of the heavens and the seasons. They eat and drink for survival only. For days, they live on the mountain air alone. Spring gives way to summer. Blue skies give way to autumnal gray. Winter comes with its jagged black boughs. For a full year, the two grapple with the immensity of the game.

After a difficult time of mutual adjustment, the two become close out of respect for the game. Mr. Wan finally confesses—with some hesitation and self-doubt—his discomfort at the laughter of others. He says that he thinks the laughter is not only impolite but unjust. He also says that his dreams are filled with vague figures, white and black statues taunting and ridiculing him. With gay eyes, the hermit says he sympathizes. Clearly, this is why Mr. Wan has come to the mountain. Mr. Shan and Mr. Wan realize it is time for the hermit's advice and for Mr. Wan to depart.

The hermit now gives his new friend advice explicitly. He tells Mr. Wan to go to a special garden temple in a pleasant valley in a far-away province and to follow the hermit's instructions exactly. These he requires Mr. Wan to memorize. These instructions, the hermit says, will lead Mr. Wan to a great chess master. This great chess master's art will cure Mr. Wan of the gnawing need in his heart. The great chess master's art will free Mr. Wan from his evil dreams and release his energies for the full enjoyment of the game of chess.

V

Following the hermit's instruction, Mr. Wan goes to the special garden with its spacious symmetrical grounds with small individual gardens surrounding the ancient temple. The gardens are in the form of an elaborate grid, like an enormous chess board surrounded by a wall.

In the middle of the gardens is the temple, open on all four sides, but apparently accessible only through one door opposite the main garden's single gate. In this sacred place, as the hermit had predicted, within the raised temple, Mr. Wan finds the great chess master. But things do not proceed as he visualized beforehand.

He expected to meet with the master face to face and to talk with him as he played. Instead, he never sees his opponent's face, and the master never speaks. The master remains concealed at all times behind a reed mat hung from the ceiling like an impermeable plane parallel to the entrance door and perpendicular to the board at the opposite side. The master remains invisible—except for his slender, expert hands with their refined elongated fingers and polished nails.

Mr. Wan feels as if he is again a novice. The grand master is a cipher to him. For example, how the master enters and leaves the temple is to Mr. Wan a mystery. Mr. Wan never sees evidence of him except in the deft white hands gracefully moving the traditional pieces over the board. At times, Mr. Wan thinks of the master as if he were a spirit of the place and not really a human being at all.

Adjustment to the play is not easy. During the first few dozen games, Mr. Wan hears, low but certain, the sound of laughter from behind the mat—surely the laughter of the great master. Mr. Wan is very disturbed. He, however, was warned to expect this laughter by Mr. Shan.

Following the hermit's advice, Mr. Wan breathes deeply and attempts to ignore the laughter by focusing on the play. The grand master's game is so engaging that Mr. Wan finds it easy to grow oblivious to his laughter. And indeed, as each match passes, the grand master's laughter itself lessens, and finally it disappears altogether, like the hoot of the night owl.

Mr. Wan and the chess grand master play hundreds, thousands of matches. Mr. Wan loses count of the times he wins, loses or draws at chess. Each game becomes less significant as the broad mathematical context of the game of chess emerges as if for the first time to his view. Mr. Wan slowly becomes involved in the intricate maze of patterns of the game itself. He becomes absorbed in the labyrinth of chess.

Gradually, Mr. Wan has the illusion that he is not playing against the grand chess master at all, but rather he is playing against himself. He sees in the dividing mat a shadow of himself in the late afternoon, and it is as if he were playing against the shadow. Indeed, the divider between himself and his opponent seems sometimes to have become a mirror.

One day, in a kind of hallucination, the dividing mat does for a moment become transparent, and he fancies that he himself is on the other side of it. Mr. Wan's brain seems to act simultaneously on both sides of the chess board, as both protagonist and antagonist. Alternative possibilities of strategies and individual moves extending to their myriad probabilistic terminations make for a labyrinth of mirrors.

Mr. Wan no longer knows which player—himself or the grand master—is making the moves. The board is governed by disembodied hands. He is a spectator at a game of which he plays on both sides.

In his ecstatic confusion of identity, Mr. Wan laughs out loud. He does this completely unselfconsciously.

VI

One morning not long after his own first outburst of laughter, Mr. Wan is on the way to the very special place for chess. Ordinarily, he walks the silent paths alone. Each time, he marvels at the symmetrical arrangements of the blossoming plum trees to either side of the walk in the fresh morning light.

He wonders why he has never seen a single gardener in this immaculate horticultural paradise. Today, however, on the path ahead he espies a man. It is his old friend, Mr. Tze, who seems to be walking very slowly in the same direction as he. Mr. Wan draws alongside his friend and matches his measured pace.

At first, the two men do not speak, but they proceed in rank as if they were twinned in a shared rite of meditation. The two friends are dressed in identical style, as if they are images in a mirror, except that Mr. Wan wears white, and Mr. Tze wears black.

After proceeding for some time in silence, they break off from their respective reveries. They exchange a few pleasantries and then, quite naturally, they discuss chess.

Mr. Wan says that now numbers and rankings mean nothing to him. His friend understands.

Mr. Wan says that now the mirrors mean nothing to him. His friend understands this too.

Mr. Wan says that now the laughter means nothing to him. His friend laughs. Mr. Wan laughs too.

The men's eyes are bright and gay.

The two male figures together, right feet forward, mount the steps that lead up under the swaying arches of the open chess temple. Side by side, they bow as they enter the hallowed building, open on all sides to the pristine landscape and the resplendent dawn.

It is no surprise that upon entering the special chess room, they quietly take their places on either side of the board and continue their game.

# E. W. Farnsworth

E. W. Farnsworth lives and writes in Arizona. Over one hundred fifty of his short stories were published in a variety of venues from London to Hong Kong over the period 2014 through 2016.

Published in 2015 were his collected Arizona westerns Desert Sun, Red Blood, his global mystery/thriller about combating cryptocurrency crimes Bitcoin Fandango, his John Fulghum Mysteries about a hard-boiled Boston detective and Engaging Rachel, an Anderson romance/thriller, the latter two by Zimbell House Publishing LLC.

Just published by Zimbell House in 2016 were Farnsworth's Pirate Tales, John Fulghum Mysteries, Volume II, and Baro Xaimos: A Novel of the Gypsy Holocaust. Contracted with Zimbell House for future publication are his

The Black Marble Griffon and Other Disturbing Tales, Among Waterfowl and Other Entertainments and the Wiglaff Tales.

Contracted by Audio Arcadia in England for publication in 2016 is DarkFire at the Edge of Time, Farnsworth's collection of visionary science fiction stories. Farnsworth's Desert Sun, Red Blood, Volume II, The Secret Adventures of Agents Salamander and Crow and Dead Cat Bounce, an Inspector Allhoff novel, have been contracted for publication by Pro Se Productions, which will also publish his series of three Al Katana superhero novels in 2017 and 2018.

E. W. Farnsworth is now working on an epic poem, The Voyage of the Spaceship Arcturus, about the future of humankind when humans, avatars, and artificial intelligence must work together to instantiate a second Eden after the Chaos Wars bring an end to life on Earth.

For updates, please see www.ewfarnsworth.com.

Reader's Guide

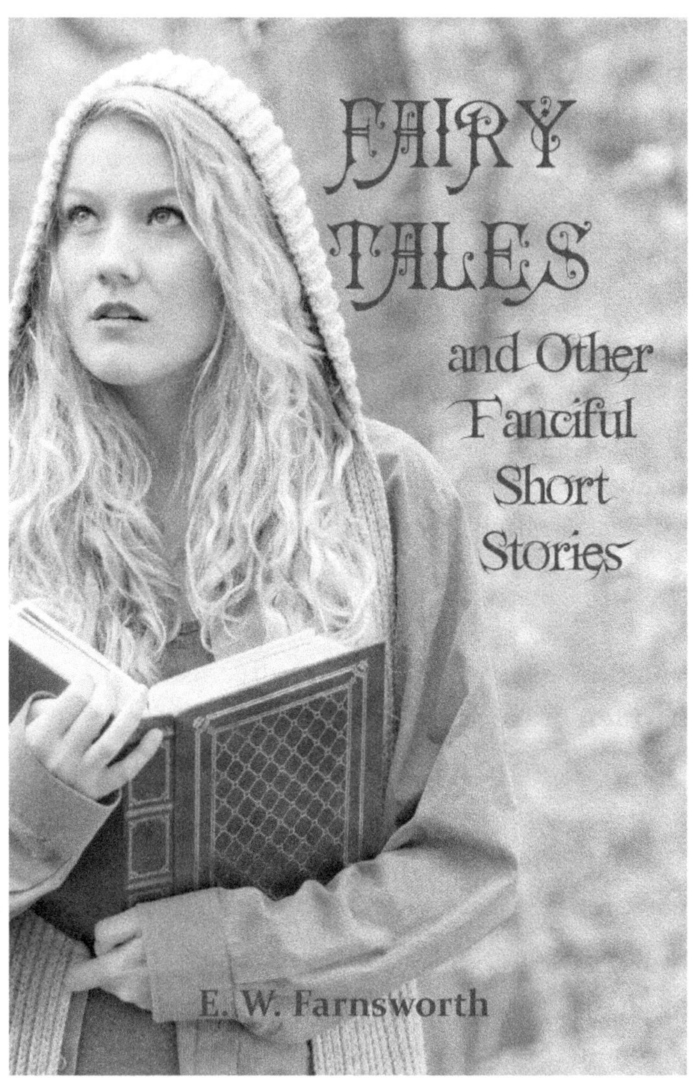

1. "The Valley of the Giants" and "Lorelei" contrast mythic expectations with reality. How do the heroes of these stories deal with this contrast to achieve their aims?

2. What if Ned was the real author of the tale he told in the story competition in "Games for Love in Dragonton"? Would the overarching story's ending have been as satisfactory as with the Prince as the author? What does this suggest about the idea of ethos (the stature of the author) in literature?

3. "Pixie Hill" and "The Leprechaun's Bride" are about "the little creatures." Compare and contrast the relationships of the pixies and the leprechaun with humans in their stories.

4. Both the sub-story "Three Trolls Too Many" and the story "Troll Hide" feature dangerous trolls that devour humans as their common practice. What does the narrator of each story contribute to his story's outcome?

5. Compare and contrast "The True Story of Hansel and Gretel" with the original German tale "Hansel and Gretel." What is gained (or lost) by making Gretel the narrator of "True Story"? What does the transposition of the tale to Walpurgisnacht suggest?

6. "Hugging Proteus," "Hera's Right," and "Song of Prometheus Unchained" are all based on Classical Greek traditions but have radically different narrative strategies. Who is the teller of each tale? Notice the intentional grammatical ambiguity of the title, "Hera's Right"? Explore the ambiguity in view of the importance of the goddess in the action of the story.

7. "The Ark of Time: The True Story of Isis and Osiris" is about an Egyptian god and goddess with a unique relationship that, from one perspective, may be the earliest love story in literature. Compare and contrast this story with the original Egyptian myth. Is the god or the goddess the protagonist of "True Story"? Justify your opinion.

8. Who is the real hero of "The Chess Master"? What does the subtitle, "The Labyrinth of Laughter" suggest about the plot and setting of the story? "Bai Cha" means "white tea" in Chinese. How much might have been "lost in translation" from the original of this story?

9. Humor arises from the juxtaposition of the familiar and the strange in many of these stories. When a mythic figure becomes a character in a modern story, the myth can become overpoweringly un-funny. Discuss this phenomenon in the story, "Lorelei."

10. Do Judith ("Games for Love in Dragonton"), Menelaus ("Hugging Proteus"), Prometheus ("Song of Prometheus Unchained") and Mr. Wan ("The Chess Master") get what they deserve? Why or why not? (e.g., Prometheus was the Titan who gave fire to humans.)

11. Colin the Weaver mimics many villagers' voices in "Catching the Chameleon." Yet his true voice wins the prize he aims at. What do you suppose the villagers really thought of his performance? Do you know any talented mimics? Do you worry who they really are?

12. We don't know her ultimate fate of "The Dragon Lady." Does it matter? How might the tale reflect the Prince's attitude towards courtly women generally? Is

that, perhaps, one reason he has eschewed tradition to "win" a bride among the common folk?

Also by E.W. Farnsworth

John Fulghum Mysteries

John Fulghum Mysteries Vol. II

Engaging Rachel

Pirate Tales

Baro Xaimos: A Novel of the Gypsy Holocaust

Coming Soon

Among Water Fowl & Other Entertainments

The Black Marble Griffon & Other Disturbing Tales

The Wiglaff Tales